CHINKS IN ARMOUR

Dr. Helen Hudson and Inspector M. J. Monahan were two strong women.

But each had her own weakness.

Helen Hudson's nerves were shattered by an act of violence that left her barricaded from the world in her luxurious apartment, communicating only on the Internet, and dulling her senses and sensuality with booze and pills.

Monahan had a fear of shooting to kill as her best friend once had done, and a fear of giving her body and her heart to the wrong man as she had done once and vowed never to do again.

It would have been much better for both ̣ they been perfect. For they were facing a killer who was.

COPYCAT

a novel by

L A U R I   M A E R O V

based on a screenplay by
David Madsen
revisions by
Anne Biderman
Jay Presson Allen
Frank Pierson
Charles H. Eglee

A SIGNET BOOK

SIGNET
Published by the Penguin Group
Penguin Books USA Inc., 375 Hudson Street,
New York, New York 10014, U.S.A.
Penguin Books Ltd, 27 Wrights Lane,
London W8 5TZ, England
Penguin Books Australia Ltd, Ringwood,
Victoria, Australia
Penguin Books Canada Ltd, 10 Alcorn Avenue,
Toronto, Ontario, Canada M4V 3B2
Penguin Books (N.Z.) Ltd, 182–190 Wairau Road,
Auckland 10, New Zealand

Penguin Books Ltd, Registered Offices:
Harmondsworth, Middlesex, England

First published by Signet, an imprint of Dutton Signet,
a division of Penguin Books USA Inc.

First Printing, September, 1995
10 9 8 7 6 5 4 3 2 1

Ⓡ REGISTERED TRADEMARK—MARCA REGISTRADA

Printed in the United States of America

PUBLISHER'S NOTE
This is a work of fiction. Names, characters, places, and incidents either are
the product of the author's imagination or are used fictitiously, and any
resemblance to actual persons, living or dead, events, or locales is entirely
coincidental.

. . . The Spartan eyes his Helen's charms,
By the best blood of Greece recaptured;
Round that fair form his glowing arms
(A second bridal) wreath, enraptured.
Woe waits the work of evil birth,
Revenge to deeds unblessed is given!
For watchful o'er the things of earth,
The eternal council-halls of heaven.
Yes, ill shall ever ill repay;
Jove to the impious hands that stain
The altar of man's heart,
Again the doomer's doom shall weigh!

      from Friedrich Schiller's "The Victory Feast"

PROLOGUE

Berkeley

"I'm reading your book, you know, Dr. H."

"What? Joe, I'm sorry. I was just looking at the water." Dr. Helen Hudson sat in the right front passenger seat of Officer Joe Shields's police cruiser, making a feeble attempt at daydreaming as they moved across the San Francisco Bay.

Joe could tell she was worrying again by the funny way she'd scrunch up her brow and put her right index finger under her nose covering part of her face. He'd seen her do that four or five times over the last few weeks just before she was about to make a public appearance, like at the talk show in Burbank and the book-signing the day before in Los Angeles.

"I picked up one of your books last week."

"Oh, Joe, I wish you would have told me. I would have given you one. I've got a stack of them sitting in my study and I've run out of relatives to send them to."

"Well, I thought since I've been doing this, I ought to know what you're talking about. I was wondering if you'd . . . ah, you know . . .?"

"You want me to sign it, Joe."

"Yeah, I've never known a real celebrity."

Helen made small talk with Officer Shields as they rode along in the big, gray Chevy. He was stocky, only about five nine; she had a few inches on him. He had a pleasant, almost vaudeville comic face. Today, he was wearing a uniform, which was a departure from the plainclothes suits he'd been sporting when they were down in Los Angeles. He was back in the territory of the San Francisco Police Department, so she guessed they had insisted on the uniform up here.

She noticed it was looking a little tight around the middle. Mrs. Shields probably cooked a big dinner for him every night with lots of meat and starches. She imagined that he sat there with a beer and the paper in front of the television news while the kids played at his feet. Helen could tell from the things he said that Joe Shields loved his wife and children. Their lives were as alien to her as the sociopaths she studied for her livelihood.

They turned off the 80 now, leaving the Bay Bridge and San Francisco behind them, moving off onto the Ashby Street exit, and down the familiar streets of Berkeley.

He had insisted that she call him Joe, but for the first week they were together, he would only

address her as Dr. Hudson. He just couldn't bring
himself to call her Helen. They had compromised
on Dr. H. Officer Shields was a bit in awe of her,
not used to spending time with women who were
so smart, so confident and accomplished. He was
a good man and she had come to appreciate his
solid nature, his normalcy. These were qualities
lacking in the men she loved and the men she
studied. Helen caught him occasionally making
sidelong glances at her, admiring her aristocratic
good looks, the sharp cheekbones, and delicate
features.

The male attention was welcome. She hadn't
had much time for relationships lately and she was
emotionally consumed on a daily basis with Daryll
Lee Cullum. He was the man of her dreams now,
a killer who had wedged himself inside her mind,
merged with her DNA. For two years she had
eaten, drank, showered, and slept with him.
Sometimes in the predawn as she sat in front of
her computer writing her book, she would close
her eyes and allow his transparent image to en-
velop her. She could feel his tattooed arms em-
brace her lightly and trace the lines of the dripping
red heart with the knife of Jesus plunged into it
below the crook of his right elbow. His head hovered above her, topped by his wavy dark red hair,
the lightly freckled boyish face that had misled at
least five women to a tortured and bloody death.
This was her meditation. She crept inside his mind
and waited there for the clues that would unglue
the mystery of this particular serial killer. It was

her job to dissect and analyze and support the irrefutable evidence that would hide Darryl Lee forever from the populace, from the supply that fed his addiction.

Helen stared out the window of the car. Berkeley. It had been at least a year and a half since she had left for her sabbatical. Six months out the book had been published. Seven months later it had crept up on a few nonfiction bestseller lists and she was an instant celebrity. Serial killers were hip now. She had already built her reputation and fortune as an expert witness and consultant, but that was strictly in professional circles. In the last few months, her agent had booked her on the talk-show circuit. Sales of the book were climbing. *People* magazine had called and wanted to do a spread with her.

This should have been her moment of triumph: returning to Berkeley after the years she spent fighting to have the department take forensic psychology seriously. Only now, her victorious pride was taking a back seat to the miasma of fear she moved in every day.

"You're not thinking about your lecture, are you, Dr. H?"

She jerked her attention back to the car.

"No, Joe. You're right. I should go over my notes." She stared out the window as they crossed Martin Luther King and glanced at the Berkeley City Hall as they headed toward Shattuck.

"Don't worry. They're gonna get him. It's only

a matter of time." He was a sensitive man, this cop. He knew where her mind was taking her.

Helen lifted up her black bag onto her lap and let the touch of the smooth leather soothe her. Out slipped the pack of note cards with the outline for her talk. Her fingers fumbled through them. This was academic; the lecture was second nature to her. She stared at the road and allowed the guilt and fear to stab at her mind again.

Darryl Lee Cullum was a free man and she couldn't shake the feeling that it was her fault. Sherman, the Oakland D.A., resented like hell the expense of assigning her protection. They had rehearsed her over and over, but the brilliant Dr. Hudson had gotten righteous and sloppy and Daryll Lee had gotten a mistrial. In the confusion afterward, he had managed to take a bailiff hostage and escape with the help of one of his trial groupies, Teresa Ann Slocum. She had hoped to play Bonnie to his Clyde, or perhaps Caril Fugate to his Charlie Starkweather. Poor Terry ended up his first posttrial victim in celebration of his freedom. He'd left a message for Helen carved on her stomach and a lovely filigree design down her arms. Daryll Lee's stylistic trademark had become tattoos left in blood by the sharp point of a stiletto. He had begun experimenting with this concept on his last victim before he was sent to trial. In addition, there was usually a tidy deposit of his sperm made sometime after death. The .44 special tucked in his belt came in handy on occasion, also. "Every artist's got to sign his work, Helen." He had told her this on their last meeting.

Sherman had almost wished her dead after the trial. Nevertheless, he knew that Dr. Helen Hudson was his only shot at taking Cullum down again. She was the death trap.

Darryl Lee had sworn his God-given right to revenge on Helen from the moment he was arrested. He was completely confident that he would have his day with her. Every day, Darryl Lee taunted her with his freedom. He sent what he called "love packages" filled with locks of young women's hair, fingernail cuttings and occasional patches of skin, schmaltzy Hallmark cards with dried drops of his new victims' blood as signature. After the escape, a handmade Valentine arrived with an original poem that had graced several of his notes since then:

> Put on your Sunday best, Doc,
> You're gonna ron-des-vous [sic] with me
> *Le bon temps* is startin—
> Darryl Lee is Free!!!

He loved to call her and whisper dirty things on the phone as if she were one of the scores of troubled young women who had begged to marry him when he was in prison. She got an unlisted number, but he was able to get it from her literary agent's secretary by pretending to be Phil Donahue's assistant. A sociopath of Darryl Lee's species had a natural-born anarchist's disregard for law or rules of any kind. Daryll Lee's genius was wasted on his psychopathology.

Joe had been her bodyguard for the last three and a half weeks. Daryll Lee had not shown his face once at any of her engagements. Her old friend, David Samuels from the FBI in Quantico had assured her just this morning, that they were closing in on him. Helen felt a little lighter thinking about it.

The gray Chevy was entering the campus now off of Telegraph, passing Sproul Hall, once the infamous site of sixties protests. Helen pretended to go over her notes. Officer Joe Shields was silent. She appreciated that, even if she knew it was mostly that he felt inside his own inadequacy at communicating with her. He knew he was there to protect and serve, and that was something he could do that she couldn't. Almost as if responding to her thought he reached down and patted his police special, resting cool and snug against his left hip. A lefty, Helen had already noted.

Silver-green eucalyptus trees floated by and she rolled down the window to allow their sweet and pungent odor to drift into the car. Pretty women lazed on the lawn between classes, sunning in the midday light. Frisbees flew by. Officer Shields braked suddenly. Helen gasped, her breath caught in her throat. It was only a golden retriever with a red bandanna tied around its neck. He'd jumped in front of the car and caught one of the plastic discs in its mouth. The retriever's young owner, shirtless and ponytailed, grabbed the dog, made his apologies, and ran for his next class. Helen closed her eyes and for a brief moment, slipped back twenty years to a sweeter, simpler time. When she opened her yes, they were parked in front of McCluskey Auditorium.

Joe got out of the car first and looked around, then nodded to Helen. She picked up her leather bag and stepped out into the warm afternoon.

"We gotta go find the other cop they have assigned here first and meet up with campus security.

"Okay, Joe."

He walked around the car and beside her to escort her up the steps.

"You look real pretty, Dr. H."

"Thanks, Joe."

◆

On the podium of polished gray metal and blond wood, Dr. Helen Hudson was deep into the flow of her lecture in front of hundreds of students in the packed hall there to see the celebrity professor-turned-author. Many of them had taken her class two years ago. She was back on her game, confident in the presence of intelligent and rapt attention.

". . . Society creates these crippled creatures and their revenge is terrible. For a short while anyway, they find a kind of bleak beauty in the torture of another human being. The screams of their victims obliterate their own pain. The act of killing makes them feel alive. But then comes depression, despair, guilt. And a loneliness that can only be alleviated by another victim."

Above and behind Helen on a screen five times her height, alternated images of notes, diagrams, and photographs. As she spoke, it was her image, a video projection that loomed over the auditorium for the benefit of the less fortunate in the back seats.

"Like drug addicts after their next fix, serial killers crave the rush they get from taking another life. Why? Because their emotions are stunted by years of abuse and rejection early in their lives. But what are the cofactors if any? Are they genetic? If so, what triggers violence in some people and not others? What we don't know about the mind of a serial killer is enough to fill a battleship and sink it."

Helen pauses deliberately and walks out from behind the podium. She is almost six feet tall, striking in her red suit and white silk blouse. Her professorial affect cannot camouflage her patrician good looks. She stands silent for a few moments, aware of the power of holding back information.

The audience grows agitated and a few students lean forward on the edge of their seats.

"Would all the gentlemen in the room please stand for a moment?"

The men in the huge crowd look around, suddenly self-conscious.

"Come on, indulge the girls and let us get a look at you. It's only fair, after all the time you guys spend ogling us."

Murmurs and laughter spread through the hall as one by one the men begin to stand.

"Okay, everybody under twenty and over thirty-five have a seat. If you're of Asian or African–American descent, you may sit down also."

There is more movement and shuffling of seats. Dr. Hudson waits a few beats to speak again, allowing the remaining men standing to grow uneasy in the silence.

"All right, girls. What d'ya see? Some pretty cute guys. If one of them invited you for a beer, you might go. Maybe dinner, dancing. Maybe even a dirty weekend in Big Sur . . . Well, let me tell you something . . ." Helen raises the intensity of her voice; she is emphatic now, almost frightening, ". . . Ninety percent of serial killers are white males aged twenty to thirty-five, just like these. Would you know if one of these cute guys is addicted to murder? Anything in their faces give you a clue?"

A few of the men start coughing. Several begin to sit. Helen looks out over the audience and smiles slightly.

There is a flash of movement in the balcony, which steals Helen's attention for a moment, and then she moves back behind the rostrum and looks down at her notes. On the big screen behind her, projected in rapid succession are the equally ordinary faces of Ted Bundy, Jeffrey Dahmer, David Berkowitz, Albert DeSalvo, and Bianchi and Buono, the killing team known as the Hillside Strangler.

"Albert DeSalvo, Bianchi and Buono, "Son of Sam," Dahmer, Ted Bundy . . . They were quiet, unassuming, even sweet. They held down jobs, made good neighbors. Their victims trusted them. They let their killers help carry groceries when they offered. Many times they invited their killers into their homes. The FBI estimates that there could be as many as thirty-five serial killers stalking their victims right now. But 10,479 agents can't find them. And 597,000 police officers can't stop them from killing."

"Okay, men you're off the hook. You better sit down before you scare everyone half to death." There is scattered nervous laughter and general sighs of relief as the men sit.

"Serial killers are a particularly modern disease. And one that afflicts the United States more than any other country in the world. But, we won't find the cure in police science, which can only hope to catch the perpetrator after he's killed. The answer lies in preventive science. In understanding the horror residing in their heads, and how it got there. Florida spent almost eight million dollars to electrocute Ted . . ."

Once again Helen's attention is drawn to the balcony and her voice chokes off. She stares motionless for a moment. In the wings, Officer Joe Shields stiffens, alert to her sudden panic. She gazes up at the front row of the balcony at the plaid shirt and a pair of tattooed arms draped across the railing.

Helen turns her head over to Joe and nods and

he moves to the edge of the wings and peeks around the proscenium with an inch of revealing his presence to the audience. Helen looks back up to the balcony and sees only the fresh-faced coeds waiting for her to speak again, thinking this is another dramatic pause before she springs some other frightening fact on them. She is confused momentarily. *God, I have serial killers on the brain. It's time for that week in Italy.* She smiles and shrugs at Joe and he slips back into the shadows.

"Florida spent eight million dollars executing Ted Bundy—money better spent keeping him confined for life, the subject of intense scientific scrutiny. Perhaps then we could have understood why that one particular baby boy, out of all the others born on November 24, 1946, turned out to be a monster. Maybe then we would be able to identify the Ted Bundys of the future . . . before they ever get their chance to kill."

There is a brief pause and the audience breaks into generous applause, unusual for a college lecture. Helen moves to the side of the stage and down the stairs and Officer Shields walks a few steps behind her. She blends into the crowd and scores of students press into her, shaking her hand, some calling out their congratulations. Shileds tries to remain as casual as possible, scanning the crowd routinely as Helen moves toward the hall, working her way through the throng. An older, balding man in a herringbone jacket with a cherry wood pipe sticking out of his pocket grabs Helen and shakes her hand.

"Good work, Helen. I know Berkeley's not much after Oprah, but we'll take you back anytime."

"Thanks John." Joe Shields watches his charge as she shakes the professor's hand, feigning warmth. He senses her distraction; her eyes flick from side to side. She wants out.

They finally make it out into the hallway and move quickly away from the mob of students waiting in the lobby to pounce on Helen.

"Jeez, you're practically a rock star here." Joe pats her arm proudly as they move down toward the exit.

"A year and a half ago they wouldn't even consider me for tenure. A bestseller and a few talk shows and they want me for department head . . . Joe, I need to find a bathroom."

They walk around a corner and on the right in an alcove is the ladies' room. Helen starts for the door and hesitates. Joe steps foward and knocks.

"Anybody in here?"

There's no answer and he enters, looks around. The bathroom is huge, very clean, a pristine white. New and modern like the high-tech auditorium Helen had just lectured in. Expensive glass bricks line the top of the sink counter below a mirror that stretches across the wall opposite to the stalls. Joe opens a door to a broom closet and finds only a dirty mop. He goes down the line of empty stalls and spots a pair of high-heeled legs.

"'Scuse the intrusion, ma'am."

He turns to Helen who stands in the doorway.

"All yours."

Feeling a little sheepish at this routine, he walks past Helen and out the door as she comes in and heads for the first stall. She carefully pulls several sheets of toilet paper off the roll and lines the rim of the toilet seat. She turns, about to sit, as a noose made of braided wire drops over her head and is yanked taut. Helen grabs her neck and tries to dig her hands behind the looped wire. Gasping, unable to scream, she kicks violently against the metal door of the stall.

Outside in the hallway, Officer Shields reacts and pokes his head in the door.

"Dr. Hudson? Everything okay?"

He enters, drawing his weapon facing the sinks. Behind him, Helen hangs in the open stall from the water pipe overhead. Suddenly, the door to the broom closet swings open. Daryll Lee Cullum emerges, incongruously dressed in plaid shirt, khakis, and high heels. His bright red hair is filthy, chopped short with his own knife and his skin is blotched with sores. He grabs Shields from behind and presses a lethal blade against his throat. Crazed and wild-eyed, Daryll Lee smiles for Helen—a rotten-toothed monster's grin. And he almost dances with his captive like a hophead hillbilly madman bound for destruction.

"That's my gun. Now what in the world are you doing with my gun?"

Daryll Lee takes Joe's weapon, then turns him around so he can see Helen hanging there, gasping for air.

"Hey, Doc, you're the expert. What does a sick

<u>fuck</u> like me do in this situation? Do I gut him or shoot him? What say, Doc? Maybe I do both?''

On the last question, Daryll Lee draws the blade sharply across Joe Shields's throat, inscribing a thin red line. He waves the blade in the air with a fluorish and smiles for his audience. Helen watches, choking, tears streaming down her face as her friend and protector's mouth opens and closes silently, his eyes bulging in stunned horror. Then Daryll Lee pumps two shots quickly into Joe's chest and he slams into the sinks and slowly slides to the floor leaving a red smear down the white tile and across the mirror. Daryll Lee turns and grins again at Helen who kicks and flails so violently she loosens the noose enough to get a gulp of air. She screams and screams until she blacks out.

Thirteen months later. . . .

1

Number Three

Jennifer Lyle pulled her new cross trainers out of the box, a birthday present from Mom and Dad, admired them briefly turning them over a few times and then delicately placed them back in the box and folded the tissue over them. These would have to wait until tomorrow. She looked out the window at the perfect San Francisco day, her mouth watering at the thought of a five-mile run. She grabbed her old Nikes, jammed her feet in them, and stood in front of her full-length mirror to check out her new running suit. It was purchased with the gift certificate her twin brother had given her. Thank God he let her pick out her own stuff; Josh had been color blind since birth. She looked great in the purple and turquoise sweats. They set off her blue eyes and fresh, no-makeup good looks. She smiled at herself as she yanked her blond hair back into a braid and grabbed her yellow Walkman and earphones as she ran for the door.

God, it was gorgeous. Seventy-five and barely a cloud—an unusual late August without rain. A cool breeze floated in from the bay. "Perfect," she said out loud this time as she headed straight for her car. She knew this was the optimum temperature and wind to dry the sweat when she hit her stride.

Jennifer debated whether she should put the top down on her little white Geo convertible. She decided she was in too much of a rush to get to her run. Parking would be a bitch today; everyone and their mother would want to be outside. She loved Golden Gate Park, especially on Sunday when they closed JFK Drive and she could fly straight across town in the light weekend traffic.

Jennifer managed to find a spot easily near the Panhandle and she walked to the entrance of the park. As she trotted slowly onto the main thoroughfare, she saw that sprinkled around the park were signs painted in Day-Glo colors in the kind of soft melty lettering once popularized by Peter Max and the collectible posters from the Fillmore West days. The signs and flyers stapled to trees announced the Festival of Love, an anniversary celebration of the birth of hippie culture in San Francisco. Jennifer knew, even though she was a few generations removed, that the Golden Gate Park itself had been home to several love-ins. She giggled at the thought that she was running over ground where couples her parents' age had tumbled in orgiastic pleasure almost thirty years ago.

She paced herself slowly as she ran by one of her favorite spots near the Redwood Memorial Grove, just past her one-mile mark. Out of the corner of her eye she noticed a young man with a video camera leaning against a tree. She pretended nonchalance, but she glanced over again, his boyish good looks registering favorably. Her hormones were raging these days ever since she'd stopped sleeping with her ex-boyfriend, and she decided she would definitely double back this way on the second half of her run. She stole another look and this time was pleased to see the guy had lowered his camera and was definitely smiling at her. Jennifer picked up steam and leaned into the wind as she felt the familiar and delicious rush of endorphins. Mr. Video would just have to wait until she circled the park.

◆

Dr. Helen Hudson lay tangled in her sheets, a sheen of perspiration glistening in the half-light of her curtained room as she tossed in her nightmare. It was the same dream she'd had a hundred times in the last year. Choking, white tiles, and terror. Floating in a sea of blood. Abruptly, she bolted awake, breathing fast and shallow, grabbing at the sheets.

"Andy . . . Andy?" She yelled as best she could, her throat still dry and ragged from the difficult night. She leaned over and switched on the halogen lamp by the bed. She crawled out of bed and began a search from room to room of the upstairs area, turning on lights in every room, flipping on television sets all over, most of them set to C-SPAN.

"Andy?" Again the plaintive cry. She looked down at her study from the upstairs balcony. Hung behind where she stood was a large painting, almost her height, of the haunting black-and-white image of a boy in Victorian garb. He stared sadly beyond her as she searched below.

The lower story of the loft was ringed by a balcony that circled the breadth of the apartment. Poles of robin's egg blue stretched up from downstairs to support the upper story. From her vantage point above, near her bedroom, Helen could look down on her study and living-room area. The design gave the impression of infinite space. There were almost no walls in the entire loft, except for the bedroom and bathrooms. In the central areas, divisions between the living room and adjoining areas were provided by screens. From where she stood, Helen could see over a delicate gray metallic mesh screen that separated the dining area from a den.

She moved around the circular balcony and looked down at her study, a sophisticated office setup with three computer terminals, one down, and two up with screen savers on. On the center terminal brightly colored tropical fish floated in an animated sea, and the screen on the right shimmered with a shifting set of colored fractal patterns. Mandelbrot sets. The desk was cluttered with books, phones, and lamps between every terminal. Set up beside the large crescent-shaped office table were a printer and fax machines. The office equipment, desk, and rolling chair sat on a circle of deep plush plum-colored carpet. Three massive bookshelves rose behind the computer station in a circle. They were over eight feet tall, custom designed of pale oak in a rounded pattern. Loaded with books, notebooks and files, they doubled as a barrier between the office setup and the kitchen and the rest of the lower loft. She stared for a moment. No Andy. She was alone.

Helen wandered from room to room, murmuring to herself as anxiety flooded her system. She absentmindedly snapped a red rubber band around her wrist. As she snapped she recited as if it were a mantra, "George Washington, John Adams, Thomas Jefferson, James Madison . . ." This was her wakeup ritual, a makeshift method to clear away the detritus of bad dreams and refocus what was left of her mind.

Scattered throughout the apartment, aside from the ubiquitous television sets were other high-tech paraphernalia, including a police scanner. All the gadgetry and technology were rigged to provide an artificial sense of accompaniment. They were windows onto the world for someone who never ventured forth.

She made her way into the bathroom, stopped in front of the medicine cabinet. Her skin was pale, the color of glue, her short hair a stringy mess, eyes sunk in dark purple chambers. For a moment she gasped, trapped by her own image in the mirror. "What you looking at?"

She reached into the cabinet, grabbed a bottle of Xanax and spilled a few into her palm. The presidential litany continued, "James Monroe, John Quincy Adams, Andrew Jackson, Martin Van Buren, William Henry Harrison. . . ."

Helen walked to the bar in the living room and poured herself a cognac. She popped the Xanax in her mouth and washed it down with the brandy, her favorite cocktail. She toasted the empty room. Her snifter in hand, she moved back into the office and sat in front of her computer station. On the screen on the far right she typed in a command and up popped the caption, "THE STRESSLINE," a subbulletin board on The WELL, the Bay area-based user group that Helen belonged to on the Internet. She typed in:

"ANYONE AWAKE? NEED TO TALK. SHE DOC."

After a moment another user responded:

"HELLO SHE DOC. PANIC ATTACK?"

Helen's fingers flew across the keyboard.

"NO. NIGHTMARE. YOU HOUSEBOUND?"

"SIX MONTHS. YOU?"

Helen typed:

"THIRTEEN AND COUNTING."

Helen's attention was diverted by her second computer, where a chess game was in progress. On the bottom of the screen, a command flashed from her opponent, who called himself "Czech Mate" on line.

"MAKE A GODDAMN MOVE."

She studied the board for a moment, then grabbed the mouse and made her move. N to f3. Czech Mate responded:

"LOUSY MOVE. LET'S DROP IT. LET'S MEET. LIKE A DATE.

Helen typed back:

"CAN'T DATE. NOT VIABLE MATERIAL. STOP FLIRTING AND MOVE."

Bored, she picked up her brandy and headed for the living room, which was a few short steps up on a raised platform covered in a woven mat, a tatami floor. Helen casually walked through the dark room over to a corner tea table and moved her white Knight to f3. The board duplicated the game she was playing with Czech Mate on the Internet. The pieces were of an exquisitely carved marble that she had lugged back to the States from a trip to Turkey years ago. They sat on a marble and onyx inlaid chess table she had inherited from her father.

The room appeared to be walled on the three sides that did not open out onto the rest of the loft. The left wall was of pale wood paneling that picked up the light straw color of the floor. Reaching halfway up were dark cherry wood cabinets. A mix of abstract and representational sculptures decorated the room, all museum quality. The two couches and soft chairs in the center seating area of the room picked up the burgundy and maroons of the cherry cabinets and of the wine-colored rough silk curtain that stretched the length of the right wall. The cushioning rested in wood frames of polished blond wood, modern in design, but still soft and feminine. The padding was covered in plush velvets and rich damask and silk fabric, with gold- and wine-colored pillows, and some embroidered ones, scattered across the couches. It was almost as if the muted colors and soft luxurious, almost hypnotic quality of the interior were intended to mask the brittle nature of the woman who inhabited it.

The centerpiece of the room and its most striking aspect was the far wall that would appear to face the street. If you walked into the apartment from outside and entered the living room, one would expect to see windows facing onto the bay. Instead, the entire wall was covered in a large abstract mural, a juxtaposition of harlequin patterns, large bold triangles of rust, gold, and gray in muted tones.

Helen picked up a remote lying on a side table and pressed a control. Suddenly, the massive floor-length painting split into five-inch vertical slats of equal width. Light crept between the slats, or wooden blinds, as they separated and turned one hundred and eighty degrees revealing a wall-to-wall picture window the elaborate faux screen had hidden. The room was flooded with brilliant sunlight. Helen stumbled slightly, winced and raised her arm over her eyes like a vampire facing the dawn. Slowly she walked toward the great window of her Fort Mason loft and looked out across the sweeping view from the bay to Marin County in the distance. The postcard vision of the Golden Gate Bridge floated above the bay. She mumble-sang to herself, "On a clear day, I can see forever," and laughed a tight bitter laugh.

On the waterfront, Fort Mason Center was once the site of a Spanish garrison during the mission days of San Francisco in the late 1700s. In the 1930s, it became an army embarkation depot. Over a million servicemen were processed through Fort Mason on their way to World War II and the Korean conflict. In the early seventies, coincident with the post-Vietnam peace fervor, Fort Mason was converted officially to a segment of the Golden Gate National Recreation area. The center had since become a haven for the arts and cultural junkies. There were galleries, museums, theatres, bookstores, coffeehouses, and Greens, a world-famous vegetarian restaurant. Tourists and city dwellers alike, loved to walk the pier for the exceptional view of the bay. The SS *Jeremia O'Brien*, a restored liberty ship, sat by Pier 3. Locals could be seen fishing for crab off the piers.

Dr. Helen Hudson was one of the very few wealthy and privileged enough to buy up space in one of the only refurbished warehouses in which developers were allowed by the rezoning to build residences. The irony was not lost on her that her home sat atop one of the most beautiful, accessible, interesting and entertaining locations in all of

San Francisco. For almost thirteen months, she had not set foot outside her apartment.

The phone rang. She turned and stared at it as it went on ringing. Slowly she walked toward the phone, picked up the receiver, and raised it to her ear.

"Yes?"

The caller spoke and Dr. Helen Hudson clenched her teeth and growled back, "You son of a bitch." She slammed down the phone and screamed, "You filthy son of a bitch" to the empty apartment. Then she crumpled to the floor and wept like a frightened child.

◆

Inspector Mary Jane Monahan moved cautiously down the graffitied corridor of an abandoned tenement building, weapon drawn. Tense, coiled to strike, she gave the appearance of a china doll with the ferocity of a pit bull. Pretty and petite behind thick safety glasses above pearl earrings, her long hair was drawn back into a braid almost the same color as her chocolate brown suit. Behind her was Inspector Ruben Goetz, also armed, following in the shadows. Dark and handsome, in a suit that seemed too pricey for the average cop, Ruben was just as out of place with the decrepit surroundings.

M.J. stopped at an intersecting hallway. Grasping her weapon with both hands held in front of her, she spun off the wall and swept the other corridor. It was empty. Ruben crossed behind her and flattened himself against the wall on the other side. They were both silent, immobile. The soft waves of their breath echoed against the condemned walls. Suddenly, a figure jumped out of an open doorway down the corridor past Ruben. Instantly, he dropped into shooter's stance and squeezed off nine rounds from his semiautomatic. The smoke cleared, and M.J. whipped off her glasses and looked at Ruben, disgusted. She walked toward Ruben's assailant, a life-size cutout of particle board mounted on a spring-loaded armature.

They were on a training range complex, inside a dummied-up building. Even though M.J. looked younger than twenty-eight-year-old Ruben, it was evident by her manner that she was his superior in age, rank, and experience. Ruben realized death at the hands of his imaginary opponent might be preferable to the tongue-lashing he was about to receive.

"The good news is you're still alive," M.J. sputtered at him as she slammed the shattered particle board in his direction.

"You see a downside in that I take it."

"This is kinda remedial stuff, Ruben. Didn't anyone at the academy teach you to shoot surgically?"

Ruben tried to shut her up, "Whoa, whoa, whoa. Let's review the scenario we're working with here."

"You shredded him."

"What can I say, I'm an intuitive cop . . ."

". . . With poor impulse control." M.J. wouldn't

let him off the hook. "Let's assume you didn't shoot a seventy-five-year-old man who couldn't hear the warning 'cause he's deaf. Let's say you greased the guy while he was trying to surrender."

"He jumped out at me."

She ignored him and continued, "Now you're on administrative leave, pending an inquiry. Your friends are wondering if you really are a psychopath. And the guy's junkie wife's hired a lawyer who slams a wrongful death action up your tail."

"All right, Smart Alice. Show me what ya got."

Another figure suddenly popped out of the corridor behind M.J. It was a man holding a hostage at gunpoint. With the fluid grace of a killer ballerina, she whipped around and put three rounds neatly into the gunman's shoulder.

"Hit the brachial nerve, he drops the weapon, you read him his Mirandas. Plus, you haven't taken a human life, so your karma's still okay."

M.J. had kept it light because today she felt this was the right way to deal with Ruben. But at the back of her mind she had a true story for him—for another day, a shooter's tale that forged her own philosophy about guns in an indelible way. The memory knelt in her consciousness like a child at communion every time she held a gun.

M.J. had roomed with Beryl Ann Mills, another young female rookie who had come through the academy with her. They called her Bam. She was six feet tall, skinny, and black, and hard as the concrete Oakland basketball courts where her brothers taught her the rules of survival. M.J. and

Bam had fought like hell together twelve years ago for half the respect the men in their class had earned simply because they had a different set of reproductive equipment. Bam was a sharpshooter, too, and proud as hell of the extra hours she had put in on the range. At home she would squeeze spring weights in every spare moment, at the breakfast table, on the toilet, bouncing the metal tool from hand to hand till they trembled from the strain. She was M.J.'s inspiration and her only real competition on the shooting range.

After they graduated from the academy, the two rookies were assigned to veteran cops as training partners. M.J. tagged a Chinatown detail and Bam was sent down to the Fillmore district, an area nasty with street crime. They had bet dinner at the Hayes Street Grill on who would make detective first.

Then the thing happened that every cop fears in their darkest dreams. Bam and her partner, Rudy Tejada, were walking through an alley on the way to check out a domestic disturbance, when out of the shadows stepped a figure with a gun trained on Rudy's back. Bam yelled for the assailant to drop, but the gun remained level. She shot to kill and a nine-year-old boy, the age of her youngest brother, fell from the shadows. His small frame had been magnified, a trick of the light and time of day. He held a bright orange plastic toy gun in his right hand.

After the internal investigation, Beryl Ann Mills was fully exonerated, but she swallowed the

weight of community outrage over a careless rookie's tragic mistake. The press had dogged her for
the six weeks she was on forced leave, and Bam
could not shake the guilt. M.J. and her friends and
family begged her not to give up, but she took a
flyer on the force and went to work for the post
office. She stayed in touch with M.J. for a while,
but every inch of M.J.'s success was a reminder of
her shame and eventually the two women stopped
seeing each other.

After the little boy was killed, M.J. trained like a
madwoman to shoot not-to-kill. Her father and
both her uncles had been neighborhood cops of
the old school, a tradition born of their Irish–
American roots. Since she was a little girl her
father had instilled in her a religious belief that
cops were supposed to save lives and that even a
criminal deserved to live until the courts could see
that justice was done. M.J. knew the absurdity of
this in light of the fact that she had seen the
ugliest of killers go free time after time from legal
loopholes. Nevertheless, she swore to herself that
she would never kill if she didn't have to and she
was bound and determined to shape Ruben in her
image, even if he was the lousiest shot she'd ever
worked with.

The cell phone on Ruben's belt bleeped and
M.J. cocked her head and stared at him while he
ignored it. He asked, "Are you hungry? 'Cause
I'm starved."

"Aren't you gonna answer that?"

"I'm sure it's nothing important."

"I'm sure she thinks it is."

"How about Moroccan? You like couscous?"

"Don't you want to know which one it is?"

He gave in and pulled the phone off his belt and answered nonchalantly, "Y'ello . . . Hey, heeeyyy. Is this mental telepathy or what? I was just gonna call you."

M.J. rolled her eyes.

While Ruben still looked to M.J. to tutor him on the ins and outs of homicide detection, he was cocksure of his sensuality and his attraction to the opposite sex. ". . . Oh, just the usual. Long days making sure justice prevails."

Another target popped up and M.J. blasted three fast rounds into it. Ruben shot her a dirty look.

"Listen, can I buzz you back? I'm kinda in the middle of something . . . No, I promise."

He hung up and M.J. stared at him while she reloaded a new clip.

"You know, I'm thinking, that you're thinking, that maybe I'm some kind of a . . ."

"Rake," she interrupted.

"Rake?"

"Rake, romeo, clam-digger, beaver boy, horn-dog, letch . . ."

M.J.'s pager beeped and she looked down.

"It's showtime."

"Saved by the beeper," Ruben chirped and jogged to catch up with her on the way to their unmarked blue Chevy.

◆

They made it to Potrero Hill in 3.6 minutes. The inside of Ruben's right hand was a reddish blue from holding tight to the car door. M.J. drove like Indy competition regardless of the import of their mission. She had Martha and the Vandellas turned up full blast and they sat in the car and listened to the end of the song, observing the movement outside the apartment building. The crime scene was taped off with the familiar yellow ribbon and SFPD stickers and personnel were swarming the area. The coroner's van and police cars clogged the street. M.J. spotted a television newsvan, with KXBU lettered on the side. She frowned as she saw Susan Schiffer emerge from the van, crisp in her navy blue suit and cream-colored ascot, her auburn hair sprayed to resist the bay wind. She had a mirror in one hand and microphone and cherry red lipstick in the other. Within spitting distance was her cameraman, also perfectly coifed. Hence, the moniker every cop knew him as—the Haircut. M.J. nudged Ruben in their direction. "Oh, Christ, the Mouth is here."

"Y'know, you have the technology to end this woman's career. Take out her brachial nerve and she won't be able to lift her arm high enough to put on all that makeup."

"It's a thought."

They got out of the car and braced themselves for the inevitable as they walked toward the tape. Susan made a beeline for M.J. and M.J. immediately started speaking over her as she moved quickly for the apartment door; she'd heard this routine a dozen times.

"Can you confirm the reports we're hearing that this latest murder fits the same pattern as the other two?"

"I can't confirm anything, Susan. We just got here."

Susan dogged her as she went in. "In your opinion, is there a serial killer stalking the streets of San Francisco?"

"As I said, we just got here and I'm not prepared to issue a statement at this time."

M.J. and Ruben made their escape into the building. "Is that idiot trying to scare the daylights out of everybody?"

They passed a plainclothes cop wearing a red plastic tag and unpacking camera equipment. M.J. stopped and leaned over to him.

"Hey, Bernie, grab me some overalls on the crowd will you? Nice clear faces."

Bernie kept unpacking, obviously annoyed. "Why don't I just ask everyone to say cheese?"

Ruben grabbed M.J.'s arm to slow her down. "Jesus, Quinn's here."

Homicide Chief Quinn stood at the top of the stairs conferring with a uniform. He was a big man, six feet plus a few inches and lanky, somewhere near fifty years old. His hair was still black and chopped short, it lay flat against his huge skull and he had a distinctively bushy black mustache. His brow was perpetually furrowed but he had a certain relaxed style about him that was misleading. He was ornery and pissed off most of the time, to be expected in a job where a small percentage of success was to be celebrated and it was rare that you pleased anyone. He no longer pretended to be giving up cigarettes and one dangled in his hand now as he huddled with the cop.

Ruben and M.J. mounted the steps toward Quinn and he turned his attention to them. "Land-lady found her. Front door was open. Tenant didn't answer the doorbell. The lady got worried, went in, saw the body. Used the phone to call 911, otherwise says she didn't touch nothing."

"Robbery?" M.J. asked, knowing in her gut that would be better news that what she was about to discover. Her cop instincts were warning her that she was about to find number three in a serial chain. She hated like hell to make Susan Schiffer right.

Quinn responded, "No sign of forced entry. Nothing else was disturbed. It's all yours, kid. I'll take care of the Mouth and the Haircut."

He headed down the stairs and Ruben and M.J. went in. At the door, a red-tagged Crime Scene Investigator handed them clear plastic gloves. They pulled them on.

The apartment was small, clean, and neat. The victim didn't have a lot of money, but she took pride in what she had. This was more than likely her first place on her own out of college, her first apartment without roommates. Ikea and Pier One furniture and nicknacks dominated with an occa-sional hand-me-down antique that didn't fit with the white-and-black modern veneer stuff. She had common framed store-bought prints hanging—not in bad taste, but nothing classic. There was a tall white bookshelf against the wall, half filled with self-help, the rest bestseller light reading. Up over in one corner, perpendicular to the outside wall, in a black frame hung a bright crimson heart silk screen print set against a black background. That's where your eye traveled from anywhere in the room. Ruben stared up at the heart.

A middle-aged woman stood nearby, gazing vacantly out the window, her face streaked with dried tears. M.J. approached a young uniformed cop with very blond hair, standing awkwardly near the door. She gestured to the woman.

"That the landlady?"

He nodded.

"Who was first on the scene?"

The young cop turned to Ruben and answered, "I was."

"Hello! Over here!" She looked at his badge for his name. "Johnson . . . what's the first bit?"

"Mike."

"You touch anything, Mike? Pick up anything? Open any doors? I don't want to get all excited about a good bunch of latents and find they're yours."

"No, I didn't." There was an odd, almost imperceptible inflection in his answer. M.J.'s radar went up.

"Ruben, want to get her statement?" Ruben walked toward the landlady and gently eased her down on the couch. What he lacked on the shooting range, he made up for in bedside manner.

M.J. walked into the kitchen and scanned it top to bottom, building a picture of the dead woman's life in her mind. The dishes were clean, stacked up on the drain board. There was a hodgepodge of pots and pans hanging on the wall. *You couldn't afford gourmet tools but you cooked for yourself, probably pastas and salads, unless you had somebody special over—then it would be chicken.* Beside the drain was a tea kettle, turned over on its side, almost upside down. *Did you have someone special over? Were you making him tea? Did he grab you here from behind as you moved the kettle to this counter?*

M.J. left the kitchen, pointed herself at the bathroom, swallowed and went in. In the beige and white tiled room, Jennifer Lyle lay in the bathtub, naked and bruised without her cheery jogging suit. She was draped in the tub, posed with her right leg over the side. A dying flower arrangement sat in a vase on the side of the tub. Behind her were some gift bottles of bath salts, oils, some bubble bath, shampoo, and several candlesticks holding melted wax stubs. The candles had been left to burn down to nothing. *Did he light the candles for you?* One of those expensive Danish mesh sponges sat beside the dead flowers. *You liked to pamper yourself—you knew how pretty you were. This was an important room for you, wasn't it?*

Bending over Jennifer's body was Frank Able, the coroner, a black man wearing the familiar red tag on his chest that signified he belonged to a murder scene. He had lain a soft white woven blanket, folded over the edge of the tub against the girl's leg, a shield between his body and hers as he had to lean into her to finish his business. As M.J. squeezed into the crowded room, he withdrew what looked like a large meat thermometer from Jennifer's side.

M.J. broke the silence, "So, Frank, got an estimate?"

"Eight hours. Give or take."

"I'm seeing ligature marks on the neck, petechial hemorrhaging in the eyes. Strangled, huh?"

"Same as the other two," Frank answered sparing no one in the room. Another serial killer had staked his claim in San Francisco. These were the kind of murderers that taunted legions of law enforcement officials with their invisibility from beat cops to FBI honchos. Men who murdered deliberately, intelligently, absent of humanity. By some trick of fate and birth, an evil pathology settled in their hearts. And the majority of them were here in America the beautiful, and San Francisco, named for the peaceful St. Francis of Assisi, had more than its share.

In the background, the phone rang. The atmosphere in the room tensed. A CSI carried it into the bathroom and M.J. picked it up with a tissue someone handed her as one of the technicians blurted, "She can't come to the phone. She's in the tub."

Nobody laughed. M.J. shot back, "You oughta fire whoever writes your material, man."

She said "Hello" into the phone. Everyone in the tiny room could hear the other end as the voice bounced off the tiled walls.

"Gina Martinez here. How are you this morning?"

"Can I ask what this call is regarding?"

"Would you like a new color TV absolutely free? All you have to do is visit Sunburst Time Share for no oblig . . ."

M.J. hung up.

Frank Able looked up at her. "All right if I move her?"

M.J. nodded, "Yea, be nice to her." She took a last look at Jennifer Lyle's body and choked back the impulse to cross herself. *There but for the grace of God go I.* She left the bathroom and headed for the blond rookie she'd spoken to earlier. He looked worried now.

"Mike, were you the first one here?"

"Yeah."

"Did you touch anything?"

"No."

"What's wrong, Mike? Something bothering you?"

"Nope,"

"If you're holding out on me, I'll get it out of you one way or another. You know I will."

He stared up at the red heart on the wall for a moment and looked back at her.

"There was some kind of stocking round her neck when I found her . . . I don't know what happened to it."

"Who else was in there before the CSIs showed up?"

"Lieutenant Quinn."

She seemed relieved and patted him on the shoulder.

"Well that's all right then, Mike. Thanks."

◆

M.J. burst into Chief Quinn's office waving her fist. The television news was on, tuned to KXBU and M.J. talked over the Mouth again.

"You mind telling me why you removed evidence from . . ."

"Shh. I wanna hear this."

M.J. leaned against the desk, hugged her anger in and watched Susan Schiffer live from the crime scene she just left.

"Tie-dye and peace signs were the order of the day in Golden Gate Park as the Festival of Love got under way commemorating the city's countercultural past. But all was not peace and love in Potrero Hill where homicide detectives discovered another grisly murder today . . ."

M.J. interrupted, pounding her fist on the desk, "You messed with the evidence."

He ignored her and kept listening.

". . . Police would not comment, but informed sources in the department say the latest death could be the work of the same killer responsible for the deaths of two other women . . ."

Quinn snapped off the television and reached

for his lit Pall Mall in the ashtray. M.J. stubbed it out before he got there.

Quinn dug in. "Somebody around here can't keep their big fat yap shut and I want to know who it is."

"What did you do with the stocking?"

"Look, I tagged the damned stocking. I just don't want some blabbermouth leaking the MO to her . . ." He pointed to the television. ". . . so she can spread it all over the airwaves, leaving us no cards to play."

M.J. came around the back of the desk and leaned on the short shelf wall behind him, up against the bowling trophies and the case files piled up against the frosted glass.

"Am I in charge of this thing or not?"

"What are you so damn prickly about all of a sudden?"

"Then I ought to be deciding what evidence to sequester . . . sir."

M.J. was wearing him down. "Detective, is there evidence you think should be sequestered in this case?"

"The stocking around the neck."

"Jesus, you're a pushy broad.

M.J. smiled. "I'll take that as a compliment, sir."

"You didn't say serial killer and I didn't say serial killer, right?"

"Right."

And Quinn relighted his broken cigarette.

2

Helen

Helen opened the door of her apartment. In the massive hallway outside, the San Francisco *Chronicle* lay a little over seven feet from her front door. Helen stretched her foot forward toward the paper, but it was still far out of reach. She began to inch her way into the hall. Her breathing intensified, growing rapid, shallow. As she slid down the pale yellow wall flattening the palms of her hands for support, the hallway appeared to elongate; the walls took on an exaggerated perspective. The newspaper seemed a distant, unreachable object. She snapped the rubber band on her wrist and dropped down on her knees and crawled across the floor that seemed to roll in waves underneath her. She grew dizzy and swallowed, her mouth dry. Pearls of sweat burst and matted her hair. Then almost hyperventilating, she gave up and crawled back into the apartment and shut the door. She sat in the foyer on the floor in her long burgundy bathrobe, her knees scrunched up to her chin, and attempted to catch her breath. A four-foot obelisk sculpture of yellow-and-black enamel stood sentinel next to her.

Helen pulled herself up and marched resolutely into the kitchen and came back with a broom. She opened the door again and stretched herself out, reaching forward with the broom handle in her trembling right hand. The business end of the broom brushed back and fourth against the paper until finally, she caught her simple prize and dragged it toward her. Helen grabbed the paper and rushed back to the safe haven of the apartment. Inside the door, she fumbled it open and looked down at the front-page headline: POLICE BAFFLED IN DEATH OF THIRD WOMAN. She leaned back against the door and sputtered in anger, "Idiots!"

◆

In the great noisy squad room of homicide division, every nutcase and confession addict in San Francisco was vying for attention. Aside from the excess humanity, the room was cluttered with detectives' desks, each of them crammed with telephones, lamps, files and whatever assorted photographs, inscribed mugs, windup toys and curios each cop kept to make their little piece of office feel like home. One whole side of the squad room faced the street and old-fashioned venetian blinds hung from the big windows. There was a water cooler in the corner and an old-fashioned gum machine that worked, except when the occasional penny got stuck. A few droopy plants managed to survive despite over or underwatering, depending on who remembered that they existed. One hearty ficus had finally bit the dust after consuming too many coffee dregs, a blatant case of plant murder. Tall gray filing cabinets jammed up against any available space and somebody had stuck a broken parking meter in a corner. Someone else had hung a dart board, but everybody who played kept their darts locked up in their desk along with their guns so that the usual riffraff would be short one less sharp pointy object that might cause unnecessary damage.

Detective Ray "Nikko" Nicoletti, sat center stage acting cool and laconic, the maestro of interrogation. Forty, with a mischievous half smile, he was an attractive mix of old-school cop and contemporary macho. He was questioning Harvey, a recurring ritual Nicoletti indulged to relieve the boredom. Across from them sat a man wearing a colander with inverted plastic cups glued around it. The colander man waited patiently for his turn at bat.

". . . You followed the girl home and then what?"

"I killed her."

"Where did you kill her?"

"In the bathtub."

"Why'd you do that?"

"Because she was dirty. Because she was a very dirty dirty girl."

"So you remember how many times you stabbed her, Harve?"

"Er . . . Eighty-seven?"

Nicoletti stood. "Get the fuck outta here, Harvey. I got work to do."

"The blood of the innocents is on these hands . . ."

"Either you scram, or I'm gonna make you stand in the corner again." Harvey backed out the door sheepishly as M.J. arrived at the next desk with an armload of files.

Nicoletti wondered aloud as to why he got all the weirdos. "Was it something I did in another life?"

"Probably something you did in this life." M.J.'s eyes never left the files as she spoke. Ruben walked up. He was wearing a forty-dollar silk tie with a bold grape cluster against a white background. Nicoletti stared as Ruben briefed M.J.

"Mercer's gone through all her receipts, medical, dental, legal, dry cleaning. Nothing in common with the other two victims."

Nicoletti flipped Ruben's tie between his fingers. "What's that round your neck, Rube?"

"I'd get one like yours, Nikko. Sadly, I don't live near a K Mart."

M.J. ignored the exchange between the two men.

"How about friends, acquaintances?"

"Zip-ola. The only thing these girls had in common . . . They all owned vibrators."

"That's not a lead. It's an implement of survival."

Ruben stuck his tongue out at M.J. and headed off. Nicoletti moved closer to M.J. "He's so mature."

"You should talk."

"How can he show up at work wearing something like that?"

"Would you lay offa him."

"Hey, cops are supposed to look like cops."

"Yeah, yeah, yeah. What's the world coming to?"

A few desks back, Detective Pachulski was on the phone. He covered the mouthpiece and called out to M.J. "It's Deep Throat again. Makes three calls today, fourteen total." Patch was plump and still married to his high school sweetheart, a victory for any cop—a miracle for a homicide man. In his midthirties with a slight receding hairline, he had an impish face to match his trickster demeanor.

"Phone company set up on our centrex yet?" M.J. queried.

"This morning."

"Let's put a tracer on her ass." She waited a beat and picked up the phone. "Homicide. Inspector Monahan speaking."

Pachulski whispered to her, "Ask her about the moonbike."

M.J. nodded and continued, "I'm really interested in your ideas. The moonbike. What is that?"

Dr. Helen Hudson sat on the other end of the line mortified that this idiot policewoman was playing her for a chump.

"Moonbike? What are you, some kind of . . . 'Lunar cycle.' I said 'lunar cycle'! I thought he might be on a lunar cycle because the first two were twenty-eight days apart . . . You want to make jokes about moonbikes?"

M.J. glared at Pachulski who grinned like the Cheshire cat. "No, ma'am. This is no joke. And neither is tying up police lines with crank calls when people . . ."

"Are you calling me a crank?"

"Do you have any evidence to report, ma'am? Do you know any of the victims?"

"I think this is number three."

"That is an opinion not evidence, ma'am. May I ask who I'm speaking with?"

Helen hung up.

Gigi, a baby-faced uniformed police clerk, came up to M.J. with a slip of paper. M.J. read it and slapped the note in front of Pachulski who was still laughing at his little joke. He read the paper and looked at M.J. innocently. "Who's Helen Hudson?"

"Who's Helen Hudson? Probably one of the top three forensic psychologists in the country and one of the few spot-on experts on serial killers around."

Nicolleti leaned into the conversation. "She's out of commission, M.J. Daryll Lee fucked her head up pretty bad. She's a drunk and she screwed up the trial. Besides, she got a cop killed. . . ."

All of a sudden Pachulski had an epiphany.

"She was the one when Daryll Lee Cullum got bagged?"

M.J. patted him on the head. "Thanks a lot, Patch. You can get on your moonbike and ride over to the morgue now. I want those autopsy results."

M.J. strode out of the squad room and headed for the library. She had research pull all the videos of the Cullum trial, as well as press clippings and whatever biographical material they had on Helen Hudson. M.J.'s fingers drummed a hardcover edition of Helen's book, *Our Sons, Our Killers: Profiles of the American Serial Killer*: she would take that home to skim later. Beside it was a copy of Helen's curriculum vitae. It recounted her undergraduate work at Columbia and her graduate research at Berkeley, the Ph.D. awarded there and subsequent professorship. For the last fifteen years, Helen Hudson had published numerous articles and four books, including her Ph.D. thesis and this last book, the first to achieve recognition outside the academic and professional community. There was a two-year stint where she was affiliated with the FBI's prestigious Behavioral Science Unit in Quantico. During the trial of Andrei Chikatilo, the Russian convicted of the sex murders of fifty-two women and children, she was flown in as a special expert witness. She had lectured around the world, and before the Daryll Lee Cullum incident she had been in Australia to supplement studies of the recent emergence of serial killers there. She had consulted on every major mass murderer or lust killer's trial in the last ten years. M.J. noted

that during her entire professional history up until
two years ago, she kept returning to Berkeley
to teach.

M.J. turned to the press clippings. Helen
Hudson had stirred up some controversy a few
years back over her stance against capital punishment. There was also a sidebar about her during
Joel Rifkin's trial; she had been pushing hard for a
special Federal Corrections Institute to be created
specificially to house felons charged with serial
rape and killing, or mass murder. Then there were
several pieces on the Daryll Lee Cullum trial. Dr.
Hudson had worked closely with Cullum for several months before the trial; M.J. got the sense that
there had been an almost obsessive preoccupation
with him from some of the more sensational articles that covered the Berkeley incident where Cullum was finally recaptured.

M.J. sat for an hour fast forwarding through the
last few days of the trial. She stopped when she
found what she wanted: Dr. Helen Hudson on the
witness stand. M.J. was impressed; she'd been
in court before with consultants and professional
expert witnesses and had watched them crumble
under the badgering of ruthless defense attorneys.
Consistently, Dr. Hudson was formidable and intense; she held her own, a striking woman with
an obviously brilliant mind. A defense attorney
questioned her:

"In your evaluation, you characterized the de-
fendant as a sexual sadist because he satisfied four
of the ten criteria in the DSM-IIIR. Is that correct?"

"Yes."

"Four out of ten. Forty percent. When I was in school, that was an F, Ms. Hudson . . ."

M.J. mumbled, "You bastard" to the television set. She knew he dropped Hudson's degree title in an attempt to diminish her testimony.

"Isn't it more accurate to say Darryl Lee Cullum has failed the test that would have classified him as a sadist?"

"DSM-IIIR is only one of the factors we look at in evaluating a subject . . ."

M.J. fast forwarded to the middle of another speech of Helen's.

". . . individuals suffering from aural hallucinations hear voices in both ears. Mr. Cullum reported that the voices he heard always spoke to him in his left ear."

Again, M.J. zoomed through to the next segment.

". . . was not driven by mad impulse. It was my conclusion that Mr. Cullum meets the M'Naughten rules for sanity. And at the time of the murders he was aware his actions were morally wrong and unlawful."

Chief Quinn walked into the library holding a manila envelope. M.J. muted the VCR.

"Lab results, hot off the press. No sperm."

"Surprise, surprise. So we've definitely got a serial . . ."

"You didn't say it. . . . Who's that? That the broad who got the cop killed?"

"I thought she might be useful."

"The woman's a wrong number! Work the clues, for Chrissakes."

M.J. noticed someone else in the library listening to their conversation. She stood up and gestured Quinn to move out into the corridor.

"Sir, what clues? We got no clues! Nobody in this department has ever worked a serial case and I need someone who . . ."

"Whoa, whoa. *I* did." Quinn towered over her.

"The Zodiac, right?"

"Yeah."

"They ever catch the Zodiac, sir? Or did he die of old age."

Quinn started to grind his jaw. Gigi approached them.

"Lieutenant, Commissioner on two. About the Chinatown thing?" M.J.'s insides were churning. Handing her those lab results was a gofer's job; Pachulski could have easily pawned them off on Gigi. Quinn wanted to get to her alone so that he could increase the pressure on her not to reveal the true nature of these crimes, which meant he was getting dumped on from above. Obviously, the city powers-that-be were desperate for this Festival of Love thing to go off without a hitch . . . even if it meant that more women would die. Now here was another roadblock. For some reason, Quinn wanted her to steer clear of Helen Hudson. M.J. needed to know why and she filed this one away to digest later. She prayed that it was just a superficial cop's prejudice.

Quinn had the last word on his way back to his office: "Work the clues."

M.J. turned back to the monitor in time to see the camera pan from Helen Hudson to Darryl Lee Cullum. He pantomimed a knife across his throat and grinned pleasantly.

◆

Of all the metropolises in America, the City by the Bay is perhaps the most dramatic in its beauty and certainly as colorful in its history as any. Perched atop a mass of hills, some points overlook the splendor of the Pacific coast and others the blue breadth of the bay itself. Hovering above the waters to the north is the infamous Golden Gate Bridge glowing in International Orange connecting the city to the green hills of wealthy Marin.

San Francisco has been one of the tourist meccas of this century. Thousands are drawn monthly to the exquisite restaurants, top-flight opera and museums, the charm of streetcars, the exotic pull of Chinatown, the literary history of the North Beach cafes, and the exceptional parks from Golden Gate to the Presidio. Haight-Ashbury with its funky Victorians was the birthplace of hippie-dom. The Paris of the West inspired writers from Mark Twain to Dashiell Hammett and it has been home to the notorious from Charlie Manson and Jim Jones to the fictional Dirty Harry. San Francisco has been a cultural and physical paradise for a hundred and fifty years.

It has also been a magnet for death and destruction.

On the morning of April 18, 1906, the earth shook the City of 400,000 by the Bay to the tune of an estimated 8.25 on the Richter scale. Several vital sections of the city were destroyed and many died, including Fire Chief Dennis Sullivan. Firestorms soon raged throughout the wooden city devastating its wealth and beauty, killing hundreds and creating a huge refugee population.

Almost immediately after the fires subsided, hearty and determined San Franciscans rebuilt their city from the ground up. Thus would begin a pattern of devastation and gutsy renewal that would repeat itself again and again as the century progressed. If the gods are warning San Franciscans, their messages have gone unheeded. Call it loyalty, love, or stupidity, the city's inhabitants have refused to desert it come hell or high water. And they have had both.

On November 28, 1978, an unhappy and unbalanced former city supervisor assassinated Mayor George Moscone and Harvey Milk, the city's first openly gay supervisor, galvanizing the homosexual population of the city. This event may be some kind of symbolic watershed in the city's contemporary history. Because from that point on, a series of plagues of almost biblical proportion have attacked the city like locusts and have drained its appeal to tourists in the extreme.

In the early eighties, torrential rains flooded northern California causing massive mudslides, destroying homes and lives. In mid-1985, wildfires swept through the local mountains, burning thousands of acres. In 1991, thousands in the hills of Oakland were forced from their homes by fire. The circle dance of heavy rains and devastating fires has continued yearly to erode the suburban hills either by fire or mudslide.

Simultaneously, from the early eighties to the present, the large gay population of the city has been decimated by the monster HIV virus. For several years, widespread public fear of the mysterious disease reduced the tourist and restaurant trade substantially, and major hotels were offering cut rates to stay afloat.

Then, at 5:04 P.M. on October 17, 1989, in the middle of a historic World Series head-to-head battle between cross-bay competitors, the San Francisco Giants and the Oakland Athletics, the infamous San Andreas fault shifted. The initial fifteen-second quake carved a hundred-mile stretch of disaster unequaled in California history for over eighty years. Buildings shattered and burned. A fifty-foot piece of the San Francisco–Oakland Bay Bridge crashed to the deck below. A mile-long upper piece of the double decker Nimitz Freeway snapped and shattered, crushing cars and passengers below. Adjacent to Helen Hudson's Fort Mason loft, a large expanse of the Marina District built on top of a filled-in portion of the Bay imploded. Buildings were shaken off their foundations; fires raged. At least sixty-five people died in the San Francisco area as a result of the

Loma Prieta quake. Over three thousand were
injured. Damage estimates were in the billions.

Over the next few years, San Francisco rebuilt
again. The waterfront was reborn. New civic projects like the magnificent Yerba Buena Gardens
and the Presidio National Park were completed.
Despite the inconvenience of a few inoperable freeway exits, the city was cooking again. Tourists had
overcome their fear of AIDS and earthquakes and
were pouring in.

The city had yet to exploit its role in the sixties
in a big way, other than routine tours through the
Haight. Local entrepreneurs and city supervisors
had watched the profits reaped by Woodstock II
and exploiters of the sixties' and seventies' nostalgia in vogue. For two years they planned, organized, and advertised the Festival of Love as the
first major reunion on the West Coast of the great
rock groups and some of the living icons of the
era. If all went well, it would be bigger than Woodstock '94.

The last thing anyone needed now was a serial
killer.

◆

Dr. Helen Hudson sat in her den watching television, absently picking at the nap on the chair. She
was out of her nightclothes, but still looking like a
rumpled hausfrau in a bulky yellow sweater and
baggy sweats. At the rhythmic rap of a comically
elaborate knock on her door, she bounced up.

"Finally! Where have you been?"

Balancing a bulky bag of groceries, Andy Friedman, a solid, pleasant-faced man of forty-two walked into the room. He was her assistant and probably her only remaining friend who could stand her presence for more than twenty minutes, even if his companionship was paid. Andy was as nonneurotic as any gay man could be navigating the waters of middle age and urban life on a minimal income. Working for a medicated diva with a Ph.D. and an acute anxiety disorder was a moderate challenge to him. Andy Friedman was a self-proclaimed recovering codependent, and he found the occasional opportunity to have the upper hand with Helen both therapeutic and amusing.

He headed for the kitchen. "It's seventy degrees out, the UV index is eight, wind's out of the east at five miles an hour and smells like chocolate from Ghirardelli Square."

She followed him into the kitchen. It was as meticulously equipped in high-tech fashion as her office. Tall, sleek blond wood cabinets stretched around the room. There were two sinks on the side counters beside the dishwasher; expensive Caphalon, copper, and cast-iron pots and pans hung from hooks in a device that descended from the ceiling. The counter surfaces were gray marble and in the center of the room, sat a five-by six-foot counter area, also marbled with another sink built into it. There was a microwave, a grill, and regular oven and stove top. State-of-the-art Braun electric coffeemakers and grinders competed for attention with an elegant little espresso machine of polished chrome and black enamel. Most of the room was spotless because Helen Hudson hadn't cooked more than a grilled cheese with Brie on rosemary bread for a year. There were empty food wrappers and crumpled aluminum foil on the counter beside the massive, gunmetal refrigerator. An open gourmet peanut butter jar sat beside some pricey English marmalade and a half-eaten sandwich.

Andy began putting the groceries away and throwing out the bits of trash. "Someone broke the antenna off your car. So I had no music all the way to the store and back. You really shouldn't leave the car out there. Particularly since you never drive."

"I'm not paying for a garage."

He began throwing all the rotten food out of the fridge. "My dear, with what you spend on pâté alone you could garage the *Queen Mary*."

"I got another call."

He ignored her and sniffed a new Camembert. "Mmm, lovely! Shall I just toss it right now?"

"This time he spoke to me."

"What'd he say?"

"You and me . . . you and me . . ."

"I hope you corrected his grammar and told him it was you and I."

"Andy, would you call again? Please."

"Please don't make me call that prison."

"Andy, if a three-year-old tells you there's a monster under the bed, you look. I'm three years old. Call the prison. Please."

He could not resist the pain and fear that shadowed her face and he put his arms around her. Helen let him hold her. Andy crinkled his nose in mock disgust.

"I know, I'm a mess . . ."

He fussed with her hair. "No, no. I'm sure the mice are very happy in there."

Helen smiled and buried her face in his soft plaid shirt. The doorbell rang. Instantly, her smile dissolved, replaced by panic. She gripped Andy's arm, white-knuckled and moaned in terror, "Andy . . . Aaandy . . ."

"It's just the doorbell, for God's sakes. We're not going to die!"

Helen folded her arms and rocked slowly. Andy gave her an affectionate pat. "Get a grip. I'll see who it is."

At the front door, Andy found Detective Inspector Mary Jane Monahan and Detective Ruben Goetz. They flashed their shields. Ruben announced, "San Francisco Homicide. I'm Inspector Goetz. This is Inspector Monahan. Is Helen Hudson here?"

"Er, look, I'm sorry, this is not really . . ."

M.J. cut him off, "We'd really appreciate just a couple of minutes of Dr. Hudson's time."

"Well, come on in."

As Andy led them through the foyer and hallway, M.J. and Ruben surveyed the elegant loft apartment, the high ceilings and floors of polished wood. They passed the obelisk sculpture by the door and another large black abstract sculpture with an African feel. There were a few collectible lithos and photographs, expensively framed and some small etchings on the wall leading into the living room. They walked past an alcove that housed an antique baby grand piano, the wood polished to mirror perfection. Two tall candles sat on the piano in silver holders. The alcove wall was of translucent frosted glass, with three birds etched in a Chinese style surrounded by a black filigree. M.J. noted the soft damask, velvet, and silk furnishings, a subtle contrast with the art, but it worked. No Ikea here. Strictly *Architectural Digest*.

Helen stood in the living room, rigid with anxiety, anticipating the worst. M.J. and Ruben were shocked at her sloppy and deteriorated appearance, but they maintained a poker-faced nonchalance by habit. Andy attempted to make introductions, but Helen interrupted.

"He's escaped again, hasn't he."

M.J. responded, confused. "I'm sorry."

"Look, is he out or isn't he?"

"I'm not following, ma'am. We'd like to talk to you about your phone calls to our office."

"What calls? I didn't make any calls."

Andy knew Helen was probably lying and also intuited that she was verging on a panic attack. He interrupted, "Well, isn't this nice. Would everyone like to sit down? Shall I make coffee?"

Ruben and M.J. sat down. Helen remained standing. "Andy, would you get me my—*stuff*?"

"Joyfully."

Andy headed for the bathroom and M.J. resumed.

"I talked to you this morning, Dr. Hudson. Do you remember?"

"Of course I remember, there's nothing wrong with my memory. You're the one who called me a crank."

"Yes, ma'am."

Helen sat abruptly and clasped her hands tightly and close to her left side in a pale effort to hide their trembling. "You see, I thought Darryl Lee Cullum might have gotten out of prison again and as you might know . . ."

Ruben spoke up, his voice pitched to calm, a trick he had learned in a family of high-strung women; he had been the peacemaker from the time he could speak. "Ma'am, if Darryl Lee had escaped, I promise you you'd be the very first to know."

Helen looked up at his dark eyes and thought they reminded her of a gypsy's eyes, brown like soothing dark whiskey. This man seemed to be pretending to be a cop. And that was the particular quality about Ruben that had moved him up on an urban police force in a decade and a city that had forced them to value sensitivity and humanity in their younger recruits. Ruben Goetz was the token sensitive male detective in SFPD homicide.

"Well, I guess I'm relieved."

"*You* called *us*, Dr. Hudson." M.J. was determined to put this meeting on track.

"Yes, I did. I'm sorry. It won't happen again."

"Would you mind telling us why?"

"Because I don't understand why you people insist on hiding the truth."

"How so?"

"There's a serial killer out there. The public has a right to know. Don't you think?"

"Even if there's a chain of evidence connecting these murders, nothing's been reported in the press. How do you connect them?"

A flash of the old Helen, her formidable power came through. "Oh, I don't know . . . Just twenty years of experience and serial killers on the brain."

Andy walked in with a glass of water and Helen's meds. He handed them off to her and headed back to the kitchen.

M.J. took her shot. "Dr. Hudson, would you work with us on this?"

"You must be joking."

"No."

"Look, perhaps you don't realize. I've not been well. I've retired."

"Is that why you called the station fourteen times? Because you're retired? Hey, why don't I just go downstairs and call on the phone and we can pretend it's not you. Come on, help me out here. I really admire your work and I feel that . . ."

Helen turned to Ruben. "She play this wide-eyed little girl routine often?"

"Sometimes."

"And does it work?"

"Yeah, usually."

"Well, not today." Helen looked squarely at M.J.

"Please spare me the bullshit, Inspector. You don't admire me, you don't even like me. None of you people do. But the beautiful part of it is—I don't give a fuck. That's the upside of having a break-down. Now I really do have a lot to do . . ."

During this speech, M.J. emptied the contents of her attaché case on the coffee table. Helen recoiled as photographs of the victims spilled hel-ter-skelter in front of her, a jigsaw puzzle of purple and blue flesh, breasts, limbs, and faces frozen in anguish.

M.J.'s voice was hard and flat. "Well, ma'am, it's a hell of an apartment you got here. I guess the books you wrote about these scumbags must have paid pretty good. Now we can't afford to pay you your usual kind of fee . . ."

Helen leaned over and frantically attempted to push the photographs back into the folders. "No. Please. I don't want those here!"

"But if you'd be so kind as to look at these pictures . . ."

Helen stood; she was shaking with panic and fear. "Look, I don't want this. Could you please go?"

"We can look at them downtown if you'd prefer."

Still playing Good Cop, Ruben added, "Yeah, I'll drive, if you'd be more comfortable . . ."

At this suggestion, Helen began to choke and gasp. She called, "Andyyy." Her glass dropped and shattered on the table. Dizzy, she weaved and snapped the rubber band on her wrist, then staggered toward the kitchen. Ruben went to help her.

"What's wrong?"

Helen flailed her arms. "Please . . . just stay away. Aandyyy!"

Andy ran from the kitchen bringing a paper bag. Helen slumped in his arms. He lowered her to the floor and placed the bag over her nose and mouth.

"Okay. Just breathe. I'm here."

As he placed the bag over her nose and mouth, she breathed in and out, inflating and deflating the bag. After a moment, her eyes gently closed. M.J. and Ruben watched, concerned and embarrassed, knowing they had witnessed a humiliating and vulnerable moment. Darryl Lee Cullum had been Dr. Helen Hudson's Waterloo. This was the shameful aftermath.

Now M.J. understood completely why Lieutenant Quinn had warned her off this woman.

M.J. asked, "Should we call the paramedics?"

"No. Just a good old-fashioned panic attack. She hyperventilates till she passes out, then her breathing goes back to normal and she's fine."

"What did we do?" Ruben asked.

"She's agoraphobic."

"She's afraid of spiders, too?"

"She hasn't left the house in over a year. Don't worry, she'll be okay soon. In a half hour, she'll be singing like a lark."

M.J. started to gather up the scattered photographs. "Well, tell her we're sorry to have bothered her."

"Did you want her to look at those? If you really do, leave 'em. I'll make sure they're safe."

M.J. hesitated, then put the bulky manila envelope back down on the coffee table. She pulled out her business card and left it on top of the crime photos. She looked up at Andy, a silent acknowledgment of thanks passed between them. Detectives Mary Jane Monahan and Ruben Goetz left Dr. Helen Hudson's apartment without speaking again.

As they walked toward their car, M.J. was the first to release her frustration. "Damn, fucking waste of time."

"That is one strange ranger."

"Quinn said she was a crackpot. He left out pill-popping, juice-head, hyperventilating, agoraphobic asshole."

"I thought she was kinda sweet."

"Sweet?! Ruben, I swear to God . . ." They got into the car.

High above them, several stories up in the building catty-cornered to the one they just left, a man stood in a shadowed room, his cherished new Canon ES 1000 camcorder with Casio offside monitor attachment trained through a window on the two detectives. The video camera had stereo sound, a 140,000 pixel viewfinder, 5.2 wide-angle lens, a built-in stabilizer, and could shoot on High 8 for two and a half hours before needing the battery changed. After the police drove away, he slowly panned up and over. He waited patiently for darkness to descend on the city. Then he would be able to see directly into Dr. Helen Hudson's apartment.

3

A Hooked Fish

Helen lay asleep on the living-room couch for two hours. During that time, Andy rummaged around the office, doing paperwork, sorting through the clutter, paying the bills. He pulled a manila folder off the desk to refile it and uncovered a pile of old family photos that Helen must have been going through. Andy picked them up and shuffled through them. He realized that nowhere in the apartment did Helen have a single framed photograph of anyone in her family.

Some of the pictures were in color, from the last twenty-five to thirty years, but several were old black and whites dating back to the forties and fifties. Andy recognized Helen's mother, their beauty was so similar. The Ashland family. Her father was tall and handsome, an American aristocrat. Andy thought of those old television shows from his childhood, *Father Knows Best* and *The*

Donna Reed Show. Lucky you, Helen. Then he flipped through a few more pictures. Andy saw that Helen's father had an imperious quality, superior with an edge of cruelty around the mouth. Her mother's eyes looked blank in some shots, sad and defeated in others. Maybe not so lucky.

In the photos from the sixties and early seventies, Helen was seen in various affectionate poses with a beautiful young boy who could have been her twin, only he was at least three or four years younger. The brother. In the later pictures, he appeared gaunt, with long, brown stringy hair that framed his hollow eyes. Eyes that had assumed the mother's sadness. He disappeared from the pictures after '74. There were a few pictures of Helen at Barnard as a gorgeous hippie girl with long hair and legs to match. A couple of pictures from the early Berkeley days with Carter Hudson. Andy recognized the face, it was one of those faces from the sixties that were indelible in his memory.

◆

In 1948, Caroline Harrington was an artist and painter of promising ability. She was also a southern debutante from a society family with a once great name and very little money left. After she was brought out into society, the family waited for her to marry the right young man with both name and money. Caroline had a wild streak that was typical of spoiled tomboys who discovered their beauty overnight. None of the soft rich southern boys who surrounded her could satisfy or tame her, even the ones who had grown up recently after fighting overseas in the war. Her parents succumbed to her yearning for Europe in the hopes she would get the Bohemian out of her system. She was sent to Paris to study painting and remain under the watchful eye of an older cousin who had married a Frenchman and had lived in Paris since the twenties.

Matthew Ashland graduated Harvard summa cum laude in 1941 and went directly to serve in U.S. Army intelligence overseas where he fell in love with Europe. He was rich, extraordinarily handsome, brilliant, a superb athlete and spoke six languages, including two dead ones. He stayed behind to do his graduate work in Cambridge and finished at Oxford on a Rhodes.

On a weekend trip across the channel in the fall of 1950 he met a beautiful young American woman who spoke a seductive Parisian French with a southern twang. She was pregnant before the end of the weekend.

After a hasty Richmond wedding, the Ashlands settled in to their new Park Avenue apartment in Manhattan where Matthew had gotten a teaching fellowship at Columbia. Helen was born six months later.

The untamable Caroline was soon broken by motherhood and marriage to a man she hardly knew. Matthew Ashland revealed himself to be jealous, competitive, autocratic, verbally abusive, and a profound narcissist. Caroline began drinking before little Matt Junior was born.

Matthew, Sr., was soon given tenure in the philosophy department. He drove his children as hard as his students. Helen was given a steady diet of Plato, Descartes, Kant, Hegel, and Kierkegaard before she was twelve. She and Matt, Jr., were expected to engage in dialectics three days a week, after they had finished their regular school homework. Father would march them down to the river or the park. They were each assigned a side to a philosophical argument and were expected to debate until dinnertime. Young Matt took after his mother, he was gentle and artistic with neither the stamina or intellect for the rigors of logic. Helen grew protective of him and sometimes she would slip into his bedroom at night and coach him for the next day; or she would purposely blow her argument or appear unprepared. Matthew, Sr., would torment his son, calling him stupid, an idiot faggot. Helen's compassion for her brother enraged him further. Caroline made several desperate attempts to stop the debates, but they only ended when Matt, Jr., ran away from home at thirteen for four days and lived in Central Park. After he came back, he was sent to boarding school and the family settled into an awkward peace for a few years.

As much as she hated him, Helen took after her father—at least intellectually. And as much as she feared him, she never stopped trying to please him. She loved her mother, but Helen was ashamed of Caroline—her drinking, her weakness. As Helen navigated the waters of her family's sea of troubles, she assumed the role of the fixer and the protector, the one who anticipated everyone's thoughts and needs. She would lie sleepless for hours at night, dissolving the boundaries between herself and the others sleeping near her. She would feel their feelings, dream their dreams. This was the beginning of her life as a psychologist.

She also became a perfectionist. No one, other than her father, would ever be harder on her than she was on herself.

Matthew, Jr., became a drug addict. He was dead before his nineteenth birthday.

As expected, Helen went to Barnard, the women's college of Columbia. Even thought she fought to go to Radcliffe, Matthew Ashland wanted to keep an eye on her as the Vietnam protests escalated. He had become that rarity on the Columbia faculty, an archconservative. The professor had even volunteered to do some consulting for the CIA, but they really weren't interested in an old OSS guy anymore. Instead, he became a weekend addition to one of the most right-wing think tanks in Washington.

His plan to control Helen backfired. Her bitterness toward her father had pushed her to become one of the prominent voices in the campus unrest. She was one of the students who took over the Columbia administration building in one of the most infamous college protests during the war. That night, she made love on the floor of the university president's office to Carter Hudson III, a graduate student and cofounder of SDS. They were arrested together the next day. Matthew Ashland forbid her to come home after that. The day after her brother's funeral, Helen Ashland eloped with Carter Hudson. They left a few days later for Berkeley where Helen would begin graduate work in psychology and Carter had decided to lend his talents full-time to the antiwar movement.

The last few years of the war raged on and Carter was drawn deeper into violent action. He flirted on the outskirts of the Weather Underground and the Black Panthers. He was never at a bombing or a robbery; he had never held a gun, but his name and face floated on the periphery of the most hard-core radical groups. As the war drew to a close, Helen immersed herself in her studies and her thesis work. She had become fascinated by a sexy new area of psychology concerned with criminal pathology. Carter had become increasingly paranoid and despondent, and Helen realized he was doing an enormous amount of drugs. She also knew he was sleeping with every radical groupie on campus. Their phones were tapped and Carter was routinely rousted by the Berkeley police. Their house had become an overnight stopover for radicals on the run. As far as Helen could tell, a lot of them had become ripoff artists, dealers, and gunrunners. The war was only a rationale for their descent into criminality.

Then the war ended. Carter Hudson's glory days were over. He was broke; his academic credentials were shot, and most of his friends had gone underground. His blue-blood family had disowned him.

Helen was close to finishing her doctorate and
had already been offered a teaching position at
Berkeley. The day Nixon resigned Carter took four
hits of windowpane and the police found him
trying to walk across the Bay Bridge. They brought
him home and Helen stared at the stranger she
had lived with for five years. Carter understood
without asking that she wanted him to leave for
good. As she helped him pack his few remaining
possessions in a duffel bag, she couldn't remember
if she had ever really loved him. She gave him all
the money she had and prayed that he would
stay alive.

Carter resurfaced occasionally over the years,
sometimes to ask her for money. She finally got
the paperwork done to divorce him six years after
he left; it took a private detective several months to
track him down to sign. She'd heard that he was
running coke for a while up from South America.
In the eighties, Carter's family had taken him back
and Helen learned that he'd gotten into rehab. He
had remarried six years ago and was teaching at a
little community college in the Midwest. He and
his new wife had two small children.

Helen never remarried. She had several relationships over the years, a few memorable ones. One
torrid liaison with a married professor that made
her feel ashamed of herself. And there was an FBI
guy, James Atwood, who she had surprised herself
by falling deeply in love with while she was down
at Quantico. Helen had broken it off knowing the
relationship would never survive her career. Above

all else, she was obsessed with her work, with getting to the root of the serial killer's sickness. And besides, Helen still had Berkeley and teaching in her blood and her old politics just never jibed with her lover's. James had been her only regret in life. She left Quantico after two years and moved back to California. She was thirty-eight years old then.

There were many days after that when Helen Hudson looked in the mirror and thought she saw Matthew Ashland staring back at her. Those were the days when she began to drink.

◆

Andy walked quietly into the living room to check on Helen and she opened her eyes. He sat on the edge of the couch and stared down at her. She winced through a Xanax-cum-cognac hangover and the embarrassing recollection of her little drama.

"Are they gone? Oh, fuck, fuck, fuck . . . Did I look really stupid?"

"No, no, no. I think you look rather good with a bag over your head."

"Thank you, Florence Nightingale. Oh, fuck. I want to die."

"I wouldn't. He'll be back."

"Who?"

"Don't be coy. You thought he was cute, too. Didn't you? Come on, I know you love those cute brutal types with the eyebrows and handcuffs."

Helen grinned and Andy started to tickle her. "Come on . . . admit . . . admit . . ."

She giggled like a little girl until suddenly, the laughter changed to tears. Andy stopped tickling.

"What? What'd I do?"

"I miss men." Uncontrollable sobs now.

"What am I, chopped liver?"

"You know what I mean. I miss having someone warm and strong to snuggle up to."

"God forbid he snores."

"And I miss sex."

He helped her up to a sitting position and put his arms around her.

"Come on you slut. No young cops for you till you get rid of those mice. Now you can sit here, look at the pictures, and I'll get the coffee."

"I can't, Andy."

"Well, why don't you just die then?" He got up and walked to the kitchen yelling back at her. "They'll find your body amongst the piles of unread papers and unread mail, and they'll say, 'That's the old hermit lady who ate cat food and Camembert. She was a really good shrink once.' "

He walked back in the living room carrying coffee and biscotti. "Here's your coffee and favorite cookies. Make up your mind. Live or die."

The phone rang. Helen stared like a frightened rabbit. Andy picked up the phone.

"Hudson residence . . . Hello . . . Hello? . . . Who is this?"

A few hundred yards away, a man with a camcorder in one hand and cellular phone in the other, severed the connection.

◆

It was 8:45 P.M. in the institutional gray squad room, Homicide Division, San Francisco PD. The dead end of the shift. Hunched over her desk, Inspector Detective Mary Jane Monahan studied photographs of dead women only a few years short of her age. She blew a wisp of bang out of her eye and chewed a fingernail absently. Under her desk, her leg swung up and down. Her long hair brushed the edges of the papers. All this gave her the appearance of an eleven-year-old girl studying for tomorrow's spelling bee. In the shadows, a man who loved her watched over her in silence.

She set aside the victim's photos and concentrated on a shot of the curious onlookers outside Jennifer Lyle's Potrero Hill apartment. M.J. felt a chill as someone moved closer to her in the empty room. Startled, she jerked up out of her chair and almost reached for her gun.

"Hey, hey. It's only me."

"You scared me."

Nicoletti stood by her desk. "Burning the midnight oil?"

"This stuff never gets any easier."

"That's why they pay us the small bucks." He put an envelope in front of her. "Here. Take a look."

She picked it up, opened it, slid the papers out and examined them.

"So you finally did it."

"Yeah. It's all legal. Finished. We just got to figure out who gets custody of the cat."

"How's Patty taking it?"

"Okay. She's okay."

"Well, I'm really pleased for you, Nik." Her voice was flat. She pursed her lips and trained her eyes on the crime scene photographs.

Nicoletti kneeled down and lay his head on her desk for a second. Then he leaned his chin on his hands and looked up at her. "Listen, when you're done here, how 'bout we go to Joe's, grab a steak? Celebrate."

"I don't think so. Thanks anyway."

"You got other plans or what? Not that it's any of my business."

"You got that right."

"What then . . .?"

"Look. We go out—one thing leads to another 'cause it always does, and we're back where we started."

"So? What're you telling me here? You . . ."

Nicoletti is interrupted by the arrival of Ruben, carrying several boxes of take-out. Ruben appeared oblivious to the intimate party he had just crashed.

"Bean, curd. Smoked eel shushi. Prawn tempura. Seaweed salad . . . You joining us, Nikko?"

"You kiss your mother after you eat that stuff?"

"No, but I'll kiss you if you like."

"Go fuck yourself, Rube."

Nicoletti tapped M.J.'s desk angrily a few times with his knuckles, grabbed his divorce papers, and stalked out.

"Who put the bug up his ass?"

"I guess he doesn't like sushi. Where's my cheeseburger?"

"I made an executive decision. Japanese. Better for your heart."

"You didn't even get me french fries? Ruben, you're really pissing me off."

M.J. watched as he deftly flipped a shrimp up out of the box with his chopsticks and popped it in his mouth.

"If you handled a gun as well as you do those chopsticks, I wouldn't worry about your ass so much."

Ruben answered by spearing another shrimp and sticking it in her mouth.

"Any word from Helen-put-a-bag-over-my-head-Hudson?"

"Not yet. But there will be."

"No way."

"Five bucks we hear from her tonight."

"Deal." Ruben patted his pocket and feigned surprise. "Now what is a Quarter Pounder with cheese doing in my pocket?"

◆

It was 8:50 P.M. Helen was alone in her study. On the desk facing her to the left of her terminals and in touching distance from the phone was an abstract bronze casting of a woman with arms reaching up to the heavens. The body had the rough unfinished look of fingers pressed into clay, molded, but not smoothed. The artist had taken the impression directly from the rough mold. There was an earthly gutsiness about the piece, a spirit of optimism, redemption perhaps. Helen felt she was wedded to it as soon as she'd seen it. As she looked at the generous body, she realized there were many reasons she kept it in front of her in the one spot in her apartment where she spent the most time. She reached out as if she were going to touch it, then she pulled back short. Unworthy. That was the word that washed up on the shores of her mind day in and day out. She looked again and pulled an ounce of courage from the bronze lady and walked into the living room.

Helen sat in front of the coffee table and stared at the bulky manila envelope, a thin membrane shielding her from a world she had eluded for thirteen months. Her reading glasses hung in the neck of her sweater. She slipped them on, took a deep breath, downed a gulp of cognac, and opened the files. Grisly photographs of the crime scenes fanned across the table. She studied each picture carefully, refilling her glass every few minutes. After an hour of this, she dropped the last photo and headed up the stairs, snifter in hand, a bit unsteady.

She stood briefly at an upstairs window and hit a button, closing the electric blinds. On the way to her bedroom, she heard a noise and froze for a second. It could have been the kind of noise all houses and apartments make when you are alone at night. She stopped and called out for Andy. Twice she called his name, but there was no answer. She knew he had left hours ago.

In the bedroom she rummaged through her closet looking for fresh clothes to wear after her shower. Helen felt like staying up tonight to work up some notes on the computer. Something had shifted inside of her today. She would put some decent clothes on for a change, even if it were just for herself. She laid out some black slacks and a crisp white cotton shirt still protected by its plastic dry cleaning bag.

She entered the shower and gave herself over to the steam and hot water, letting it cleanse the grotesque remains of the killer's legacy and burn through the fog of alcohol that had enveloped her.

Out of the shower, she toweled off and headed for the chair where she had left her clothes. She froze in front of the bed. Laid out on her white cotton duvet was her red suit. It had remained out of sight at the back of the closet since the day of her lecture at Berkeley, the day Joe Shields had died, the day of her "ron-des-vous" with Darryl Lee. She hugged herself and tried to make sense of this through the remnants of fatigue, meds, and alcohol. She stumbled back from the bed and looked around the room. Nothing else was disturbed. Did she do this? She couldn't remember. She moved toward the big gray velvet chair that sat in the corner of the bedroom. It was empty. She thought she had put some slacks there.

She sat on the chair and stared at the red jacket
and skirt and rocked back and forth for a few
seconds. She squeezed the arms of the chair for
strength and pulled herself up. She walked out
and downstairs to the living room slowly, forcing
herself to take deep breaths. She picked up the
white business card that was on top of the photographs and walked to the phone and dialed.

"Inspector Monahan, please."

◆

Detective Inspector Mary Jane Monahan drove
down the street toward her bungalow in the perpetually fog-enshrouded Sunset District. Street
lamps glowed through the late-night mist. All the
sleeping houses were painted bright pastels—
white, pink, green, and baby blue—perhaps in
defiance of the sun's refusal to shine on their little
neighborhood. M.J. unlocked the two deadbolts
and the lower lock of her one-bedroom house and
closed the door behind her. She kicked off her
shoes, dumped her suit jacket and briefcase on a
living-room chair, and walked over to some bookshelves that housed her modest stereo system. A
Chieftain's CD was already in place. She turned on
the power and the lilting sound of Irish traditional
music filled the tiny house. M.J. headed for the
kitchen. She opened her refrigerator and flicked
on the overhead light; the refrigerator bulb had
been dead for months. A flat half bottle of Anchor
Steam shared a shelf with a week-old burrito in a
wrapper. On the second shelf, was leftover Chi-

nese. She knew the contents of the produce drawers without looking: one shriveled lettuce head and a potato ready for planting. A homicide cop's refrigerator.

She grabbed the beer, headed for her hand-me-down couch, and plopped her feet up on her coffee table. She had constructed the coffee table herself from a two- by four-foot slab of tinted glass and an ancient lobster trap that the Monahans had inherited from the New England side of the family. M.J. was more than happy with it. The rest of the apartment was sparsely furnished, but comfortable. It wasn't that she didn't have the money, although certainly she would never have the kind of digs Dr. Helen Hudson lived in. She just didn't have the time or inclination. Martha Stewart, she wasn't. She thought of her sister Karen in San Jose, pregnant with her fourth, in her split-level ranch house with her fat husband Harry. Karen was happy as a clam. To M.J. it was like living on Mars.

The only object in the apartment that made her uncomfortable was the big Sony TV with the VCR tucked underneath. Nikko had bought it for them because he couldn't stand her little portable Zenith. They had watched every De Niro movie ever made at least three times. She couldn't bear De Niro now and the television was the only object she had kept that reminded her of her ex-lover. There had been a night where the pain had been so great, she had almost emptied a round into the thing. Only her Irish thrift, something akin to

Catholic guilt, held her back. Nevertheless, she rarely turned it on.

Nikko. What she would give to go one day without seeing him, one day without thinking about him. He had finally gotten his divorce. Too little, too late.

A melancholy Gaelic ballad teased her down deeper into her memories. She would give herself a few more minutes of this particular kind of torture, then she would get back to work.

Several years back, when she was only twenty-six and still bucking to make detective, M.J. had met Nikko for the first time. It wasn't that he was especially good looking or brilliant or anything. And certainly he was married—she had always drawn the line at married men. M.J. had ridden with him briefly when her partner had been laid up for a while. Nikko had been a detective for eight years and he was cop through and through. He just got her. He understood what made her get up in the morning, what drove her through the day, and what darkness she carried into her sleep. Riding around with him for those few weeks, the sexual buzz ricocheted inside the car underneath every piece of conversation, every story, every argument. On top of that was the secret language they shared because police work was in their life's blood. She never forgot it until the day almost four years later when he walked into her little Potrero Hill apartment for coffee and ripped off her skirt in the kitchen before the water had boiled. The pot whistled on and on while she came until the water had evaporated to a thin layer of steam.

M.J. had been dating a varied assortment of losers and good guys since high school. None of the civilians she dated, from the car salesmen to accountants, really understood what she went through on a daily basis. They didn't understand what it felt like to hold a baby while it turned blue and died in your arms. To have to shuttle a homeless family from a filthy gutter into a rickety shelter. To be one of six cops trying to hold down a thrashing man in the insane throes of PCP. To watch a three-year-old die in the streets, the innocent victim of a driveby. To see frightened children huddled in a corner after their parents have shot each other. They didn't understand that most of what she dealt with day in and day out was death and desperation. Every day she crawled under the dark belly of humanity, forced to face each moment without judgment or fear in order to survive. It was only at night that she could let the fear and disgust rise to the surface. That's why so many police marriages failed. They didn't know how to talk about it with their spouses or the spouses just couldn't handle it. That's also why so many police had started to intermarry since women had become more active on the force.

Nobody had ever been able to really get close to M.J., except in the last year there was a guy in the D.A.'s office, Tom Brame, who had fallen hard for her. He was a solid, caring guy with a compatible career and he would do anything to get M.J. to marry him. She was just starting to consider him seriously, to compromise, thinking she would never find anyone who she would really love. Until Nikko came up for coffee that day.

For weeks she felt tremendous guilt over dumping Tom and Nikko's cheating on Patty even though she knew the marriage had been over for a long time. Within three months, Tom had moved to Sacramento so he wouldn't have to see M.J. anymore. As the news of their affair trickled into the department, she worried about the effect on her career. So did her father who was counting the days his weak heart would hold. Secretly, Mick Monahan was pleased. For some odd reason he had never worried about Mary Jane professionally. He had taught her she could be anything she wanted to be, regardless of the fact that she was female. Perhaps it was because he had no sons. Regardless, Mick had always raised her to be a cop knowing from the time she was little, that was what she was meant to be. The thing was he worried that Mary Jane would never find a man who was strong enough for her. And as he was dying, that was one of his greatest concerns.

Ray Nicoletti had come up on the force while Mick was godfathering some of the younger guys. He had always liked Nikko, respected him. He may have been a little rough around the edges, but he was a good cop. He knew M.J. would be in for a tough road getting involved with a senior detective who'd be going through a bitter divorce, but he figured that he and M.J. belonged together.

Mick died the day after Nikko and M.J. moved in together.

She got up from the couch and went over to the chair and grabbed her briefcase. That was enough time spent on Nikko. He had cheated on her just like he'd done to Patty with her. She knew it was in him and could never trust him again. It didn't matter that he still loved her or that she still loved him a little. She thought about Tom Brame for a minute and shook her head. No regrets, just the usual pain.

The Chieftains stopped playing. Silence. She opened the briefcase and pulled out a pile of hard-covers. Gigi had gone to the library for her and brought back everything they had on agoraphobia. M.J. sat on the couch with her beer and skimmed books with titles like *Living with Anxiety*, *The Anxious Self*, *Phobic Syndromes*. "Agora" was from the Greek root meaning "marketplace" or "open space." Fear of the marketplace. As she read on it became clear that the syndrome was one of the worst of the anxiety disorders and was sometimes known as fear of fear itself. Agoraphobics feared their reactions as much as they feared the specific circumstances. The anxiety of knowing they might faint or lose control in public was as frightening as being in public. No wonder Helen Hudson had an attack at the mere suggestion they go down to the station. They avoided any place where escape might be difficult or impossible—crowds, tunnels, bridges, elevators, public transportation. The first attack was usually so humiliating they would never

want to repeat it. Eventually, they would be housebound and lose their ability to function in the
world resulting in complete dependence on a
spouse or caretaker. Hence Andy. M.J. flipped
through the books and noted the frequent mention
of Xanax or alprazolam, a second-generation minor
tranquilizer. *No mention of cognac.*

The interesting thing that struck her was the
unanimous determination that in more than 90
percent of the cases there was no particular causal
event. The first panic attack almost always came
out of the blue. Patients might have a history of
childhood phobias or separation anxiety, but the
syndrome was seldom the result of an acute post-
traumatic situation. *Not too many agoraphobes have
hung from a noose and watched a sadistic murderer get
his rocks off.*

As M.J. read further, other bits and pieces led
her to believe that Helen Hudson didn't fit the
whole bill. She made a mental note to call Jackie
Singleton, a psychologist she talked to occasionally
when she needed a consultation regarding the
various sickos it was her pleasure to do business
with.

Once a while back, she had talked to Jackie
about her own problems. Mary Jane was as stoic
and closemouthed as any Monahan. Her dad always said, "Mary Jane, you never air dirty laundry
outside the family . . . or inside the force." Mick
Monahan would have sooner died than visit a
police shrink and his daughter would do no worse.
Every cop knew that if the department sent you to

the psychologist, every word you said could be reported back to them. None of the confidentiality guaranteed in a civilian therapeutic situation applied here. Supposedly, if a policeman or woman chose to go on their own time, it was completely confidential. But, most of them never revealed anything in those situations that couldn't get back to management if they could help it.

Even when M.J. had first started sleeping with Nicoletti and she was the object of vicious gossip and derision, she kept her turmoil to herself. It was only after she kicked him out, when she ached for him in the night, that she turned to a private psychologist for help. Her trust for Jackie Singleton ran deep, as if they were blood-related.

It was 1:30 P.M. M.J. was exhausted. Her last thoughts as she sank beneath her quilt were of how delicately she would have to handle Helen Hudson. Then a quote from Karl Menninger in one of the books floated through her mind: "It is hard for a free fish to understand what is happening to a hooked one." Then Nikko. Nikko's face dissolved into Ruben's. And after she shut her eyes, a picture of a dead girl in a bathtub, like a strangled mannequin sent her to a fitful sleep.

4

A Festival of Love

M.J., Ruben, and Helen sat in Dr. Hudson's living room. She reclined on the couch shuffling through crime scene photographs, reading them like tarot cards.

As soon as the police investigators had entered the apartment they realized Helen Hudson was in a completely different frame of mind. She had showered and made herself up, her short hair was perfectly styled. Her casual chic outfit, a dramatic cardigan of blue-black velvet flowed over an almost floor-length skirt of the same material. Helen ensconced herself royally on her velvet couch. M.J. stared at Helen and the soft plushness of the clothes and the chair, trying to reconcile the images of the imposing professional from the courtroom videos, the fragile neurotic from yesterday, and the prima donna sitting in front of her today.

Ruben worked closely with Helen; M.J. listened

and observed, silent. The two detectives had decided on this configuration before the meeting. It was evident that Ruben was the better equipped of the two to handle Helen and she had already responded to his natural charm.

Helen worked with four files. She set one aside. "These three are the work of the same man. This one is different. Did you put it in to test me?" She held up a picture of a dead woman sprawled naked on the floor, her body wounded and bruised, her face covered with a bloody towel.

Ruben fumbled, "Well, not exactly. We had reason to believe . . ."

"God, I have to pass tests now! Is this an ongoing case?"

"About six months."

Helen ran it down fast, impatient with the insult and the distraction. "The scene is very disorganized. The guy probably lives nearby. He would have been too disoriented to drive. Look for someone with a history of mental illness, probably on welfare. Look for a lover, family member, or friend. Someone who knew her and cared about her."

This was not what Ruben was expecting. "The guy beat the shit out of her!"

"Yes, but he felt remorse. He covered her afterward because he felt bad about what he'd done . . . Not like this one." She spread the other three folders in front of her, records of the current unsolved murders. She pulled the picture of Jennifer Lyle in the bathtub and held it up in comparison beside the shot of the battered woman with her face covered. "This is a very different kettle of fish. These are highly organized. There was no blood, no prints, no stains. No nothing, right?"

"Right."

"He's very fastidious. Probably barely even broke a sweat. No signs of forced entry so he probably charmed his way in. No rape. These aren't about sex. They're about power. See the multiple thumb marks on the throat. Were the tracheal bones broken?"

"Yes, they were."

"He strangles them face to face so they can see his power. Then he revives them and begins again. For that period of time he feels like God. You're looking for an intelligent, white male, probably aged twenty to thirty, socially functional, with a major interest in American History."

For the first time during this exchange she looked at M.J. "So, did I pass?"

M.J. remained silent and Ruben jumped in. "What exactly did you mean by American History?"

"Where is the stocking that was tied round this one's neck?"

"M.J. leaned forward and spoke finally. "How d'you know about that?"

"Tied in a bow like this—right?" Helen pointed to one of the other folders.

"Yes."

"Oh, for God's sake. It's the Boston Strangler!

He's imitating Albert DeSalvo right down to the fine details."

Ruben grabbed one of the photographs. "Whoa! You're telling us this guy's copycatting a serial killer who's been dead, what . . ."

M.J. bit off the words, "Twenty years."

Ruben continued, up pacing now. "And why DeSalvo? Why not someone who's been in the news recently like Gacy or Ramirez?"

"I don't know. These guys are like viruses. There's always some new mutation."

M.J. was mobilized. She gathered her things and nudged Ruben to do the same. "Thank you for your help, Doctor. Very much appreciate it. Ruben, we'll start by getting the full records, Boston homicide files, autopsies, everything we can dig up on DeSalvo. Doctor, perhaps if we could call you tomorrow . . ."

She stopped dead. Dr. Helen Hudson was grinning, a hint of condescension tagged her smile.

"What?"

"Nothing . . . it's just that you think you can catch him by being intelligent and working hard. You'll take statements and search the files and work the evidence. But you know how he'll get caught? He'll run a red light, or there'll be a bad smell in the basement. It'll be dumb luck—and nothing you or I or any of us did will have counted for anything."

The detectives were at the door. Once again, M.J. had had just about enough of Dr. Hudson.

"Well, ma'am, all I know how to do is get up,

take a shower, go to work and hope if I don't nail
the little shit today, I'll nail him tomorrow and
they'll spell my name right in the papers."

M.J. walked out and left Ruben to deal with the
niceties. Helen had not finished her diatribe.

"Or you know the worst? The killings go on,
month after month. They get more vicious, more
bizarre. Then one day they just stop. Like the
Green River killer. And you wonder what happened? Did he just decide he'd had enough? Did
he get sick and die? Did he have an auto accident?
It's like he walked off the edge of the earth. And
you never know. But, every time there's a body
found you wonder . . . Is he back?"

Ruben stood frozen, pinned to the doorway by
his inbred courtesy. He finally remembered himself and grabbed the door handle. "Well, good
night. And thank you."

"Good luck. You're going to need it."

And she closed the door behind him.

◆

The green grass of Golden Gate Park had disappeared beneath a sea of tents, blankets, and
swarming bodies. There was an eerie counterfeit
resemblance to a bygone era. Kids who weren't
even born until the seventies wandered around
stoned in tie-dye, bell-bottoms, and beads. They
intermingled with folks old enough to be their
parents who were there to catch a glimpse of the
few groups from their salad days performing, and
to sneak a few hits off a joint while the baby-sitter

watched the kids. Grunge and alternative bands shared the stage with fat, balding, middle-aged rockers. Video monitors sat on stands throughout the crowd simultaneously transmitting the action on stage. Deadheads sold bootleg tapes and Ecstasy, maybe even a little old-fashioned blotter. Four pristine columns of blue plastic Porta Potties could be found at each point of the compass. The park was ringed by hefty security guards in navy "Festival of Love" windbreakers with walkie-talkies and cellulars attached to their belts. Kiosks were sprinkled throughout the park selling "Festival of Love" T-shirts, mugs, Frisbees, posters, CDs, etc. An "Alcohol Here Only" area was cordoned off on the south side of the park. There were no antiwar signs. Blatant commercial nostalgia.

It might not be Woodstock, but it was the closest thing to a love-in Randi Salvino had wandered into in her nineteen and half years—worth the price of a blow job on that dickhead dealer friend of Julie's. Randi was happy now, winding her way unsteadily through the blankets, smiling shitfaced after three hits of the ganja Dickhead had shared with her. The munchies had her by the tail and she was taking a shortcut to the pizza vendor in the food stands. As she tripped along, she was getting a lot of lingering looks from some really excellent-looking boys. She was pleased with herself that she'd picked this flowy white Mexican wedding dress with the lacy bottom. It was kind of see-through and of course, she wasn't wearing a bra. A string of clover flowers rested in her hair that she'd made lying around in Julie's yard waiting for her to get dressed, like when she was a kid. Her soft, strawberry blond hair flowed down around her shoulders. She carried her sandals in each hand out of respect for the yuppie picnickers and their blankets. She wandered through Golden Gate Park, a barefoot angel on a confused cloud.

Halfway to pizza, she became aware of a guy trailing her with a video camera. Then he started circling her. She giggled, a bit shy, then he lowered the camera and smiled. He was really cute and his hair kind of fell down in front of his face and he had on wire-rimmed glasses. Randi loved guys with wire rimmed glasses. She mugged a little in front of the camera, then put her hands on her hips, kind of sexy. Remembering she was at the Festival of Love, Randi held up her hand and stuck out her fingers in a peace sign. He gave her the peace sign back and then kept following her. Cool . . . he was doing a whole home movie just on her. Maybe he'd buy her a slice. This was the cheapest fun time she'd had in a while. Now if she could only remember where she was s'posed to meet up with Julie.

◆

"The three most over-rated things in the world are regular exercise, young pussy, and the FBI."

Lieutenant Quinn, Chief of SFPD Homicide held forth to a captive audience as he strode down a corridor toward the conference room with M.J. She groaned, "Oh, maaan . . ."

"What? I talk like a cop. This is how I talk. I got the commissioner up my ass saying we could use a little help."

"We *could* use a little help. We need the ViCAP, we need their database thingies. . . ."

"The FBI bury you with fucking help. With the Patty Hearst thing, some snotnose in a crewcut took over my desk for a month."

"So you're saying . . ."

Quinn cut her off. "Look, you want help? Nikko is nearly done on the Chinatown thing. I'll put Nikko in with you."

M.J. swallowed her fury. She knew that Quinn was signaling that he would put her in her place if she didn't run this investigation the way he wanted, sans the FBI and sans Helen Hudson. There was a killer on the loose and Quinn was worried about saving face. She knew that putting Nikko in meant that she would be second banana, which in essence meant lame duck. It was also Quinn's personal fuck you at her for the five-year relationship he had never approved. Well this was her case and she intended to fight for it.

"That really won't be necessary, sir." She hit the "sir" extra hard and they headed into the conference room.

Seated around the table were Ruben, Pachulski, and Inspectors Kerby, Kostas, and Landis in rolled-up shirtsleeves and loosened ties. M.J. was the only woman in the room. Nikko stood up and put his jacket on while Ruben continued debriefing.

". . . So, I'm checking anyone who lives like

DeSalvo, psychatric hospitals with anyone who has a similar profile, anyone with a German wife, anyone wearing green pants . . ." M.J. and Quinn sat down. "Hey, we just started."

M.J. took over. "Files in from Boston yet?"

Ruben answered, "Fedexed this morning. Be here tomorrow first thing."

Quinn looked at Nikko as he headed for the door. "Hey, where you going?"

"Chinatown."

"Sit in here for a minute, will ya?" This was as offhand and casual as Quinn could manage, but not wasted on anyone in the room. M.J. and Ruben exchanged looks. Nikko eased back into his chair. M.J. picked up the reins again.

"Patch, what's up?"

"Still running phone records." Pachulski wouldn't look at her.

"On this last one?"

"No . . . the ones before."

"For Chrissakes, Patch, you been on this a week."

"I put in for overtime, but nothing doing."

M.J. turned to Quinn, her lips pressed tightly together. He was making her life hell.

"I'm on the hook here, M.J."

"Gonna make a great headline. 'Investigation stalls, budget cuts blamed.' "

He relented. "Whatever you need. Put it together any way you want. Just don't call it a task force, okay? Draws the press like flies to shit."

Nikko stayed quiet. He was still smarting over

M.J.'s rebuff the night before, but in no way would he upstage her. He secretly hoped that Quinn wasn't planning to put him in, but he knew that Quinn was probably dangling him over her to keep her in check.

Ruben gestured to Kerby. "Herb, anything turn up off registered sex offenders?"

"So far on the nights in question all the rapists, child-molesters, weenie-waggers, and toilet-seat lickers were tucked up safe in bed. Only have several hundred cases to go."

"Any recents for animal mutilation?"

Kostas spoke up. "Only case I got is juvenile, so the records are sealed. Gotta go to the court with a name."

Quinn decided to end the formal meeting. "Okay. That it? Thank you lady and gentlemen. Let's do it."

He stood. Chairs scraped. Everyone gathered their files.

Quinn spoke under his breath to M.J. "You getting anything from the Hudson broad?"

"Besides a headache?"

He raised his eyebrows in an "I told you so" and walked out. Nikko glanced over at her, shrugged his shoulders, and headed to China-town. She knew he was trying to tell her that he wasn't behind Quinn's powerplay. *Thank God he still loves me that much.*

◆

At the same time the meeting of San Francisco homocide detectives was breaking up, across the Pacific Ocean on the twenty-fifth floor of a thirty-story Hong Kong high-rise, a nighttime gathering of a brotherhood of a different sort was taking place. A gorup of eight teenagers stood in a ring around their *dai lo*, or big brother. The young gangsters had been recruited the year before as they played in their local video arcades and soccer fields. For the last year, they had been "hanging the blue lantern" or waiting to prove themselves worthy of the initiation that was about to take place. Against the wall of the otherwise bare white room rested a small shrine draped with gold and red silk, home to a statue of an ancient Chinese warlord smothered in smoky incense.

Each of the boys held a stick or two of lit incense. One by one they repeated after their big brother the thirty-six oaths that would guarantee their membership for life in the Wo Hop To, a triad which lived by mystical and fanatical principles of a three-hundred-year-old tradition. The triad was named for the triangle of heaven, earth, and man used as their symbol. Each of the oaths swore the boys to brotherhood, loyalty, revenge, secrecy, etc. After each one, they pledged obedience to the oath on pain of death if they betrayed the pact. "I will be killed by five thunderbolts." When they finished, a pungent cloud of incense shrouded the solemn gathering. Another brother came around the circle and pricked each boy's middle finger and squeezed the blood into a bowl of water. The bowl was passed around the room and they each drank. They were now and forever a Forty-Nine, a triad soldier, until promotion to higher rank . . . or death.

Two of the boys would be on their way to America in a few days. They both spoke English like many well-educated Hong Kong Chinese and one of them had lived in Los Angeles for five years with his wealthy importer father. They had been chosen to enhance the Wo Hop To's ranks in San Francisco.

Since the early eighties, the Triads had increased the percentage of Southeast Asian heroin in America from 5 percent to over 80, perhaps 90 percent. Considered by most American law enforcement experts to be several times more powerful and treacherous than the Mafia, they controlled a worldwide empire of prostitution, heroin export, gambling, money laundering, and the mass smuggling of illegal immigrants.

In 1997, when Hong Kong reverts to the control of the People's Republic of China, the Triads will no longer be nurtured by local politicos. That is why they are systematically infiltrating Chinatowns across America and other Asian enclaves around the world. By 1977, their new power bases will be intact and they will move the heart of their crime operations out of Hong Kong. San Francisco is the linchpin of their American plan.

For several years, the Triads have been pouring illegal Asian immigrants into North America through the same routes they channel their heroin.

The illegals pay them exhorbitant sums of money for this service and then owe them obeisance for life, which usually includes further extortion and dirty favors.

Ironically, it was the extreme and violent oppression against the Chinese by white America that had led them to refuge in the tongs, legitimate protection brotherhoods. Like the Africans who were brought here as slaves, the Chinese were brought here in the 1800s as coolies, or "bitter labor," who did the dirty work in the gold mines and on the railroads. In 1882, Congress passed the Chinese Exclusion Act, which barred further immigration and forbid their becoming citizens. The tongs became powerful lobbyists, protectionists and business entities, and were eventually inextricably linked to the Triads.

A little over a year, back when Nikko and M.J. had finally settled into a good thing, Nikko got a little restless. He watched M.J.'s career take off like a Fourth of July firecracker and he realized that she was a lot more savvy as a leader than he ever would be. He knew he was a good detective and could run an investigation with the best of them. But what Nicoletti craved about the life was the back street work, the occasional undercover, the really sleazy lowdown stuff that used to scare the hell out of his wife Patty when they were together. He would come home in the middle of the night and she would say that she could smell it on him, the stink of lowlife crime. Patty would make him shower before he got in to bed with her, and sometimes she would refuse him altogether because she hated what he was doing. She hated the cop hours and the cop danger and she didn't understand why he just couldn't let it go and get a real job.

That was what had driven him to M.J. It took a cop to understand a cop. What they had was emotional shorthand. M.J. had grown up in a police family and the life was in her genes and her blood. The first time they made love, Nikko felt he had come home for the first time in his life. Something let go inside him, the part of him he had always had to protect Patty from could come out into the light with M.J.

The essential problem was Nikko had never been a domestic kind of guy and that included monogamy in its definition. Even though his life with M.J. could hardly be defined as traditional, he still bucked at anything or anyone that might tie him down. The other glitch was deep down inside Nikko was your basic old-fashioned macho narcissist. He was raised in a blue-collar family—where his longshoreman father's word was God and his mother and sisters served the men with passive devotion. For every minute he put in with M.J. on her career, an inch of jealousy and resentment built quietly inside him. He still loved her more than anyone he'd ever loved in his life, but there was an incurable bastard under his skin that after four years together reared its nasty head.

Nikko had just started easing into Chinatown then. He was looking for a sideline, something to take him out of straight detective work and out of the way of M.J.'s rise through the ranks. He had been hanging out with a couple of cops from Daly City that had solved the murder of Henry Liu, a Chinese writer who had been assassinated by the Triad. The case had made international news because the Taiwanese government had been implicated. The Daly City boys led him through the labyrinthine maze of local Chinese power. On the surface, Chinatown obeyed the laws of the city. Beneath that, the Triads were everywhere.

Nikko started hanging out in the Chinatown nightclubs and restaurants, plenty of them fronts for gambling and mah-jong parlors. He couldn't hide the fact that he was a *low fan*, or white policeman, or "number four" as the Triads referred to him. But what he could do was start gathering a network of informants, sympathetic locals afraid of the growing power of the Hong Kong gangsters and the strangling grip of the drugs and gambling sickness over their community.

He started to close in on a particularly nasty young gang that was funneling heroin into the streets. Quinn and the commissioner were impressed and started to throw some weight behind Nikko as it looked like he was close to a major source of opium traffic.

And then he met Tina Leung. She sat across from him in the Red Bamboo restaurant one night with a girlfriend. They spoke Cantonese together giggling like schoolgirls over their dumplings. She had thick black hair that flashed the light like raven feathers, skin of beige marble, and the face of a Chinese princess. She was nineteen years old. Nikko flirted across the table using the few lame Chinese words he had to get her attention. The girls giggled louder. He pretended not to know what to order and got Tina Leung to help him with the menu. Within a week, he learned that her breasts smelled of jasmine and the soft skin of her stomach tasted like almonds and honey. Her tiny nipples rolled under his tongue like loose pearls and for a short time he forgot who he was.

Nikko rationalized his unfaithfulness to M.J. with the benefits he was getting for the case. Tina was indispensable. She understood Chinatown and how it worked and she spoke Mandarin, as well as Cantonese and perfect English. Soon he had begun to confide in her and seeing that she seemed to be from a good family, he revealed the horrible truths he had learned about the Triad.

What he didn't know was Tina Leung was mistress to Wu Lee, or Little Dog, the local Triad chief.

For some unknown reason, perhaps owing to fate or the mysterious laws of the universe, the gods of luck had decided to shine down on Ray Nicolleti. Two hours before a rendezvous with Tina, he learned from another informant that he was about to be set up. With backup in tow, the date turned into a gun battle and Wu Lee and three of his wounded brothers were arrested. Tina died three days later of her wounds.

When M.J. found out, that was the beginning of the end of their relationship.

Now, over a year later, Nikko had closed in on an illegal immigrant smuggling ring, also Triad controlled. He sat in a dark corner of the Green Dragon, an empty noodle house at midnight. Beside him, leaning in to the shadows was Kwok Tung, a young Forty-Nine who had broken his oath out of fear for his life and anger at the assassination of one of his brothers by Triad order. He was bartering information to Nikko in exchange for witness protection. The two men held their whiskey glasses in a ritual toast, right hand holding the glass, left palm raising it from below.

"You know we are both dead, Number Four, if they find out we're together."

Nikko had worked through three levels of informants and had done intricate negotiation to get this meeting. He smelled paydirt. Kwok ran down the details of what would be a big shipment of humanity in the next two weeks.

At a nearby table, sat a hunchbacked old widow looking shriveled and innocuous. The restaurant owner's mother, Mrs. Ng, had thick salt-and-pepper hair pulled back in a sloppy bun. She sat at the table snapping the ends off of snow pea pods, shoveling the pods in one pile and the useless green strings in another. Her face was expressionless and anyone in the vicinity might assume she was old country and spoke only Chinese.

The meeting ended and Nikko brushed by her table on the way out the back door.

The old woman grabbed Nikko's arm, her grip as hard and sharp as a dragon's talon. "Stay away from here, *low fan*. You do this thing and a ghost of your making will follow you till the end of forever." Nikko jerked his arm away. He wasn't one for fortune cookie superstition. Even still, a cold chill penetrated his skin.

"Thanks alot, Grandma."

She spoke to his back as he walked away, "Chinatown's gonna be bad luck for you, cop."

And he walked out the door into the cool San Francisco mist and pulled the collar of his leather coat jacket up to shield himself from the fear that followed him into the night from the Green Dragon. Perhaps his luck had run out.

Nikko had no idea that Mrs. Ng was Tina Leung's great-aunt. She prayed to the gods that her curse would be enough to take him down.

5

Ruben

Helen sat in her office ringed by her three monitors, all alive. The far right computer was tuned in to the ceaseless flow of chatter on an Internet bulletin board. Her body faced the center terminal, a chess game in progress. Helen made a move, White Bishop to g5, sat back pleased with herself, and waited for her invisible opponent's counterattack.

Andy walked in, dressed in a sport jacket, turtleneck, and cologne. "You winning?"

"Bet your ass."

He is relieved to see her so unusually cheerful. "I'm off then."

"Have fun."

Andy left. Helen looked up and saw that Black had moved his bishop to e7. She made another move. She typed in "I'M CREAMING YOU." Then she turned to the far left terminal and started scrolling through an article from the Forensic Medicine Institute. On the right-hand monitor, the tiny mailbox icon flipped up with a small "ping." She ignored it, engrossed in her reading. She finished the article and slid her chair back on its rollers. She stretched and rolled her neck. The mailbox icon caught her attention. She clicked into her message. The screen read:

"A GAME FOR YOU. PLEASE RUN 'TOMOR-ROW.AVI' FILE ON YOUR PLAYER."

Helen clicked on the AVI player icon that activated her audio-visual software, typed in "TO-MORROW.AVI" and hit enter.

A photographic image filled the screen. It was a shot of Jennifer Lyle in the bathtub. Slowly the image started to morph. Jennifer's arm flipped up in an almost comical fashion. Her face transformed into the smiling face of Randi Salvino. The image danced spasmodically as the body decomposed; the face began to dissolve and suddenly froze on-screen.

Helen looked on paralyzed with horror. She shouted for Andy, but he was long gone. She reached for the phone.

◆

Inspector Detectives Monahan and Goetz stared at the distorted face on the computer screen. Helen sat with her chair and back turned away from them.

"She's next."

"How do you know?" M.J. asked.

"Because I know! I watched her face change to that."

"How did he send this to you?"

Ruben answered, "He's hacked into her Internet address."

"Can we trace it?"

"Not unless he's actually on the line."

"Can we play it back?"

Helen had begun rocking back and forth in her chair. She gestured to the monitor. "At the bottom of the screen there's a rewind icon. Click on that."

"Sure."

M.J. saw a glimmer of salvation for the first time since she'd begun the investigation. "Christ, Ruben. Maybe, just maybe we can save a life here."

"It's too big a file to copy to disk."

Helen reached into a drawer and pulled out small tape. It appeared almost cassette-sized, only thicker and the tape was sandwiched in metal, not plastic. "Back up to tape."

"What?" This was all Greek to M.J.

"She's got a tape backup. We can make a copy and take it with us."

"How do you know about all this stuff?"

"Misspent youth in video arcades." He reached out to Helen for the tape. "Want me to do it?"

Helen handed the tape off to him. Ruben went to work. M.J. looked at Helen.

"Why would he send this to you?"

"Why d'you think?"

"I don't know. Nobody's mentioned your involvement in this."

Hysteria and anger launched Helen out of her chair. "There is no involvement! I am not involved! This is a game they play. They hang around at the scenes watching the cops. He's watching you— and you've led him straight to me!"

"But he didn't write to me, he wrote to you. Why?"

"Because I'm their damn pinup girl, that's why! They all know me. They collect clippings. I'm their muse. I'm their worthy opponent."

Ruben stood up and muttered at the screen. "Hello! . . . What the hell?" The two women stared over his shoulder. A legend appeared on the monitor:

"NOW YOU SEE ME . . ."

A grinning skull metamorphosed atop a pair of clawlike hands. It turned and scuttled away with the sound of derisive laughter and suddenly, the whole picture dissolved, replaced by the words:

"NOW YOU DON'T."

Helen pushed Ruben out of the way and maneuvered the mouse and made a few desperate jabs at the keyboard.

"It's gone! The file's not here. What did you do?"

"I didn't do anything! I just set up to copy to tape, but the damn thing never ran. It just did that. . . ."

"Jesus Christ Ruben, that was hard evidence. How can it be gone?" M.J. was furious with him.

Helen worked feverishly, getting nothing for her efforts but error messages:

"CANNOT FIND. FILE TOMORROW.AVI DOES NOT EXIST."

"It's not Ruben's fault. It's gone. It's not on the C drive, it's not in list. None of the utilities are retrieving it."

"You think he put a virus in there?"

"Has to be."

M.J. was lost. "Would somebody mind . . .?"

Ruben explained, "He wrote a self-destruct virus into the program. You try to copy it, it erases itself." Ruben was impressed in spite of himself. "Gotta hand it to him."

M.J. turned to Helen. "Do you remember what she looked like?"

"She was a girl! She looked like a million other girls. I barely saw her."

"We should get back to the office. Get Mercer into this. There's got to be a way . . ."

Helen reached behind the computer and started pulling plugs out of sockets and connectors.

"What are you doing?"

"I'm not leaving this on. This thing's like a fucking open window. He can get in any time he wants!"

"So he comes in the window. We grab him. This is the only lead . . ."

"Great! So what am I? The lamb tied to the stake here? You don't understand. This is the only space I have in the world. I am not going to let you . . ." The words tumbled out of Helen in a crescendo of fear.

"I'll get a guard over here first thing."

"I'm not having anyone else here!"

Ruben stood up and put his hand on Helen's arm gently, grounding her. His voice was soft and low, weighted with compassion. "Hey, hey. We're on the same team. We'll turn the monitor back on. I'll stay and watch it till we can figure something out, okay?" He looked at M.J. "Go on."

M.J. watched Ruben and Helen together; she understood there was something operating between them that demanded her exclusion, like a child locked out of her parents' bedroom on Sunday morning. For a second, she had that weird tight feeling she used to get when she saw her best junior high girlfriend talking in a hallway to a boy M.J. had a crush on. She shook it off and grabbed her trench coat.

"Catch you later."

M.J. walked out of Helen's building and out to her car. Suddenly, she felt a chill through her body that set her teeth on edge. Someone was watching her. She whipped around to find a video camera in her face. The Mouth had been waiting in ambush with the Haircut in tow. Susan Schiffer shoved a microphone at her. M.J. pulled her keys out and jammed them in the car door, fueled by her anger over the lost computer evidence and intensified by the realization that Susan Schiffer had discovered Helen.

"Detective Monahan, sorry to startle you. Does the fact that you are leaving the home of Dr. Helen Hudson mean you are now treating this as a serial case?"

M.J. unlocked her car and got in. "I have no statement to make at this time. Now, I'm sorry I have . . ."

"Is it true that a task force is currently being set up to investigate these killings? Will you be heading up . . . ?"

"I have no statement to make at this time."

"Look, gimme a break, M.J. We're both girls trying to do a job here."

"I'm sorry, Susan." M.J. slammed her car door in the reporter's face, fired up the engine, and screeched away from the curb.

The Mouth muttered into the exhaust fumes. "Bitch!"

◆

Ruben sat mesmerized in front of the reactivated Internet monitor in Helen's study. The mundane and lonely outpourings of the "chat" rooms scrolled down the screen. There were millions of people out there online who downloaded the contents of their hearts and minds into the infinite reaches of cyberspace. Their anonymous communications floated disembodied like a message in a bottle sent across the sea. A high-tech breed of lonely hearts.

Helen poured herself a cognac and paced behind Ruben. She was thinking about the fact that the killer had taken a picture of Jennifer Lyle in the bathtub—he liked to take pictures. Helen was building a mental picture of the killer in her mind based on every piece of knowledge they had gleaned so far and on her intuitive ability to sense his particular makeup, his particular pathology. Aside from the new fact that they had learned that he was a probably a cyberjunkie, not an unusual avocation for a loner with a vivid interior life, the Copycat liked to record his victims on film, probably before and after death. The photo of Jennifer Lyle was framed almost exactly like the police crime scene shots. The new girl's photograph was taken while she was alive. It could have been a still frame from film or videotape. Helen had a feeling that this guy loved technology: he owned cameras, editing equipment, and computers with sophisticated software, and he was definitely on the Internet. He had taken the time to study a famous killer and was imitating him down to precise details. And the most frightening piece of data was that he knew who she was. He knew how to get to her and he was showing off specifically for her—challenging her, intentionally pulling her into his game.

It was hurting her head to think about all this; she couldn't get clear tonight. She just wanted a last glass of brandy and sleep. Helen leaned down to Ruben and put her hand on the back of the chair as she spoke.

"He's not going to send anything else tonight, is he?"

"I doubt it."

"Want a drink?"

"No, thanks."

"Always on duty, huh?"

"Always."

Helen sat down next to him. "So . . . how about you and M.J. then?"

"How about us?"

"Are you . . .?"

"We're partners."

"Partners in every way?

"Not yet."

"You're pretty sure of yourself, aren't you?" Helen was surprising herself with this line of questioning. She found that she couldn't help her attraction to the young cop. He was intelligent and charming, and she had been cooped up without heterosexual male attention for over a year.

"No, actually I'm shy and selective. The problem for me is . . . Well, I find myself . . ." Ruben looked at her. She was not a twenty-three-year-old secretary from Oroville. He could not play her, nor was he capable of it. ". . . Well, you're in the witness category."

Helen Hudson was exactly the kind of woman he wanted eventually, if not now. The same qualities that drew him to M.J. were there in Helen, the toughness, the acid tongue, the mind that pierced to the heart of the matter, and the aching femininity. They were both beautiful and sexy as hell and untouchable. An old rhyme popped into Ruben's head: "Water, Water, everywhere, but not a drop to drink."

"Well . . . in better times maybe." She kissed him lightly on the cheek and moved closer to the Internet terminal. "Now, what if my hand were just to slip and turn off the computer? Just for tonight. Could that be our secret?"

Ruben gave her the scout's honor sign. The computer flicked off. He gathered his coat and some papers. Helen walked him to the front door and stood in the door frame to say good-bye.

Outside in the hallway he asked, "Sure, you'll be okay?"

She smiled and nodded.

"We'll have someone here in the morning."

"I'm really fine. Really."

He turned and headed off and she watched him go. About ten feet down the hallway, he stopped.

"Hey . . . The number of my cellular, in case you need me." He turned and reached for his wallet and took out his card and stretched it out to her. But, he did not move closer to the door.

Helen didn't budge. A look of mischief played across his handsome features. This was her Rubicon and he knew it.

"Any time. Day or night." He held out the card and stood his ground.

"Another test?"

Ruben, ever the naughty boy, grinned. Helen gathered herself, summoned all her nerve, let go of the door frame, and took a shaky step toward him. Then another and another. Ruben felt the same mixture of pride and elation watching her take those baby steps that a parent does watching their eleven-month-old walk for the first time.

Helen nailed her sights on Ruben's open hand, the small white card like a holy communion wafer beckoned her forward. She kept her breathing steady, easing each foot down over the rippling waves. She reached for the card and took it. She smiled into his eyes and he acknowledged her triumph without speaking. Then Ruben walked away and down the corridor. Helen turned back to the door and realized with horror and rising panic that the door's sure-close device had done its job. The door was of thick, massive gray steel with a long steel pole for a handle extending parallel to the door frame. Helen grabbed the pole and shook it frantically. She was locked out of her apartment. Verging on hysteria, she swung around back to Ruben who now seemed a vast distance away. The hallway narrowed and expanded, a fun-house nightmare in rough yellow plaster.

"Oh, God . . . help me!"

Ruben raced back to her. Helen's breathing became more and more labored. Her eyes rolled back in her head. The mixture of panic and circumstance crossed up her synapses. Flashes of the day in McCluskey Hall assaulted her. *Joe Shields running into the bathroom.* Ruben held her as her body convulsed. *A noose tightened around her neck.* Her hands fluttered up to her neck grabbing and pulling. Ruben got up and kicked the door. It wouldn't give. He moved back to Helen, trying to support her.

"Ruben . . . I can't! Please, I'm falling." Her legs buckled and she fell to the floor in the hallway. *A high-heeled shoe teetered on the edge of a toilet seat.*

"I got you. I'm right here." Ruben held her tight

up against the wall in a kind of frisk position. The effect was awkward but reassuring. Helen's breathing seemed to ease a little. They stayed frozen in this strange tableau for fifteen interminable seconds.

Sometimes in the oddest, or most inappropriate moments, we are snagged by beauty or desire. Ruben stared at the nape of Helen's neck and felt the brief and powerful urge to kiss her.

Instead, he unholstered his gun. "Put your hands over your ears." He took aim and fired at the lock. *Darryl Lee's gun fired and Joe slammed against the wall, spraying blood.* Helen passed out.

Ruben picked her up and carried her into the apartment. He put her down on the couch in the living room. The Xanax bottle was nearby and he gave her a couple and pocketed the bottle. Helen lay there for a moment, pulling herself together.

"Oh, God. My door!"

"Yeah, sorry about that."

She started giggling uncontrollably, the result of the neurobiological interaction of shock, brandy and medication. "You shot off my lock."

"I'll call a locksmith." Ruben rose to go to the phone.

Helen grabbed his arm hard. "Please don't go. I'm afraid."

He pulled a chair up next to the sofa. She lay back, momentarily relieved, consumed by exhaustion.

"You're nice, aren't you? *Niiicce.*" She pronounced the word as if it were a disease.

"Yeah. I suppose I'm just a nice Jewish boy."

"Do you know the root meaning of "nice"? It evolved from the Latin, *nescius* for *ignorant*. Not the best survival tool for a cop, huh?" She was laughing and slurring her words now.

Then Helen put her hands up, held the sides of her head tightly and muttered, "He's in my head . . . I don't want him in my head . . ."

"Who?"

She shook her head from side to side and the tears came for a few moments and then she fell dead asleep.

Ruben sat in the chair next to her with its post-modern European curves and velvet upholstery that he knew he could never afford on his cop's salary. He was stung by what she'd said to him, even though he knew she wouldn't remember it the next day. *Nice*. The funny thing was he thought it did work for him, most of the time. And the thing she hadn't seen yet, that he knew existed at the core of his being, was a piece of him that was tough as nails; it was the thing that authenticated him as a cop—and it was always available when he needed it.

Some people will tell you there are two kinds of cops. There is the traditional Dirty Harry variety who define the word macho, live to carry a gun, get off on the adrenaline, and stuff their feelings as far down as yesterday's garbage. The second kind truly believes that their utmost duty in life is to protect and serve, to watch over the weak and less fortunate, to make it safe for the rest of the world to function. Ruben was the latter kind. All his life he wanted to be a cop. Like M.J., it was in his blood, as unlikely a candidate as he appeared on the surface.

When other kids were trading baseball cards and comic books, Ruben used to go to the library and check out books on Sir Robert Peel, the founder of law enforcement in England in the 1700s and the forerunner of the American police system. He knew when every cop show on television ever made was on, from first episodes of *Starsky and Hutch* to reruns of *Dragnet* and *Adam-12*.

The blood part came from Ruben's dad. Sid Goetz wanted to be a cop from the time he was a little kid running errands in his father's store in downtown San Francisco, Goetz Clothing for Men, up until he defied his pop by secretly enrolling in the police academy. In 1960 that was not a profession that Rose and Joe Goetz would tolerate for their only son and the entire family badgered poor Sid with their shame and fear for four years until he succumbed and left the force. He went back into the family business for the rest of his life like the three generations before him.

But there was a tiny cop light inside of Sid that refused to go out. From 1964 until twenty-five years later, he was a reserve officer in the Richmond Sheriff's Department. He kept a big sheriff's motorcycle in cherry condition in the garage and Ruben would spend his favorite weekend afternoons with his dad polishing up the big bike and testing the lights and siren.

Of course, the same family pressures that came down on Sid twenty-five years earlier descended upon Ruben when he announced during his senior year in high school that he wanted to go into the academy. Grandpa Joe was still the family patriarch and over his dead body would Ruben's destiny be anything other than Goetz Clothing for Men. After two years of local community college, Ruben went to finish his undergraduate degree in economics at the University of California in San Diego. There he met Cheryl Licht, a beautiful, if spoiled-rotten temptress from Beverly Hills and they were engaged by their senior year. The immediate summer after graduation, after a month-long series of terrible dreams and mysterious stomach ailments, Ruben came home with his head shaved in preparation for his first day at San Francisco Police Academy. The lovely Cheryl took a powder. Sid Goetz was secretly pleased as punch. Grandpa Joe died a month into Ruben's training.

Ruben's ancestor, Jacob Goetz, was one of hundreds of German and Bavarian Jews, like the most famous of them, Levi Strauss, who traveled the terrifying sea-and-land journey from Europe to the American West in the mid-1800s. Most of them had come to find their fortune in the great Gold Rush. Nearly penniless, Jake worked the mines for ten years until he finally struck a small vein. In the meantime, he sent enough money and enticing correspondence back home to draw the rest of his brothers and several of his cousins, too. There was even a family legend that had grown out of the exploits of Samuel Goetz, great-great-great-uncle to Ruben, who settled as a lawman in Cripple Creek, Colorado. (He never made it to San Francisco.) Supposedly, Sam cleaned up the little town without shooting his gun once. For those who say 90 percent of all cops have it in their blood, Sid and Ruben probably owed theirs to Uncle Sam.

The Goetz family soon settled in and around San Francisco, and invested their tiny gold fortune into the menswear business. Ironically, once Ruben became a cop, he realized retail was also in his blood and became infamous on the force for his sartorial splendor from the first day he made it to plainclothes.

The six months he was in the academy was the hardest time of his life. From what they called "O Dark 30," or 4:30 A.M. when they started physical training, every teaching sergeant he had tried to break the pretty college boy down. For the first time in his life, Ruben saw what he was made of.

But it wasn't until he got out into the streets that he discovered the piece of him that had been locked inside him waiting. The first week on the job he was backup on an armed robbery, shot at in a hostage situation, and he rescued a four-year-old girl from the father who had been assaulting her. He just did the work without fear completely focused on the immediate. There could be no place for fear in action; fear was your death warrant. The fear had to wait till you got home at night and talked to your wife or girlfriend or best buddy over a beer. Ruben realized that was the thing that made it work for him. He could function above the fear.

And he loved the life with all his heart. When you are a cop, no day is ever alike—it beat working for a living.

Ruben looked down at Helen moving restlessly in her medicated dream state. He peeled off his jacket, loosened his tie, and moved over to the other couch and stretched out. The skin of his face was already shadowed with late-evening stubble. It would be dark and itchy in the morning and he didn't have a clean shirt with him. He figured if all went well he could get to his little apartment in South of Market for a quick shower and change of clothes.

He looked again at Helen and he immediately thought of M.J. The only thing missing in his life now was someone to love, someone to release him at night from the weight of the unspeakable acts of humanity he witnessed by day. There were dozens of women in his life lately who meant nothing, just juggling for practice. Cheryl Licht was a fleeting blip in his consciousness. He had the perfect San Francisco single life—morning cappuccino in the North Beach cafes, foreign films in Japan town, quick dates from the pickup scene at the Marina Safeway on Monday nights, and a great job. But recently, every night he spent alone made him conscious of the empty space in his heart.

Ruben picked up his most recent tie acquisition and looked at the piece of a Chagall painting that decorated the front. It was an image of old country newlyweds dancing through a kiss, the husband floating in midair ecstasy. He ran the tie through his fingertips, turned out the light, and closed his eyes. He remained in a shallow slumber until his cellular phone rang at 6:30 A.M.

6

Peter

—

"Peter? . . . Peeeter!" Georgette Foley sat braced against a stuffed magenta husband wedged between her body and the bed frame. It was a squat device like a big pillow with stubby arms. She allowed it to hug her in a way she had not allowed her flesh-and-blood husband for five years. In her lap, a brown toy terrier with a rat's face framed by a pink velvet ribbon attempted to burrow beneath her robes, an atavistic impulse carried from his ancestors who had been bred to hunt animals that lived beneath the earth. She fondled the little ratdog with a tenderness and intimacy also absent from her relations with her husband. "Where is Daddy now, precious? Has he forgotten all about us?"

Although it was already late evening, Georgette had remained in bed all day despite the glorious northern California weather that had fluctuated between sixty-eight and seventy-four degrees. She lounged in her Laura Ashley flannel nightgown dotted with tiny pink and green roses, further tucked inside a thin, calf-length cotton robe trimmed with lacy ribbon and embroidered above her left breast with a large pink and magenta rose with green leafy filigree. Her bedspread and sheets were another pink floral celebration in polyester cotton. On either side of her, on identical cherry wood bed tables rested pink ceramic lamps with pink canvas shades. The wallpaper echoed the rose motif. Around the room were framed watercolors, needlepoints, and prints—all portraits of flowers. It was as if Georgette existed as a subset of the genus *Rosa*. She had not entered a garden in months. Nevertheless, she had rendered this cheap, cloying imitation where the air sat dead and still. Her garden flourished without natural light and required no nurture. This allowed her to focus all her maternal energies on the ratdog and her remaining attentions on her afternoon saps and paperbacked bodice rippers.

Georgette subsisted on her husband's modest salary, disability and the fruits of her fourth lawsuit in that many years. This suit she had filed for worker's compensation for the extreme stress she had endured at the hands of that ridiculous woman at Foxwood Insurance Company, Inc. Even though Georgette white-lied and stole pens and paper and was often absent or late or on personal calls, she justified all these indiscretions because of her delicate nature. No one understood how sensitive and intelligent she really was, least of all that twenty-eight-year-old Ivy League bimbo with her perfect fingernails. Foxwood had finally settled and Georgette had languished in semiinvalid bliss for sixteen months.

In walked a man who appeared to be much younger than Georgette, maybe twenty-eight or twenty-nine. He wore a white lab coat over a conservative light blue shirt and tie, and dark gray slacks. His straight, light brown hair fell down over his ears and framed his wire-rimmed glasses. He was boyishly attractive in an oddly plain way. A nerdy awkwardness dulled his good looks. There is a quality certain people acquire as they attempt to socialize themselves and adapt to the status quo. Perhaps against their true inner desires, invisibility becomes their dominant feature. Peter was one of the invisible people, and currently in the process of executing an extreme method of overcompensation.

"I've been calling and calling. Didn't you hear me?"

Peter held a glass of water in his hand. He walked to the edge of the bed and sat down. "I'm sorry, my love, I was just . . ."

"You completely forgot about her, didn't you?"

She took the proffered glass and stuck it in the little dog's face.

"She was very thirsty, weren't you, my little sweetie?" Her voice lowered a half octave and lost its icky-sweetness when she addressed her husband. "What are you doing? D'you want to watch Letterman with me?"

"Well, I . . ."

"You know I hate watching talk shows on my own."

"Yes. Well, I . . ."

"Oh go on, get back to your silly computers."

Peter, clearly relieved, started to leave.

"Haven't you forgotten something?"

Peter leaned over her, ignoring the ratdog who yapped at him jealously, and avoided his wife's lips already pursed for a smoochy kiss. He kissed her on her dry forehead. Her skin was colorless like the pale background her two-dimensional roses inhabited. He absently stroked the fringe of over-processed mousy-brown hair back from her forehead. She appeared ancient beyond her thirty-five years, her face pinched and lined without wisdom or warmth to temper the effect.

"Wuv you," she said.

"Love you, too," he answered.

He left the bedroom and headed through their dreary little living room toward the kitchen. Fortunately, Georgette's obsession with froufrou had not spread to the rest of the house; she'd neither the money nor inclination. He unconsciously savored the cheap, dark furniture and drab renter's curtains. He reached the kitchen, which was a mess. She never cleaned up after her canned soups and macaroni and cheese, but he didn't care. A half-empty can of dog food sat on the Formica counter in a pool of toast crumbs. His mood lifted with every inch he put between himself and his wife and her pet. He began to hum to himself as he locked the cellar door off the kitchen behind him. It must have been one of those old sixties songs he'd heard at the festival yesterday.

He walked down the stairs to the basement and headed to the center of his favorite room. Like a child skipping beside a hedge, he ran his hands over the lineup of sleek, gray high-technology equipment and gadgets, camcorders, modems, copiers, VCRs, home-built hard drives and monitors that filled his underground lair. Hard plastic and polished metal. He loved each and every machine. Meticulous research had gone into every acquisition. They were specific, predictable, dependable, efficient, and returned his attentions with equanimity. The Human Factor, a substance Peter Foley had never comprehended or mastered, was pleasingly absent here.

On a small video screen, suspended in freeze frame, Randi Salvino posed, one hand on hip, on extended in a peace sign. On a lab table nearby, cushioned by plain white folded sheets long since abandoned by fussy Georgette, lay the real girl poised on the edge of lifelessness. Makeshift restraints harnessed her to the table. An industrial-strength plastic bag, salvaged from Peter's day job was pulled over her head and secured tightly at her neck by silver duct tape. Another strip of tape held her mouth shut. She was semiconscious, eyes closed, asphyxiating by degrees.

Peter leaned over her and put his left hand

gently on her forehead. In his right he held up an Exacto knife that hovered over her face. Her eyes fluttered open, saw Peter and the knife, and she tensed with horror, struggling in vain with her last remaining strength against the straps that held her.

Directly facing Peter, a bulletin board extended the breadth of the wall. On it was a collage of photographs, some taken with a variety of cameras, others edited from video footage. There were several pictures of each of his three previous victims, including Jennifer Lyle. Some were taken before capture, others during the actual "seduction" and the rest from the aftermath. A second collage was building on the right-hand side of the bulletin board. There were several shots of crime scenes and some featured M.J. and Ruben. In a place of honor were photographs of the interior of Helen's apartment, a few with Helen and Andy in the shot.

Peter lowered his body closer to Randi's so his lower arm rested lightly between her breasts. "No, no, you don't understand." With a single deft stroke, he made a slit through the plastic and the tape across her mouth. Randi gasped and sputtered, hungry for air. "There. Didn't I tell you I'd take care of you?" He stroked her forehead, just as he'd done with Georgette. His white lab coat draped the folds of her white Mexican wedding dress. Like strange angels making love, he cradled her as she breathed, awake again in a mist of terror.

◆

Inspector Mary Jane Monahan stood on a stony windswept hilltop high above the city. The early morning fog still embraced the landscape like a swatch of gray tulle. M.J. stood on cold, barren ground that matched the color of the panorama below. It could have been the day after a nuclear incident.

Behind her the body of Randi Salvino lay facedown, naked except for her white bikini underwear. Beside her, a No Dumping sign jutted against the sky, guarding the dead girl with its irony. Dr. Frank Able was packing up his things. The coroner's men with their yellow body bag stood idle, waiting like grave diggers on a cigarette break. M.J. turned to a uniformed patrolman, the first on the scene.

"You isolated the kids who found her? They claim they didn't touch anything?" Over his shoulder, she could see a small crowd of civilian onlookers huddled at the bottom of the hill. Nicoletti took statements from a ragged group of leftover Festival of Lovers. Ruben arrived nearby in a taxi and made his way up the hillside. Seeing Ruben, Nicoletti broke away.

"Morning." Nicoletti took in Ruben's crumpled suit and unshaved stubble. "Stand too far from your razor?"

"Up all night with a sick friend," Ruben responded, his voice tight with exhaustion. He didn't have the patience for Nikko's razzing today.

He kept walking up toward the lonely figures on the hilltop. Nicoletti grapped his arm.

"Hey, come here, I wanna talk to you."

Ruben pulled his arm away irritated, but he paused for the senior officer to have his say. "What?"

"You got a thing going with M.J.?"

"I don't believe this!" Ruben, astonished by the question, not to mention the timing, turned and headed up the hill.

Nicoletti dogged him; he wouldn't let up. "You stink, man. Where you been last night? You screwing around on her?"

"What's wrong with you?"

Nikko waved his finger at Ruben. "You treat her right, okay? Don't go running around on her. She don't deserve that."

"It's none of your business, Nikko."

"You mess her all up—I'm gonna make it my business."

"Hey, Nikko. Remind me why she gave you the boot, will you?!"

Nicoletti hung back as Ruben approached M.J. Ruben pulled her aside. "What the hell's he doin' here?"

M.J. ignored the question. She also didn't seem to notice Ruben's appearance. She was all business, focused on the dead girl. "So, what do you see?"

Ruben squatted down beside Rnadi's body. M.J. stood over him. Nicoletti hovered in the background. "Well . . . looks like she's been sexually assaulted. No defense wounds. No ligature marks or bruising like the others, but she's very cyanotic. Asphyxiation, maybe? This ain't our guy."

"Look at her heels."

Ruben's eyes wandered down to the dead girl's feet. "No bleeding. You think maybe she was dragged up here postmortem?"

"Maybe. On this stuff," she gestured to the rock terrain, "we're not gonna find tracks." The acrid scent of expelled wastes from some nearby factor rode a blast of bay wind. Or perhaps it was only the lingering vapors from the coroners ministrations. M.J. resisted the urge to breathe deep; the poisonous air was a perfect punishment for her inadequacies. *I failed another one. I let her die.*

She leaned over Ruben, still on his haunches, and pulled a hair off his shoulder.

"Long night?"

'Don't *you* start."

M.J. shifted back to business. "What about her arms?"

Ruben, momentarily thrown by the sudden change of subject, recovered. "Needle marks . . . But she doesn't look like a user."

Nicoletti came up behind them. "Probably so stoned she didn't know what hit her, eh, Rube?"

M.J. cut in, her voice clipped. "I hope so."

"All these little hippie-dippies. All wanting to be happy. All wanting to make love. Your type, hey, Rubie?"

Ruben slammed into Nicoletti. The older cop pushed back harder on reflex, and Ruben almost went sprawling on the stony hillside. M.J. put herself between them, her arms blocking. She was furious. "What the hell you think you're doing? You want to be on the six o'clock news?"

And indeed down below them, Susan Schiffer and the Haircut had set up shop and were interviewing Festival of Lovers.

M.J. turned to her ex-lover. "Nicoletti, you want to finish taking their statements? Now!"

Nikko gave Ruben one last hard look and headed down the hill.

"Let's get out of here." She turned and started down a few beats behind Nikko. "Goddammit, Ruben."

"Look, I'm sorry, okay?"

"I ought to put you on report."

"I'm sorry. I can't stand that bastard."

As they attempted to move quickly past the group at the foot of the hill, the Mouth cornered them.

"What's all this about the Boston Strangler, M.J.?"

"I'm sorry, Susan, you're on the wrong side of the tape. We're looking for evidence here. We'll be making a formal statement later."

"Inspector, will you confirm that someone is copycatting the Boston Strangler and this is his fourth victim?"

"We're going to review all the evidence very carefully before making any statement."

M.J. and Ruben headed for their car. Susan

handed her mike off to the Haircut and ran for her car.

In the car, M.J. drove in stony silence. Ruben looked at her, hangdog. In her rearview mirror, M.J. caught Susan's car pulling toward them. She barked at Ruben, "Put the light up will you?"

"What for?"

"Just do it, okay? I don't want the Mouth tailing us to Helen Hudson's."

"We're going to Dr. Hudson's?"

"I am."

The police emergency light flashed on top of the blue Chevy. M.J. began to ease the pedal to the floor. Susan accelerated behind them, staying on their tail.

Ruben looked at M.J. confused. "What am I . . .?"

"You're gonna lean on the labs for a really fast prelim on the sperm."

"Is this a trust thing? Because if it is there's one thing you need to know."

"No, there's one thing *you* need to know. You never, never, never, never, *ever* mess with somebody inside the case."

"Excuse me? Excuse me?! What do you . . ."

"You damn well better start working on that impulse control. A woman who is implicated in this case?"

"She might be a source, she's not a suspect."

"Someone who's practically a piece of evidence? It's page one, man. Page one."

"It's page one to try and comfort a witness who's scared shitless?! Who's . . ."

"Oh, you comforted her, did you?"

"Damn right I did."

"Well I'm sure you made her very comfortable."

M.J.'s anger was pushing her hard and she poured her adrenalin into her driving. Susan Schiffer's crew was keeping up behind her.

"Look, I swear, nothing hap . . ."

"Don't try to lie to me, Ruben. You don't have the face for it."

"You're jealous! I can't believe it. My dreams come true."

"Jealous of you? Rube, you are your own biggest fan. The woman's unstable. You could wind up with a harassment charge. Anything. You're like some horny little teenager."

"I can't believe this. Nikko thinks I'm in the sack with you. You think I'm screwing Helen, and I haven't been laid in weeks."

"Put your seat belt on, for Christ's sake."

Ruben buckled up. "And what the hell is Nikko doing? He's acting like he owns you."

"Nikko is my business. You stay out of it."

"You're never gonna get a social life with him acting like . . ."

"Like what?"

"Like some . . . bull moose in heat."

In spite of herself, M.J. smiled. "What the hell do you care if I have a social life? We're talking about your social life, okay? Leave mine alone."

M.J. took another screeching two-wheel corner.

Ruben hung on for dear life. In the rearview mirror, she watched Susan lose control of her car as she tried to follow. M.J. grinned triumphantly.

"Anybody who's ever watched TV knows about that corner."

◆

Helen was in her bathroom. Her hands trembled as she shook the contents of a bottle of pills into the palm of her hand. She replaced two and swallowed the remaining four. The doorbell rang.

"Andy, where in the hell are you?" she called out knowing the question was rhetorical. Andy was out.

She opened the door to M.J. who took in Helen's disheveled appearance.

"I know you found another one. Was it the Dancing Girl?"

"How d'you know? Ruben told you? Oh, man."

"No, I heard it on the scanner."

"Can I come in. I need . . ."

Helen let her in. "Yeah, they want you to call the office cause your radio's down."

"Lady, you are some piece of work."

Helen followed M.J. into her study. Desperate for company, she chatted obliviously. "I turn my damn scanner off and then I turn it on again. I can't listen to it, but I can't not listen to it either. So I make Andy listen to it. Only he's not here so . . ."

"Are you on medication? Because I need your whole brain on duty."

"I'm not on duty. Nor is my brain."

M.J. dialed her office and caught Helen up at the same time. "Everything's different. It's a different guy. She was asphyxiated, not strangled, dumped outdoors, sexually assaulted . . ."

"So nothing like DeSalvo's."

"Completely different." She spoke into the phone now, "Monahan, messages please."

"So why are you here?"

"Because I think I'm wrong. There's something artificial about it. Like it was posed. Why drag a body all the way up a hill where it's going to be found by tourists at first light?"

"Do you think he's changed his routine? That doesn't happen."

M.J. is forced to ignore Helen for a moment; someone has picked up her line. "Hello . . . Yes . . . No . . . Monahan."

Helen continued. "These men are robotic. The murder is like a ritual. The method itself is part of the pleasure."

M.J. noticed the Internet terminal was dark. Beside it, the monitor that Helen played chess on was alive, a variety of nature scenes dissolved into each other on the screensaver. "Why is that computer turned off?"

"I turned it off."

"You can't do that."

"I believe I can. Would you like me to turn it back on?"

"Yes." Then into the phone, "Okay, thank you."

Helen sat in front of the down terminal and with

the care of someone handling a rattlesnake, she booted up. M.J. dialed another number.

"Hello. Ruben . . ." She listened and nodded.

Helen looked up when she heard the mention of Ruben's name. "Please thank Inspector Goetz for taking care of me last night."

M.J.'s jaw tightened and she delivered the message straight-faced. "Ruben, Dr. Hudson wants me to thank you for taking care of her last night." She hung up.

"Lab report on the new one. There were two kinds of sperm." M.J. frowned and narrowed her eyebrows. Something still didn't sit right. "So— well—it looks like a gang thing. Thanks for the use of the phone."

She started to leave, but Helen had come alert. "Two kinds of sperm? They said one was a secretor and the other wasn't, right?" Helen swung over to the terminal on the far left and started typing fast and purposefully, only pausing for her system to catch up with needed data.

"How did you know that?"

"There were needle marks? On her left arm?" M.J. was frightened at Helen's uncanny knowledge of the facts.

"So far nothing they test for comes up positive."

"Was the body found near a 'no dumping' sign?"

"Yes."

"Like this?" Helen turned the monitor so the detective could see better. She leaned over Helen's shoulder. M.J.'s body shuddered as a grainy image materialized on the screen: a dead girl spread-eagled facedown in an empty field. The sign beside her read NO DUMPING.

"I could have taken that picture, this morning."

"He's switched from DeSalvo to Bianchi and Buono, the Hillside Stranglers. Two guys, so two kinds of sperm. His idea of a joke!"

"But you said they're robots. That's not consistent with . . ."

"Consistency is the hobglobin of small minds. Tell them to test for the chemicals found in Windex. That's a product for cleaning win . . ."

"I know Windex, for God's sake, I clean my own windows."

"It's what Bianchi and Buono injected into one of their victims."

"Why Bianchi and Buono? Why in such detail?"

"He's a perfectionist. And he's getting bored. He needs to up the stakes . . ."

"Last night, for just a while, I thought I had a chance to save a life. Find the sequence, crack the code, save a life. Now, all I know is that I don't know a damn thing."

Helen stayed glued to the monitor, her fingers still flying over the keyboard. "I wish I could give you some better news, Inspector. But he's very smart. He likes his work and he's going to do it again."

She swiveled around to look at M.J., but she was gone. Helen shrugged, then reached over and severed her link to the Internet.

7

Daryll Lee

———

". . . in an apparent attempt to reenact murders committed in the 1960s by Albert DeSalvo, the infamous Boston Strangler. In response to growing public alarm, informed sources report that a special task force is being set up inside the police department to direct the manhunt for . . ."

Peter Foley lifted the remote at his elbow and disconnected the power to the nineteen-inch color television he had jerry-rigged a few feet up and to the right of his terminal. This was the 6:00 P.M. KXBU evening news, and he had heard all that was necessary. He smiled at Susan Schiffer's image as it imploded. A few moments were required to consider whether the present rate at which the media were absorbing the facts and reporting them to the public were appropriate to the overall vision of his work. They were at least one step, one "killer," behind in their comprehension of his process. This, of course, gave him no indication as to whether the inspector, Ms. Monahan, and her posse of subliterates were further along in their investigation. He reasoned that they had caught up with the concept of the switch, the metamorphosis as it were, from one exterminator model to the next. This had nothing to do with having extraordinary detection ability or even God on their side, and certainly from all appearances they had not the gumption as yet, to call in the FBI Behavioral Sciences Unit. However, Ms. Monahan had somehow found Helen and touché for that discovery. In all likelihood, Helen was in synchrony with him now. Without her, he would be Van Cliburn or Itzhak Perlman without an audience. He knew there was one woman who understood his music. And now he wished only to play for her.

He patted his copy of *Our Sons, Our Killers: Profiles of the American Serial Killer*, which he kept by his side whenever he was in the planning or creative stages of his work. Helen was his touchstone, her book was his primer, his Bible as it were. He wanted to get it all right for her. And the beauty part was, he could put in his own little twists and trademarks, just skew things a slight bit. Then she would appreciate his own particular brand of genius.

◆

". . . this latest killer. Aiding the police in their search is noted criminal psychologist Dr. Helen Hudson. Jim, you may remember Dr. Hudson from the Daryll Lee Cullum case a few years back. It was on the strength of her expert testimony that Cullum was sentenced to die for the slayings of a dozen women. . . ."

The TV set was on in the SFPD squad room and Pachulski, Kerby, Kostas, and Landis watched as the Mouth continued her rundown of their case on the six o'clock news. M.J. sat apart from them going over her files. Her phone rang.

"Monahan."

"You lied to me!" It was Helen on the other end and she was in an hysterical fury. Obviously, she, too, had been watching the news.

"I did not; Susan Schiffer got it. I don't know how."

"You agreed to protect my privacy. I made the mistake of believing you. Now every psychopath in town thinks I'm involved. Don't you ever come to me asking for help again because . . ."

"Helen . . . Helen . . . What do you want me to do? Life's a bitch. Go take another pill, okay?"

M.J. slammed the receiver down. The men gathered nearby turned and stared at her for a moment, and then looked back up at the television. M.J. felt a flash of shame at the way she had spoken to Helen. But she was frustrated as hell with cracking this case and she would be damned if she would give in to the egocentric, neurotic ravings of this woman. *Jesus, they had provided her with a twenty-four-hour guard and Ruben was practically on call for her. No, she had done enough for Helen Hudson. There were women dying out there, and there would be no Catholic guilt over this agoraphobic has-been.*

◆

". . . the slayings of a dozen women. During that trial, Cullum escaped from custody, killing a police officer assigned to protect Dr. Hudson. Meanwhile, police continue to remain tight-lipped about the progress of their investigation. Today's discovery of yet another murder victim is causing San Franciscans to wonder if there's been any progress at all. Back to you, Jim."

"Thank you, Susan, for . . ."

Daryll Lee Cullum ground out his cigarette and got up and snapped off the miniature television that sat up on the shelves across from his bunk, a gift from one of his many female admirers. "Well, good for you, Helen," he spoke out loud to the empty cell and the blank screen of the television.

"Hey, good for you, Daryll Lee." Daryll Lee ignored the sarcastic commentary from the dimwitted Joe Dellums in the next cell. Joe continued to laugh brainlessly for the next five minutes. Then suddenly he stopped, completely clueless as to why he was laughing in the first place. Joe might be dumber than a mattress, but he'd managed to slice and dice one of his fellow inmates during his last incarceration and that was no mean task in San Quentin where prisoners were strip-searched regularly and cells were turned upside down almost as often. Apparently, the thought of doing more time was meaningless to Joe, since he was

serving three consecutive life sentences for an assorted bag of break-ins, rapes, and murders. Daryll
Lee, who had a good fifty IQ points on Joe, kept
his distance.

Anyone who believes that hell is only experienced in the afterlife, has not walked through
the gates of San Quentin. The 140-year-old state
penitentiary sits across the bay from San Francisco
on the other side of Paradise Cove, that stretch of
water being all the geography that separated Daryll
Lee Cullum from Dr. Helen Hudson. However,
Helen had little to fear from Daryll Lee these days.
Escape from one of the most finely tuned and
impregnable maximum-security corrections insti-
tutes in the world would be like walking out of the
fires of hell itself. To walk the yard at San Quentin
is to know terror and danger in every moment.
Five to six thousand of the darkest, most brutal
hard-core felons in California's penal system live
within its walls. Guards and prisoners alike
breathe the air of constant vigilance.

The most stringent unit of San Quentin, the
prison within a prison, is the Adjustment Center.
The guards call it the AC, but it has been better
known as "the hole." This is where "the animals"
are kept. The most infamous inmate to share the
hole was Black Panther George Jackson who led a
bloody mini-insurrection in 1971 that left six dead.
He was shot to death before he made it across the
yard. No one has ever escaped from the hole. In
room number twenty-three of the North Tier,

Daryll Lee Cullum had made his home for the year
since his capture and new trial.

Daryll Lee, like most of the residents of the
Adjustment Center, was not considered safe
enough to hold a prison job. Only on the rare visits
to his lawyer was he able to walk the great yard
and glimpse the two administration buildings, the
gun tower above the main gate, and the armed
balcony towers. He walked as slowly as he could
to prolong the delicious feeling of sunlight on skin.
His complexion had grown as sallow as Helen's,
also a shut-in since their last meeting. Sometimes,
as he walked the metallic stairs beneath the cat-
walks overhead where the guards stalked with
their rifles ready, he heard the inhuman wailing of
the prisoners in the strip cells, windowless concrete punishment boxes with a hole in the floor for
a latrine. Daryll Lee was obsequiously obedient to
every bull, or guard, on the North Tier. He had
vowed to assiduously avoid the strip cells. In essence, San Quentin had turned Daryll Lee Cullum
into the model prisoner and this had been an
exceedingly productive time in his life.

Daryll picked up a copy of his Holy Bible and
the hard cover first edition of *Our Sons, Our Killers:
Profiles of the American Serial Killer*, by Dr. Helen
Hudson, and lugged them both over to his bunk.
He reached down under the bed and pulled out
the original, handwritten copy of his book that he
had tentatively titled *Daryll Lee, My Story: The Truth
About Why I Had To Kill*. The entire manuscript
had been penned longhand with the only writing

implement he was allowed, a felt-tipped plastic pen. Writing allowed Daryll Lee to escape the dull metallic grayness of his cell and the screams and rantings of his tiermates. He had spruced things up the best he could with magazine pictures and photos of the best looking of his correspondents tacked up on the wall. But anyway you looked at it, he was in a claustrophobic inferno surrounded by concrete and bars the color of oatmeal and cold blue steel.

Of course, there had been plenty of time to write; the only other activities at San Quentin he had been allowed this past year were eating, showering, shitting, and Bible class. And even that had been temporarily suspended since Harold Hooks had hidden a homemade knife in his New Testament and had used it to cut off the ear of his new cellmate who had the misfortune of being a recent convert to the Nation of Islam, a religious affiliation that Harold could not abide in a home-boy.

The typewritten version of *Daryll Lee, My Story* had been diligently transcribed by another one of his "girlfriends," Ms. Sherry Diane Wannemaker from Sioux City, Iowa, an aspiring paralegal and sometime Sunday school teacher.

It had been Sherry who had sent the manuscript off to one of those publishers who specialize in books of this nature; it was quickly accepted. After working a few things out with his lawyer, they had popped out *Daryll Lee: My Story* in paperback. It would be out on the newsstands any day. It did sort of irk him that he wouldn't see any of the profits from the book; the victims' families would now receive them by law. But Daryll Lee had long since sacrificed any prospect of wealth for the more accessible reward of notoriety. He had just made arrangements for a signed advanced copy to be given to the one person in the world whose opinion Daryll Lee most admired, and he would give anything to see the look on her face when she saw that book.

Sherry thought it was a work of genius and would be a must-read for every young person in America. She even said it would do better than O.J.'s book. Actually, he owed the last chapter on his coming to Jesus to her. He probably never would have included it, seeing as how it might distract people from seeing the true error of his ways if they thought that a guy like him might have a shot at redemption.

No, he had felt it was his God-given duty to reveal the horrors of his childhood and to tell how Satan had compelled him to do all those wicked things. Besides that, Daryll Lee always felt that he didn't fit the classic, mild-mannered boy-next-door-turned-psychotic serial murderer mold that Helen Hudson and her ilk had made legendary. Daryll objected to being lumped into a pool with the average sexual sadist or lust killer. He felt he deserved a category unto himself. He wasn't some quiet repressed nerd that all of a sudden starts to whack prostitutes like that wimpy gardener, Rifkin. As he thought about this he looked in the little shaving mirror he kept by the sink. His bright red hair was thick and wavy and he kept it trimmed up so it stood high on top, sort of like a redheaded Elvis without the excess grease. He even kind of liked the way his eyes seemed extra blue set against his prison work shirt and indigo denims. His skin was bad and his teeth were rotten and yellow from too many Dr. Peppers and Snickers bars, chewing tobacco, and cigarettes. He ran his right index finger over the puffy lips that he mistakenly imagined girls just loved to chew on. As grotesque-looking as he was, Daryll Lee had developed a fantasy that he was some kind of jailhouse sex symbol. After all, he had never really had any problem getting girlfriends, even though most of them were borderline psychotics themselves. He might have had a problem keeping them, but that was just because he couldn't help cutting 'em up once he got close to them. This had posed a problem in terms of maintaining a longterm relationship, but that was just because he hadn't had a healthy parental role model. After all, when Daryll Lee was only four years old, his daddy had gotten shot in a bayou bar brawl, and before that his daddy used to beat his mom and sister up regularly.

Daryll Lee's mother had made him bathe with his older sister, who was retarded, up until he was eleven. Mama constantly ranted and raved that sex was evil and that God had done her a favor by taking his daddy like he did. After Daryll Lee's first wet dream, his mother was furious. She tied him to his bed without food or water for three days and left him to sit in his own waste. After he was released she forbid him to masturbate. Not only did she take the locks off of every door inside the house, so that he had no place for privacy, she removed the door handle from the bathroom and his bedroom so that she could see into both rooms. He was timed every time he went to the bathroom, and was allowed only one minute to do all his business, no matter what it was. After the minute passed, she would burst into the room and watch him finish up whatever he was doing.

Needless to say, one of his great pleasures at San Quentin was his toilet, although that was hardly a private affair in the prison setting.

Unfortunately for the other teenage girls in his southern Louisiana parish, Daryll's homicidal fantasies and building rage toward his mother were thwarted when she got hit by a truck when Daryll was fifteen. Therefore, poor Daryll took out his sexual confusion and anger toward women on whomever was available before the first time he was popped into an adolescent reform program. He would have killed his sister, too, but the state had decided to institutionalize her a few weeks before Daryll had come completely unhinged.

Writing his autobiography had posed a great and welcome challenge for Daryll. He had always been a very bright kid, considering that he was from what was impolitely called a po' white trash family with very little formal education. At the adolescent security farm, he had managed to get

his high school diploma and was just starting to
get into the classics when he was released that first
time. (Wood carving, the other special skill he
developed in shop class had come in handy when
he decided to start leaving his mark, so to speak,
on his victim's skin.) However, in prison he decided to model his writing style on a combination
of Helen's straightforward prose, the Holy Bible,
and his favorite television shows, *Hard Copy* and *A
Current Affair*, which he especially liked because
they had both done feature pieces on him. He
loved that Jewish guy Maury and it tickled him to
think he was married to that hot Chinese girl on
the CBS news. Daryll Lee's favorite evening ritual
before beginning his writing was to watch Connie
on the news while he masturbated under a copy
of Helen's book. Then he would switch channels
and watch Maury and get his style down all the
while knowing he'd just had this big hot bloody
fantasy over Maury's wife. Then he would read
one chapter from the Bible and pick out juicy
quotes to head each chapter (i.e., ". . . *do you know
that your body is the temple of the Holy Spirit who is in
you, whom you have from God, and you are not your
own?*" I Corinthians 6:19). Then he would choose
a particular killer to study in Helen's book. His
idol was Ed Gein, who made lamp shades and
wastebaskets from human skin, used emtpy skulls
as dinnerware, and made mobiles from body parts.
Now there was a guy who had really turned murder into an art form.

Daryll Lee Cullum had felt compelled to reveal

the whole and complex truth in *Daryll Lee, My Story*. And besides, it had really burned him up that after all the time he had spent with Helen, spilling his guts out to her, she had only given him six lousy pages near the end of her book. Her big excuse had been that he hadn't come to trial yet before her publication date, and she was a primary witness for the prosecution. An inch beneath the surface of his newfound born-again persona, the real Daryll Lee longed to take his big hunting knife and carve a few pretty pictures on the good doctor's skin. He would just love to have her alone with him for a special honeymoon weekend in some motel room where he could tie her up and really give her a firsthand glimpse of what this pathological stuff was all about. He could just kick himself for getting caught up at Berkeley. Oh well, this new dream of revenge against Helen whispered to him at the back of his brain and gave him a reason to keep on living. Daryll Lee dreamed the impossible dream: one day he would get out of San Quentin and reunite with the one woman who was worthy of his genius.

He looked down at the bulge in his prison grays. Damn, if thinking of doing Helen didn't give him a hard-on every time.

◆

It was 7:30 P.M. now. A floor above him, Peter Foley's wife and dog napped. He sat at his workstation, enveloped in a pale circle of white light, the source of which was a $14.99 full-spectrum bulb that he had recently purchased from an artists' supply store. After extensive research, he had learned that full-spectrum light provided the optimum effective source for both acuity and comfort. This single bulb provided the only illumination in the large basement structure. Most of his machinery lay dormant in the semidarkness like Gepetto's toys asleep at night. The gentle hum of the one live hard drive and monitor blended with the minimal electric purr of his scanner and the underlying buzz of the refrigerator and central heating unit upstairs. White noise. If he paused and concentrated, he could isolate each sound and describe the tonality and wavelength of the vibration that belonged to the source. Since he had passed through what Dr. Helen Hudson referred to as the first, or aura phase, of his development, the time when his quietly cultivated homicidal fantasies had birthed themselves, he found that each of his senses was extraordinarily heightened. Colors were sharper, sounds were brighter; his skin was ultrasensitive to the touch. Time had slowed down.

He was between kills now. He had that empty postpartum feeling, a slight depression that would pull him down deeper and deeper as each hour progressed until he could achieve his next creative act. There had been several weeks between the first Boston Strangler re-creation and the second. He had been very depressed before the second kill and vowed not to wait so long before the next. So he had increased his vigil, his stalking (phase two as per Dr. Hudson) by several days until he found the jogger in the park. Phase three, or the seduction, had been so easy with her. After her death, he sensed it was time for the change. This was a critical time, because he had so much to do: i.e. locate the dumpsite; acquire the sperm samples, the hypodermic needles; secure the subject; and edit the video footage for the transmission to Helen. In the end, he was immensely pleased with himself. The Hillside Strangler. Bianchi and Buono. Two men. A nice blueprint for an interesting experience, although he realized the Windex was nothing more than a flourish and had contributed little to the extermination process.

Now, he would not wait another day for the next. He was sleeping only two or three hours a night; there was so much to do. He ran down his list for tonight: ammunition, music store, note for Helen, gas, etc. He had quite a bit of driving to do. But first things first. He had e-mail to prepare.

He squatted down and lifted up a large wooden orange crate stashed underneath his drafting board. He slid out a metal lockbox that fit snugly inside the crate. He unlocked the thick gray box and reached into his totem file. Within the lockbox were shoe boxes housing the remains or souvenirs of each kill. Opening Pandora, as he called the motherbox always made him chuckle. He would have never thought to save an item of clothes or lock of hair from each of his victims, but Dr. Hudson had meticulously outlined this practice as the totem phase, or phase four in the serial murderer's cycle. Peter Foley took great pleasure in choosing a different remembrance from each woman. When he would feel the blues coming on between kills, it sometimes helped him to rummage through Pandora. He especially liked the cool metallic feel of a stolen lipstick or silver compact. There was a perfume bottle, hair barrettes, an earring—small items he could slip in a pocket, rub his fingers over. Small and insignificant enough that they would not be missed, except by the one person who couldn't care anymore. They were treated with the delicate and respectful handling reserved for ancient artifacts of grand historical import. And in fact, an element of Peter's fantasy was that his collection would one day be featured in some kind of odd museum exhibit, the Smithsonian wing devoted to the great genius killers of the world.

Most important to him was a box simply marked by an artist's rendering of Helen of Troy torn out of a children's book of mythology. Beneath the taped-on illustration was another torn page from a library book. Between the ripped edges of paper was a verse from Schiller's poem "The Victory Feast":

> . . . The Spartan eyes his Helen's charms,
> By the best blood of Greece recaptured;
> Round that fair form his glowing arms
> (A second bridal) wreath, enraptured.
> Woe waits the work of evil birth,
> Revenge to deeds unblessed is given!
> For watchful o'er the things of earth,

The eternal council-halls of heaven.
Yes, ill shall ever ill repay;
Jove to the impious hands that stain
The altar of man's heart,
Again the doomer's doom shall weigh!

Somehow Peter had gotten the meaning of the last part of the poem all fouled up in his head. In his backward universe, the world itself was evil and long overdue for punishment. He himself was the judge and avenger, and he alone was due fair Helen, the prize of battle.

He reached into Helen's box and let his fingertips lightly grace the contents. There were several photographs he had taken on his telephoto lens and some High 8 footage, all of which were shot from the building diagonal to Helen's. In addition, there was an audiocassette in a clear plastic holder simply labeled "Berkeley." The word had been typed by his computer printer and cut out and taped on. Underneath the loose items were a stack of papers and articles, some of them old college term papers.

His hand brushed against something soft and warm. For a moment he resisted the urge to pick it up. It was so far the only item of clothing in his totem collection. Peter closed his eyes for a moment, the touch of silk taking him back to a recent night when he had entered a woman's apartment uninvited, something he rarely needed to do these days. There was the waiting in the dark while she closed the downstairs lights and the living-room blinds. When she called a man's name he had resisted the urge to answer her, to come upstairs to her, take her in his arms and hold her. He had wanted to slip his hands around the soft skin of her long neck and squeeze her to him, to take her life inside his.

But he had to wait. It would have to be enough to move among the air she breathed, to touch the furniture that held her. It was a revelation to find her home and office neatly filled with hard drives and monitors, modems and fax machines, scanners, printers, electronic remotes. They were so much alike in their love and appreciation for electronic magic. He relished the kinship.

Peter had listened to the muffled rush of water from the bathroom. Again he wanted desperately to enter, to touch her wet skin, to watch the blood and water mesh in a waterfall of transparent crimson. Instad, he had gone to the closet searching until he found the red suit. He had quickly hung the clothes in the chair back up in the closet. He stood in the center of her bedroom, the center of his universe, and let time go limp like a broken girl in his arms. Gauze curtains like pale white film billowed slightly in the air-conditioner breeze. A slow motion walk to her dresser. Reaching underneath the pile of bras and teddies produced a thin, gray silk camisole. He had slipped it into his pocket and disappeared into the night.

Peter let go of Helen's underclothes and picked up an old newspaper clipping out of the box with a photograph of her and ran it through his scanner. He chose not to use any of his own photographs at this time; the moment wasn't right. He congratulated himself on his self-control. Helen's picture revealed itself on-screen on the terminal in front of him.

From shoebox number four he pulled out a photograph of the No Dumping sign. He shuffled through the contents, looking for a few other things while he was in there. Then he scanned the picture of the sign, along with a picture of Andy Friedman he had taken through Helen's apartment window. On his second terminal, which was networked to the first monitor to which his scanning device was now connected, he had his morphing software up. On the "morph" terminal was the base image of the dancing girl who he had created through the juxtaposition of the image of dead Jennifer Lyle with the once alive Randi Salvino. He started transferring, one by one, the scanned images from the other screen to the dancing girl screen. The first piece to join them was Helen. Then using a special electronic pen, he placed a red dot in the corner of the dancing girl's left eye. As he brought new images over, he placed red dots in a seemingly random manner over each one, so that eventually the screen looked like a macabre collage with red pushpins all over it. He worked fast under the pressure of his self-appointed deadline, savoring the anticipation of his next evening adventure.

8

Number Five

He had been driving through the San Francisco night for one and a half hours. Breathing calm. Heartbeat steady. It was a cool, clear night. Orion the Hunter beamed down on him from between feathered shards of clouds.

He saw the gas station on the corner of a residential area. Horgan Street. He liked that name. It was one of those mixed-up neighborhoods that had small-roomed, modest, middle-income houses sprinkled between apartment buildings. A few California oaks still stood on scattered lawns.

He circled around the block twice, the first time registering the phone booth on the corner of the gas station illuminated by a streetlight. The second time, he pulled up to the curb and went into the booth. Anyone observing from the street or the gas station, if they had any reason to observe, would have seen a nondescript young man wearing glasses and a black windbreaker using the telephone. He left the booth and got in his car and circled the block again. On only the third circuit, just as he rounded the corner from Sixteenth onto Horgan, he saw what he had been waiting for all night. An attractive young woman, probably around twenty-six or twenty-seven said good-bye to her girlfriend at the door of an apartment building. The two women hugged and the one leaving tucked her wine red silk scarf around her neck, zipped up her leather jacket against the evening breeze, and walked toward her brown Honda Civic waiting for her halfway down the block.

The watcher caressed the chill dark metal of the heavy gun that sat on the seat beside him. It was a Bulldog .44 Special—squat, fat, and nasty, extended by a makeshift silencer. He drove a little farther down Horgan, flipped his car around, and pulled up to the curb about ten yards away from the Honda. Then he waited for the girl to approach her car. Time breathed and stretched like a Siamese cat in a pool of afternoon light. He looked up and down the empty street.

Casually, as if he were strolling across the street to greet an old friend, he opened the door to his car and walked over to the Honda. He slipped a small flat object from his black-gloved hand into his left pocket. He held the Bulldog in his right hand low against the back of his leg.

She had just shut her door. He tapped on her window. Slightly surprised and as suspicious as any urban-wary single woman, she looked up and saw an attractive young man smiling down on her. He looked charming and lost; a lock of his sandy brown hair fell down over his wirerim glasses. She hesitated, then rolled down her window.

"Hey, sorry to bother you, but can you tell me how to get to Pier One Fort Mason. I've been driving around for hours."

"Oh, sure." She leaned out the window slightly to point him in the right direction. He saw the streetlight catch her profile just right, his senses so sharp the pale peach fuzz of her cheeks appeared soft and inviting. He lifted the gun and shot once. His body sprang back a little, surprised at the recoil. Then again. Two quick popping sounds in the night.

He opened the door and gently nudged her over so he could lean into the car. He pulled the small flat object out of his left pocket and fiddled around inside for a few seconds. Then he closed the door and walked back to his car. As he walked, he tucked the dead woman's scarf into the pocket of his windbreaker. Then he drove down Horgan, carefully observing the speed limit.

He knew the way to Pier One Fort Mason without anyone's help.

◆

Officer Burt Benoit drank the last few cold sips of bitter coffee and looked down at his watch. He picked up the *Chronicle* and turned to the sports section. The apartment door next to where he had placed his folding chair opened abruptly. Dr.

Helen Hudson poked her head out. She looked haggard and her eyes were dull from brandy and meds.

"I was just checking to see if you needed anything, Officer Benoit. I'm going to bed."

"No thanks, Dr. Hudson. I'm all set out here." He already had a pretty good buzz going from the coffee and none of the junk she had in her refrigerator was up his alley. Burt was strictly a meat and potatoes kind of guy, with the occasional Dunkin' Donuts break because he was a traditionalist. Burt didn't trust a cop who didn't like donuts. If you saw Burt coming down the street, the old cliché, "you are what you eat" might come to mind. Burt was a beefy guy.

"All right. I'll see you in the morning."

"Yeah, okay, Dr. Hudson. You get some sleep. Everything's okay out here." Helen nodded numbly and closed the door. *Jeez, this babe is cooked.* Burt shook his head and adjusted his rear end, trying to make himself comfortable in the inadequate chair. It was going to be a long night, but it beat the hell out of busting liquor store banditos, which was the detail they'd pulled him off to do this guard dog thing. He closed his eyes and tried to visualize Helen Hudson looking cleaned up and rested. Then he looked at his left hand and stared at his wedding ring. *Nah, she's too skinny anyway.* He picked up the paper and went back to getting the lowdown on the 49ers new lineup. It looked like they were on the way to the Super Bowl again this, probably another predictable finale.

Outside on the street, a man parked a silver-gray Caddy, popped the hood and got out. He was dressed entirely in black: black T-shirt, jeans, sneakers, and windbreaker. He moved like a two-legged panther. He eased around the car, propped up the hood and with a Maglite, located the car alarm, made a few adjustments, then clsoed the hood. As he stood up, he glanced around; the street was empty. He pulled off his wire-rimmed glasses and held them up to the streetlight. He removed a small square of yellow cloth from his pocket and wiped a spot of grease off his lens. Then nonchalantly, as if it were part of his nightly routine, the man strolled by the side window and smashed the glass with the butt-end of the Maglite. The car alarm began cycling through a piercing repertoire of warning sirens. The man trotted silently to the side of Helen's building and disappeared into the shadows. Under his arm he carried a small rectangular object, about four by eight inches. It slipped inside his jacket as he melted into the darkness.

Helen lay awake upstairs, staring at the play of city lights on the ceiling of her bedroom. She lay on top of the sheets in a long, clingy, silver-gray knit tank dress. The soft crackle of her police scanner was alive in the background. Underneath the continuous catalog of a troubled San Francisco night, the muffled drone of the car alarm sang outside her locked bedroom window. She focused her restless mind on the feed from the police scanner.

". . . Suspect vehicle proceeding eastbound on Bay Bridge, Three–Charlie–Fifteen in pursuit . . . Shots fired, request backup . . . Domestic disturbance, 2116 Castro. . . . Female DOA at Sixteenth and Horgan, request CSU and coroner . . . Roger that. Do you need additional units for crowd control? Affirmative . . . Victim was found in vehicle, '91 Honda Civic, California license number Baker–Apple–Seven–Three. . . ."

Helen bolted upright in bed. She padded across the room to her dresser where she had placed the scanner and turned it up. She stood still for a second and then ran into the study and pulled Ruben's beeper number off her cluttered desk.

◆

On the corner of Sixteenth and Horgan, the brown Honda Civic was swarming with uniformed police and coroner's assistants. The coroner was leaning over the dead woman's body. Yellow tape had already been stretched around the perimter of the crime scene. A forensic technician was using a measuring device on a tripod, much like a surveyor's tool, to track the trajectory of the bullets. Another Crime Scene Unit tech removed a large slug from the passenger side car door and held it up in the streetlight for inspection. "Gotcha. It's a beauty."

The CSU techie dropped the slug into a Baggie and continued his survey. Nearby Ruben and M.J. were getting the lowdown from the uniforms and trying to pin down witnesses. A crowd of locals

had gathered around the car. The dead woman's
friend was crying, and a female uniform comforted
her. Dr. Frank Able unfolded himself from the car
and stretched up. A weary look passed between
him and M.J. At least this didn't fit their serial
guy's MO. Probably a drive-by gang initiation,
although this was not the usual neighborhood
for it.

Ruben's cellular rang. "Yeah? Hi! . . . Look this
really isn't a great time . . . No, looks like a drive-
by. Victim's in a parked car, no sexual assault." He
covered the receiver with his hand and mouthed to
M.J., "Helen."

M.J. still annoyed by her earlier phone conversation with Helen, rolled her eyes. She continued
her inspection of the driver's side area of the car.
Ruben stayed on the line. "Look, I really got to
go. . . . What? . . . She was on the passenger side
. . . I don't know." He called out to one of the
uniforms who were first to arrive on the scene.
"Hey, Ed, was her cassette player on when you
guys got here?"

"Yeah, I turned it off. Couldn't hear myself
think."

"Yes, it was . . . okay . . ."

Ruben walked over to the car. M.J. was inside.
He leaned in to her. "Would you mind putting the
tape player on a second?"

"Are you kidding me?"

Ruben felt a little sheepish, but he knew he
couldn't afford to ignore the instincts of the

woman on the phone. "Helen thinks it might be ABBA."

M.J. gave him a withering look, but she complied anyway and turned the keys to initiate the accessory power. Then she flicked the tape player power knob on; the tape was still inserted. The sound of the Swedish group that had topped the charts in the seventies spilled out into the night. M.J. stared at Ruben. They were both only beginning to sense what Helen was intimating.

On the other end of the line, Dr. Helen Hudson sat at her computer, scrolling through a data bank, the phone receiver cradled against her shoulder. As she heard the unmistakable pop confections of ABBA, her face darkened. She closed her eyes and dropped her head, as if a shroud of profound dread had descended upon her. She opened her eyes and keyed in a command to call up a specific file. A picture of a man's face appeared on-screen.

Helen remembered Ruben on the other end. "Oh, God! I thought so . . . Hold on . . . don't hang up! Are you near a gas station? Is there a phone booth nearby?"

"Here, M.J., I've got to go check the phone booth." Ruben handed the phone to M.J., who was now sitting very still. Her mind was running over the facts and cross-checking them with the memories of another crime that resonated at the back of her mind. Ruben jogged over to the phone booth at the gas station on the corner.

M.J. spoke to Helen. "It's Berkowitz, isn't it? He's doing Son of Sam."

Helen didn't answer immediately. She stared at David Berkowitz's face in front of her. Then she tapped into the rest of the file. A series of crime-scene photographs flashed on the screen, each one the handiwork of Son of Sam."

Helen didn't answer immediately. She stared at David Berkowitz's face in front of her. Then she tapped into the rest of the file. A series of crime-scene photographs flashed on the screen, each one the handiwork of Son of Sam. She acknowledged M.J. "One of his victims was listening to ABBA in a parked car when she was shot with a Bulldog forty-four."

M.J. called the forensic tech over who had rescued the bullet from the door. "Tony, lemme see that slug." Then something over the phone connection to Helen caught her ear. "What's that siren I can hear?"

"I think it's one of those obnoxious car alarms that wake up everybody in the neighborhood but the person who owns the car," Helen answered.

"Yeah, they oughta be banned."

Tony handed M.J. the Baggie. She examined it.

"It's banged up, but it looks like it's bigger than a thirty-eight. Could be a forty-four."

While the two women talked, Ruben searched the phone booth. Under the phone, on the shelf above where a shredded phone book hung from a chain, Ruben found a handwritten note. He snapped on a latex glove and carefully picked it up by one corner, examined it, then headed back to the crime scene.

As Ruben walked toward M.J. he shouted some orders to one of the uniforms to yellow-tape the phone booth. One of the CSU techs immediately ran over to start lifting prints.

Something in Helen's Son of Sam file jogged her memory. "M.J., look in the crowd. Berkowitz liked to hang around and watch the cops work."

M.J. walked over to Bernie, the photographer, and grabbed his arm. Together, they walked the crowd. As the police photographer's strobe popped and flashed into the looky-loos, they started to disperse. After one bright flash, a tall young man ran away quickly. M.J. bolted out through the mob to go after him. Then she realized he was just a jogger on his nightly run passing through.

M.J. walked back toward Ruben. She was still holding the phone, their link to Helen. She saw that Ruben held up a piece of paper in his hand. M.J. deadpanned to Helen, "We found a note."

Ruben took the phone from her and read it to Helen. "It reads, 'Police: Let me haunt you with these words, I'll be back.' "

Then Ruben held the back of the note up so M.J. could read it and put his index finger over his lips indicating she shouldn't say anything about it to Helen until she finished reading it. It began "To Helen." M.J. became extremely concerned. She took the phone back and Ruben headed for his car. She tried to sound as nonchalant as she could. "Yeah, Helen, listen. I know it's late, but Ruben's

going to drop by with a couple of questions. Yeah
. . . have to go now. 'Bye."

She hung up and immediately barked at the
nearest detective. "I need a unit to Pier One Fort
Mason now, approach code two, wait for instruc-
tions. And see if you can raise the goddamn officer
who's on security detail over there."

◆

Outside Helen's apartment while she was on the
phone with the detectives, Burt had become increasingly unnerved by the persistent shriek of the
car alarm. He got up again and peered through the
hallway window. Several annoyed neighbors had
gathered around the defiant Cadillac and were
trying to silence the alarm to no avail. He looked at
the apartment door as if to ask permission,
shrugged his shoulders, and threw his paper
down. He trotted out into the chilly night to take
care of the nuisance once and for all.

By the time the beeper on Burt's belt went off,
his head was stuck under the hood of the gray
Caddy, siren still blaring. Simultaneously, the man
in black had crept up the stairs to Helen's apartment and picked the lock of her door while resting
his right knee on Burt's abandoned chair. He now
wore a black ski mask that covered his face and
hair and pressed his glasses tight against his face.
He placed a small wedge between the door and the
frame to keep it from closing.

Helen was in the bathroom applying makeup in
anticipation of Ruben's arrival. A bizarre melange

of feelings and sensations juggled for attention in her psyche and body. Building anxiety over the increasingly complex pattern of the copycat killer. Exhaustion from consecutive sleepless nights. Muddy confusion from the cognac and Xanax. And an underlying erotic tension that the thought of Ruben inspired. Strangely enough, Helen felt alive. Something was shifting inside her; something she did not wholly comprehend.

As she leaned into the mirror to apply her mascara, she heard a noise. She left the bathroom and crossed the loft catwalk and looked down to the hallway. She could see a crack of light coming through the front door.

In the darkened living room, the man lifted the receiver of Helen's phone and placed it on the table. He wore very fine black leather gloves.

Helen slid through the darkness and into the kitchen where she grabbed a knife. She glided along the wall of the living room and around the corner to the foyer. She opened the door and saw Burt's empty chair. She picked up the phone on the table near the front door. It was dead.

As she crept back into the living room, she heard another noise and ducked behind the couch. Then she saw the man in black for the first time. He darted past her, paused in the middle of the room, looked around, and headed toward the stairs to the upper balcony of the loft. Helen, staying low to the ground, quietly headed back toward the front door. She made it halfway there, then gently bumped into an end table, home of an antique

Tiffany lamp. The lamp's pull chain swung against its ceramic base making a slight tinkling sound. The figure on the stairs froze midstep, and turned toward the noise. A moment passed and he continued upstairs.

Helen crawled on her hands and knees back to the hallway. She hoisted herself up by the front door handle. Adrenaline pumped through her system. The silky nightdress clung to her moist skin and nipples hardened with fear. She was trembling and gasping for breath now, using every resource of her being to ward off the incipient panic. She took a few steps out into the hall, then sagged against the wall. The walls began to breathe, expanding and contracting, taunting and suffocating her like a giant, malevolent rubber band. The floor rolled toward her in waves. She slumped down, nauseous, hyperventilating, in the nascent throes of an agoraphobic attack.

The man in black walked along the loft catwalk over the living room and retraced his steps toward the stairs. He hesitated as the sounds of Helen's gasping echoed through the apartment. He turned around and descended the stairs to investigate. He crossed the living room staying close to the side of the room that faced the street. He reached the front door and stared out into the empty hallway.

Unseen in the darkness, Helen had managed to crawl back through the foyer and along the opposite wall of the living room and hide behind the couch as the prowler slipped into the hallway. Then she made her way down the corridor off the living room and stumbled into the study. The knife was held blade up and away from her body as sword and shield. Trembling out of control, she bumped against her desk knocking a bottle of cognac and a snifter onto the floor with a loud crash and shatter.

The man in black turned again and started toward the source of the noise. Helen made a desperate lunge back into the living room, grabbed a remote-control device near the couch and started opening and closing the mural blinds that covered the front window in her own version of a semaphore distress signal. The man spun around in the center of the room, alarmed.

Outside in the street, Burt and the neighbors were oblivious to the flashing blinds, still hypnotized by the unstoppable alarm. Ruben's car screeched to a stop in front of Helen's building and Burt finally looked up. As Ruben charged in Burt abandoned the car alarm and ran in after him.

As Ruben raced up the front hallway, the man in black rushed into the upstairs bedroom.

Ruben burst into the apartment through the open front door. Burt arrived seconds later and stood in the doorway. Ruben moved carefully through the apartment, his gun stretched out in front of him.

Burt moved behind him, his gun now drawn. He realized this had been his watch and he'd blown it. He'd be lucky to get garbage detail now, much less the liquor store beat.

Quickly convinced that the prowler was not

downstairs, Ruben jumped up the stairs to the loft. He slipped sideway down the circular wall. Reaching the bedroom door he flipped around quickly and covered the room with his gun, skipping to the other side of the door frame. He saw that the bedroom window was wide open, the gauzy white curtains bellowed gently in the ocean breeze. He ran to the window and peered down. The alleyway was empty. He ran his hand along the window ledge. A ragged chunk of wood had been ripped out, probably by the kind of three-pronged hook climbers use to repel on rock faces—also a favorite of cat burglars.

Ruben shouted, "Helen, are you okay?"

After a moment, Helen emerged from the darkness, dazed and disoriented. She smiled weakly. "Yeah." Then she slowly made her way up toward the bathroom.

Burt screwed up his courage and blurted up from the bottom of the stairs, "Backup's here. What the fuck happened?"

Ruben glared at him contemptuously. "Turn on some lights, will ya?" Burt reached over to a Tiffany lamp and yanked the chain. Then he looked around the room for switches, trying to make himself useful, all the while anticipating what a setback this evening was going to be on his record.

Ruben went to find Helen.

The bathroom door was locked. "Helen? Open the door. It was probably nothing. A burglar." There was no answer. "Open the door. Please."

Through the door he heard her muffled reply.

"Why don't you shoot off the lock?" Then she started laughing. It was an awful sound, the sound of hysteria on the verge of collapse. Ruben stood outside and waited. His thoughts were the closest thing to prayer he had ever mustered. Finally, she opened the door.

Her legs were wobbing. She sunk down to the floor of the bathroom, her knees pulled up to her chest. She began rocking herself mindlessly. She was trembling and crying, the carefully applied makeup had become a muddy stew. Ruben lifted her up and sat her down on the marble sink top as he would a four-year-old who had skinned her knee. He grabbed a washcloth and wetted it under the sink and gently wiped off her face.

"He was in my apartment!"

"I know, baby, I know."

Then without warning, in some sort of manic phase of a breakdown, she broke away from him, shot out of the bathroom, and ricocheted through the bedroom, and up and down the hallway, literally bouncing off the walls. Ruben attempted to follow her and catch her, but she kept slipping away from him. Finally, he grabbed her.

"Where am I safe?" She cried. "Where am I safe in this world?"

"It's okay . . . You're safe here." He pulled her down into a chair with him, his arms tight around her, holding her still. He smoothed her hair and massaged her neck, once again as he would a child who had just faced one of those great unjust occurrences in life that remove us from innocence and build a shell around our hearts. He whispered to her softly. "When I was a kid, and I'd be in a state, my dad would hold onto me like this, till all the fight would go out of me."

Suddenly she broke free and whacked him across the nose. "You think you're my daddy?" Helen had pulled herself up to her full height, almost six feet of defiant raw energy in her sexy steel-colored gown. For the first time since he had known her, in that moment she burned with her full power, like Athena ready to go into battle. She was beautiful, alive, and enraged. Ruben stared up at her in awe. There was something so perverse about all this, so erotic, that he got up and kissed her. She kissed him back, then again, she collapsed sobbing.

Ruben's nose began to bleed, the latent result of Helen's blow. Tears ran down her face and blood wetted his full lips. It tasted rich, bitter, and salty. He smiled. The things between them that had been waiting to be had finally happened. There was release, connection. An unspoken agreement.

"Helen . . . honey, I gotta go."

He reached down and pulled up his pant leg. He dug out a small gun from an ankle holster, what cops call a sneaky gun. It is not departmental issue or requirement; it is personal insurance.

"You know how to use one of these?"

"Point and shoot."

"Up like this, it's on safety." Holding the gun pointed away from them, he demonstrated. Click,

click. "Like this, you're ready to rock and roll."
Click down.

She nodded her acknowledgment and took the gun.

"Stay put, Helen." He kissed her on her forehead and left.

"What else?" she stated to the empty apartment, knowing she could not leave. She must accept an eternity of self-imprisonment. For tonight when her life depended on escape, the borders outside her cell had tried to swallow her and squeeze her into nothingness. No, she would probably die here.

Outside the bathroom, the apartment was being carefully combed by backup and a few CSI's. As far as Burt could tell, nothing had been disturbed, added, or taken. There would certainly be no prints. They guy had been pretty slick.

Ruben got authorization to keep one of the new uniforms at the door. He sent Burt home, despite his protestations that he would be a good little watchdog.

Helen stayed locked in the bathroom for several minutes after Ruben left her. She looked down at the pistol in her hand, small, elegant . . . lethal. With expert hands, she emptied out the bullets. Dr. Helen Hudson understood guns and how to use them extremely well. She had also seen a friend and protector blown apart with his own gun. She opened the bathroom drawer and pushed the cosmetics and ointments to the front and shoved the pistol and bullets to the back.

Helen washed her face, left the bathroom, and went to her office to comb through the Son of Sam files while the police finished searching the apartment. Her system was still charged with adrenaline and anxiety. Finding not a clue from the prowler, the last CSI left. Helen logged off the system and walked into her bedroom, exhausted, finally prepared to face her dreams.

She undressed and walked to the head of the bed. For a few moments she collasped on top of the covers, too weary to pull down the sheets. She moved her head to rest on her pillow and felt a hard, slightly wet object underneath her face. She sat up quickly and pulled back the covers. There, resting on the pillow, was a brand-new paperback copy of *Daryll Lee, My Story.* His face leered up at her from the shiny cover, surrounded by tiny photographs of his victims' faces, the kind of high school wallet photos dad's carry proudly in their soft leather wallets. A smear of fresh red blood marred the surface and stained the sheet that had been carefully laid across it.

Helen screamed so loud and long that the new guard rushed in from outside. She cried in his arms until the CSI's came back to get the book.

◆

After he had murdered the woman in the Honda, Peter Foley drove to Twelfth Street and parked his car. There he found waiting for him the Caddy he had stolen and outfitted with a security alarm. Stuffed under the seat were the few items he needed: ski mask, a roll of rope and pick, Daryll Lee's book, a tiny vial of mouse blood.

He could not resist driving by the crime scene on Horgan on his way to Helen's. He longed to slip into the confusion of civilians milling about, another curious, but bland young man. The Son of Sam had loved to stand in the crowd after the murder, to ask questions, just another concerned citizen. Peter hated to give up a chance to mimic another detail to perfection, but he had essential work to do that night. He had a delivery to make.

He drove to Helen's for his second visit.

After he left her place, Peter walked several blocks before he took public transportation back to get his car at Twelfth and Horgan. He drove the streets of the city all night until dawn. His body vibrated with pleasure. His mind was pure and clear, like polished Irish crystal. Then he went home and slept for two hours on the dull brown couch in the living room.

9

A Stone Heart

"Once that you've decided on a killing
First you make a stone of your heart
And if you find that your hands are still willing
You can turn murder into art . . ."

Detectives Monahan, Goetz, Nicoletti, Pachulski, Kerby, Kostas, and Landis sat around a conference table in the Task Force Room. The room was smaller than the squad room—cluttered, all business, with a variety of high-tech audiovisual equipment stacked against the wall. A blank white board and Magic Markers were positioned in the corner. The homicide team was huddled in semidarkness listening to a recording from the eighties, "Murder by Numbers," sung by Sting in the now-defunct band, The Police. Behind them on the wall, the copycat killer's note was projected on a large screen. The words appeared to be done in several different types of font, as if the killer had spent a meticulous amount of time on the typeface. Some were larger and bolder than others in no particularly obvious pattern. The lyrics to the song were part of the note:

> "Now you can join the ranks of the illustrious
> In history's great dark hall of fame
> All our greatest killers were industrious
> At least the ones that we all know by name."

Lieutenant Quinn entered the room with Police Commissioner Victor Petrillo. The detectives immediately sat up in their chairs, the air tense with the unexpected arrival of the heavy brass. Petrillo could have been fifty or younger; vanity and ambition had kept him handsome in a bureaucratic way. He wore an expensive gray trench coat, not the department-store variety, and Italian leather shoes. Quinn looked shabby and meaningless next to him in his cheap brown jacket and Sears tie. Most of Petrillo's cop instincts had long since disintegrated as he navigated the Machiavellian waters of city politics. They had been replaced by the ability to kowtow, lie, manipulate, and threaten at the proper moment. Every real cop in the room knew the commissioner was there because he lost face with every day this investigation remained fruitless.

Suddenly a bit self-conscious at the seemingly recreational nature of the meeting, M.J. turned off the compact disc player. As this was her show, the other officers waited for her to speak. She looked up at the commissioner. "Good morning, sir."

Petrillo nodded his acknowledgment and gave a sort of don't-mind-me-I'm-just-one-of-the-boys signal. She continued, "The song is 'Murder by Numbers' by The Police. Obviously the killer wants us to hear this song for reasons other than music appreciation. Familiarize yourself with the lyrics and let's put our heads together and figure out what the guy's trying to tell us. Anything else?"

Pachulski answered, "We're set up on Helen Hudson's phone line so we can monitor calls and anything coming into her modem."

"Anybody else?" M.J. looked around the room and then nodded to Petrillo. "Questions, Commissioner?"

"Lieutenant Quinn's given me a status report, so I'm pretty much up to speed." He paused for effect and paced a little, his head bowed down, hands behind his back. There was a rehearsed quality about this, as if he'd risen to commissioner on dramatic skills alone. "I don't need to tell you that this case has captured the imagination of the national media, so not only do we have a serial killer on the loose, we have a public-relations nightmare for the city. Don't discuss the investigation with friends, family, or neighbors. No telling who'll peddle your remarks to the tabloids for a buck. We got a great team here, doing a great job. Just nail this motherfucker ASAP." He punctuated this last statement with a fist in the air, let it hang for a second, and then dropped his hands into his pockets satisfied that just by the fact that he had spoken, there would be a major break in the investigation.

The meeting was over. The detectives started gathering up their materials. Quinn walked the commissioner to the elevator and the two men spoke in low tones for a few minutes. M.J. emerged from the Task Force Room carrying an armload of files. She could tell Quinn's ass was on the line by the way Petrillo patted him on his shoulder.

Quinn fell in with M.J. as she headed toward her desk.

"Well, he's not a happy camper. Wants the fuckin' FBI in. I guess I can say good-bye to my desk again."

"Hmm." M.J. appeared preoccupied. She wanted the FBI's crackerjack Behavioral Science Unit to take a look at the original of the Copycat's note. So far, SFPD forensics had not come up with anything substantial on the paper, the ink, or the printer, all common ones and as expected, no prints. She knew this was a bad time to push Quinn on the FBI issue, and she sensed that he was about to tell her something she didn't want to hear.

"Also . . . I'm gonna have to put Ruben in with Nikko for the Chinatown thing tomorrow."

She stopped dead and faced him. "Sir, I really can't spare Ruben at this time. We're at a really critical stage and . . ."

"M.J." He pulled her into his office. "You got

jack shit. You know it and I know it. Worst is the commissioner knows it."

"Look, if this is the first step in kicking me off the case, sir, why don't you just tell me, to my face."

He ignored her, and could not stop himself from looking away. "One other thing . . ."

"What?"

"The Hudson broad."

"What about her?"

"The commissioner thinks, and I agree with him, that she's leaking like a rusty bucket. Probably wants to start a bidding war on her next book. Anyway, she's not reliable. 'Specially after lunch."

"She takes tranquilizers her doctor prescribes."

"And who prescribes the brandy?"

"Sir, she is the one person who has been useful to us on this."

"You are not to discuss the case with her in any way, shape or form. Do I make myself clear, Inspector?"

"Crystal, sir. And if I disagree?"

"Mary Jane. Your dad was the best cop I ever knew. You're gonna be better. But you won't get the shot if you don't play it right."

Outside Quinn's office the homicide team bustled about their desks settling in for the long day of tedious phone calls and checks and cross-checks that is the backbone of policework. Not much glamor or glory, just repetitive routine and attention to detail. The guys goofed around a little to ease the tension after Petrillo's visit. Somebody told a dirty joke. Somebody else beat him to the punch line. Ruben groaned in mock disgust and suddenly Quinn materialized next to him.

"Goetz. My office." He disappeared again.

"What's that about?"

Now M.J. was beside Ruben. "You'll find out." She looked down over his shoulder at a piece of official-looking paper, a document headed with the Coroner's office logo. "What you got?"

"'Tox' report on that drug test on the Salvino girl. It *was* Windex." She looked at Ruben. He was the only other person in the room who understood as she did that they had access to the one woman who could comprehend the mind and actions of the killer. M.J. walked over to her desk, her stinging conversation with Quinn fresh in her mind.

M.J. looked down at the framed picture of her father on her desk with his arms around her mother, her sister, and herself. Then she looked to the right of it. She had framed another photograph of just the two of them. It was of the day she had graduated from the academy and she was in full-dress uniform. Mick Monahan was also in full dress, just for the occasion. He had long since abandoned the beat cop's day uniform for the nondescript coat and tie of the plainclothes detective. Mick had his arm around his daughter and looked down at her as she looked straight at the camera, a petite ball of fire and ambition. Pride and love encased her like a protective shield. He could send his oldest daughter out into the mean streets believing in his heart that God would take him before any undue harm would befall this child. Mick Monahan had been dead for five years.

Did you always play by the rules, Daddy? Somewhere in the back of her consciousness she remembered someone telling her that laws were meant to be bent and broken, if the Law had come to replace Right. She also knew she would have never been allowed to become a cop if everyone had played by the rules, and certainly not a detective. She picked up the phone and dialed Helen Hudson's number.

◆

Dr. Helen Hudson and Inspector Dectective Mary Jane Monahan sat in the former's living room. It rained outside, not the kind of storm that cleanses and purifies. But a cold, relentless shower that alternated between a mad downpour and indecisive drizzle. Color receded in fear. The streets and cars, people and vegetation faded into an X-ray of movement, barely perceptible, hanging on to life. Even the plush velvets, expensive damasks and silks of Helen's furniture were ashamed to reflect their luster in the wash of gray light.

Helen sat on the couch reading a copy of the killer's letter. She turned it over and saw that it was addressed to her, faltered and dropped it on the table. She took a swig of cognac. "Sorry . . . I . . ."

"That help any?" M.J. referred to the brandy. She could not contain her contempt for Helen's escape into alcohol. There were women dying all over San Francisco and this privileged and gifted person who held the key to saving them buried herself in a high-tech designer cage and a sea of drugs and alcohol. M.J. had reserves of compassion, but she saved it for the victims. She prayed that a hard approach might get Helen on track.

Helen smiled at her, a smirk pasted on with irony. "You don't feel fear, do you? You're probably one of those people who think everything happens for a reason and we're all God's chillen'. How nice for you." She drained the remaining liquor for effect and continued. "Truth is, the engine that runs the universe is terror. How can you be a cop and not see that?"

"I talked to a doctor friend about you."

"Oh yes? And . . ."

"No names. Just Patient X. The way she told it, there are your full-on, full-time agoraphobics and there's someone like you. Kind of a temporary agoraphobic."

"How reassuring."

"What you have are panic attacks. And what I'm wondering . . ."

"Look, please don't try to shrink a shrink . . ."

"What I'm wondering is . . . What do you feel so bad about that you've kinda put yourself under house arrest here?"

"Let me guess. Is this the she-can-walk-out-of-here-anytime-she-likes theory?"

M.J. slogged on, ignoring the sarcasm. "Is is about the death of that cop?"

"Brilliant, my dear Holmes!"

"Because Daryll Lee pulled the trigger."

"It might just as well have been me."

"You think people blame you for that?"

"I damn well know they do."

"I'm a cop. I don't blame you."

"This is absurd . . ."

"Well, lady, I put my ass on the line to bring you that letter. You gotta tell me what it means or not?"

Helen took a deep breath. She picked up the note as if it were drenched in a lethal virus. At first, she was tentative, almost stuttering. M.J. had to lean in to hear her. " 'Helen, don't lose your head.' He writes like he knows me. Does he think he's my equal? Is it a threat? Does he want to cut off my head? Dahmer cut off heads . . . Who else? Kemper. Rifkin? Did Rifkin . . ." She was disoriented for a moment. She crumpled the paper and looked to M.J. for rescue. "This is very difficult."

"Take your time."

" 'First you make a stone of your heart.' Textbook psychopathology of a serial killer. Disassociation—the first step." As she studied the verse and commented her voice grew stronger and more certain.

"Somewhere along the line, something terrible is done to a child that makes him think he can do terrible things to other people." She smoothed out the paper and took another deep breath. Her eyes closed. M.J. watched Helen disappear for a few moments, lost inside a killer's mind. Then M.J. ught to herself. *How wrong I was. She is extraordi-*

narily brave. In truth it was probably this uncanny ability to empathize with their pathology that drove Helen into her shell. She could share their demons, become one with them.

Helen came out of her trance a little. "Gacy's father beat him for fun. Kemper's mother locked an adolescent boy with his hormones running wild in a cellar that smelled of death because he was embarrassing his sisters. I'm sure our copycat has his own horror stories." M.J. had once read about a psychic who weighed three hundred pounds. She ate to drown out the feelings and thoughts of others; her fat was a shield against the pain and horror that poured into her at random from the world. M.J. understood now watching her, that Helen's true genius was also a mechanism that bombarded her with evil when she worked at this level.

"What made 'a stone of his heart'? Rejection and humiliation, I'd guess. If he fights back the punishment is usually worse. More humiliation. A child trying to regain control uses the only means available . . . bed-wetting, fire-starting, cruelty to animals. Rage and control, control and rage."

"Sounds almost like you're making excuses for the guy."

"No, it's just that everything is cause and effect. First you need to see the damaged child. Then you can see the man behind the monster."

M.J. watched Helen's face begin to glow with the intensity of the work. She bent to look at the letter again. " 'When you first decide upon a kill-

ing . . .' Are these his first killings? Yes, I think
they are. He's fantasized about them for a long
time though. He's attacking what he feels he can't
have. What's beyond his reach. Kemper said that
in order to have the experience he needed with
women he first had to evict them from their bodies.
Then and only then does he feel he has control."
She looked at M.J. "You want more?"

"Yes, please. Go on."

" 'If you find your hands are still willing, you
can turn murder into an art.' Art . . . Why does he
want us to think that what he's doing is art? I think
we're looking for someone who is desperate for
approval. He probably has a poor academic record
and he probably does a routine kind of job. Possibly one that brings him into contact with women.
The primary focus of his life is his anger, mostly
against women. Any woman will surrogate for a
mother who was cruel or absent. He's delusional
and grandiose. In his fantasies he'll believe he has
the power of life and death over women. With his
victims he will."

M.J. sat in awe. As Helen broke down the meaning of the note, M.J. felt as if the other woman was
cracking some kind of psychological hieroglyphic
code. " 'Flushed with your first success, you must
try a twosome or a threesome before your con-
science bothers you much less . . .' A twosome?
Does that mean two in the same day? Who did
that? Kemper killed the two coeds. The Gainesville
er a few years ago. And Bundy at Chi Omega
hree. 'You can join the ranks of the illustri-

ous, In history's great dark hall of fame.' Well, he wants to be a hero. He wants to be famous."

"Maybe he's doing the murderer's hall of fame. Boston Strangler, Hillside Strangler, Son of Sam. Helen, does the order mean anything?"

"It's not chronological. Son of Sam was before Hillside."

"He's sending you letters. Like he's daring us to nail him."

"If he wants to be famous, he has to be caught. . . ."

"So you can write a book about him. Maybe he wants you to make him a hero."

"Sad thing is—he will be. He'll get his face on a bubblegum card with all the other little shits. If you can't be a football player or a film star, be a serial killer. Ramirez kills eight women—gets a hundred marriage proposals a mouth."

Something in this last revelation propelled M.J. up from her chair. She walked to the window. The rain had stopped. Off in the distance, Mount Tamalpais had broken free of its cloud cover and split the sky into two patches of blue. The detective kept her eyes on the emerging horizon as she queried the doctor. "What do people do when they idolize someone?"

"Ask for an authograph."

"Right. Or send fan mail."

"You think he's writing to them?"

"Worth a try."

◆

Dr. Helen Hudson understood what had created
Peter Foley, even if she had only her training,
instinct, and imagination to construct a killer's life.
She knew very well that there are people in whose
hearts good does not exist, where soul or spirit or
love is alien as the stars. Peter Foley came from
that chain of ancestry where pain and lovelessness
were handed down like religion or family heir-
looms.

When Peter's mother was very young, she had
reached out for her father's love, like all little
children do instinctively—opening her heart to the
cozy daddy smell and warmth. Instead, she was
raped, the rancid smell of two-day-old beer and
Old Spice lingering on her skin, a reminder of
forced humiliation. She would carry that smell for
days even when her mother would finally scrub
her in the bath, her face turned away from the
sickly bruises that covered her three-year-old's
thighs. Little Sandra soon learned to hate her
mother who would lie in her own bedroom alone
at night while Daddy would come into Sandra's
room. In addition, she learned something else:
how to leave herself. She left Sandra behind and
entered a place of no thought, no feeling . . . a
soulless place where she soon resided almost full-
time. She felt nothing. And when she had her own
husband, she would lie there as he entered her
and go to that place again.

The result of that soulless connection was Peter.
Uncannily he was a beautiful child with pale questioning eyes and a certain cast of his head that

made him appear a little philosopher or statesman. He was a smart and engaging child, despite his mother's anger and unhappiness. His father took pride in him and that in itself made Sandra despise the little boy. When little Peter reached the age of three, something clicked inside of grown-up Sandra, Sandra the mother. Perhaps, it was a genetic code that locked into place. Perhaps, it was the habit of hatred and abuse that was so ingrained, she was compelled to pass it on to another generation. From then on, for each attention paid her son by her husband, she would meticulously plan her revenge the next day. As Peter's young life progressed, the horrors she would visit on him grew deeper and darker. At first he loved Sandra, her white skin and dark hair. She was Mommy after all. And after she would beat him or lock him in the closet for a few hours, she would always hold him and kiss him and feed him milk and cookies and dry his tears with kisses and gently whisper that she would drive him far away and leave him to starve if he should ever tell his daddy about their playtime together.

Soon enough, the father noticed his son's sullen and agitated demeanor. Peter would play outside alone for hours. His father and mother would have screaming fights at night about it, and the father would end up on the coach. Finally one Sunday, the father took his little boy fishing and Peter confessed to his daddy, "Mommy hates me." He couldn't get much more than that out of his son, but it was enough that he would lay down the law that night, maybe even move out with him for a while.

So Sandra made a choice in the middle of the night. Did she really need a husband? What would she prefer: a man in her bed or a little son she could play with, the kind of games of cruelty and pleasure that had finally given her life meaning?

On Monday, when her husband was at work, she ran away with Peter. All the way across the country to the West. She changed their names. Peter never saw his father again, nor did he ever know how to find him. Soon, after many beatings and days locked away, he believed Sandra when she told him his father had abandoned them. She also began to teach him about how dangerous and disgusting sex was, and that women and men together were evil. After a while, he could not remember his given name. All he knew was that he was sad, and lost, and very angry inside.

So he looked for ways to take care of the big hurt he carried inside him. He liked to go into the woods and find bugs or worms or little animals and beat them with sticks. That made him feel a little better. But not enough. One day, he went a few blocks away from his house and found Mrs. Harvey's cat with her new litter. He took three of the kittens into the woods and played games with them the way his mommy played with him. Only the kittens dies, one of fright, the other two of torture. Peter found this gave him a certain kind of pleasure and release, something he hadn't felt for many years. He was six years old.

Soon, he discovered matches. Sandra smoked and she would leave the matches and cigarettes around carelessly. Peter would go out in the driveway and light little piles of leaves. Sometimes he would go out in the woods and make fires and throw bugs and stuff in them. He loved to hunt through the woods. He would stalk an animal or even a neighbor's pet for hours before the actual capture. Then he would devise an intricate death for each subject, usually a slow and painful one. He loved to analyze the process and sometimes he would dissect the dead animal after the fact, or what was left of it. Peter's strangeness did manage to cause some problems for Sandra; the neighborhood children were frightened of him. But she preferred that other families shunned him as a playmate; that left their private world intact and inviolate, special. However, they moved a few times during his childhood, after the violent and suspicious deaths of several cherished pets were traced to Peter.

As he grew further into childhood, his love affair with fire increased. Once, after a bed-wetting incident—there were many of these—his mother locked him in a closet under the stairs, while he still clutched his most recent matchbook acquisition. He found some old newspapers and lit them. Suddenly, the crawl space was on fire and Peter screamed and screamed until his mother got him out. She kept him at home for weeks, nursing the burns on his hands. Soon after, they moved again.

As Peter grew into adolescence, the beatings

began to subside. He was growing taller than Sandra, and she was forced to change her tactic.
Psychological torture became the order of the day.
He stopping lighting fires. He stopped torturing
animals. Peter became quiet, and studious. He
would spend as much time as he could hiding in
his room pretending to study to stay clear of his
mother. Or he would wander the malls for hours
on end, watching the gangs of kids having fun
together as he walked alone. He never brought
other teenagers home. Peter was actually not bad
looking, but his painful shyness and inability to
talk to girls marked him as a geek. One or two
friendships were formed, also with oddball types,
in his favorite classes—math, biology, and chemis-
try. He liked anything that was precise, orderly,
controllable like numbers. And of course he loved
to dissect. Unfortunately, his creativity and imagination had been stunted by fear and his tremendous lack of self-esteem. He was eager to please
his teachers, but he just did not have the personal
drive or spark to catch their attention. Deep inside,
he knew that would change one day.

The best thing about high school for Peter was
he was learning how to appear unobtrusive, normal. He began to understand conformity and its
value. If you put on a certain mask, no one would
bother you, or be bothered by you. You could
think terrible things in your mind, but no one
would ever know or care.

When he was seventeen and close to graduating,
he took a girl home. She was a little chubby and as

shy as Peter, but very smart. Sandra was nice for a while, then she started asking the girl why she would want to spend time with a loser like her son. Couldn't she tell he was a nothing like his father and probably lousy in bed, too, like his father was? The girl got scared and went home. After she left, Sandra railed at Peter. Couldn't he tell she was a whore? What would a girl like her be doing with him anyway, except that he was so stupid he couldn't see what she was?

Peter never asked another girl home while he was still in high school. Instead he began to have fantasies. He wanted to do things to get back at his mother. They were strange, elaborate fantasies about the girls at school. In these daydreams he would do the things to them that he had done to the animals in the woods when he was little. Afterward, he would feel an incredible sense of elation. He always became sexually stimulated; once, he even ejaculated. What he didn't understand was why he couldn't put Sandra in the dreams. He knew he hated his mother and she was the source of his pain. But, he couldn't kill her, even in his mind.

Peter barely managed to get into Berkeley. It wasn't too far from home and he could come home on the weekends and visit Sandra. As he was still incapable of approaching other coeds, this was where he spent a lot of his study time. The girls in college were even more beautiful, and they were smart and self-confident and highly sexed. They were like an ancient foreign tongue, complex and incomprehensible. It made him even angrier inside that no one had taught him this language.

He decided to be a psychologist, and expressed a strong interest in the pathology of the criminal mind. This is something in which he knew he could excel. He worked hard to please his teachers, but his grades were mediocre or worse. Graduate school was out of the question without scholarships and the proper recommendation. Soon his quest for higher learning became irrelevant. Sandra had taken ill with lung cancer. By the time he was in his senior year, she had become extremely sick. Peter never graduated. Instead, he returned to Oakland to take care of his mother until the day she died.

After his mother's death, Peter drifted back to Berkeley. He got a job in a biology clinic lab; they specialized in fertility. One day he met one of the secretaries, a fragile, eccentric woman almost ten years older than him, Georgette. Eventually, he lost his virginity to her. She didn't seem to care that he had no idea what to do. Sex meant little to Georgette. Neither did conversation or experience. They all interfered with her television shows and romance novels.

Georgette lost her job at Berkeley and they decided to move to Daly City where they could rent a house cheaply. Peter found another clinic job at nearby San Francisco State. They settled into a perfect middle-class life. Two snug little hearts of stone. He saved his money and bought lots of special toys. And he floated in a fantastic dream-world of sadistic pleasure and sexual torment. On his lunch breaks, he would watch the coeds bouncing in their tank tops and bikinis, the happy students playing their guitars and spinning their Frisbees. And he dreamed that he was king of their world, that they would crawl into his pleasure palace on their hands and knees, and he would grind their little lives up with his bare hands. Their youth and power would be his forever. And he would grow bigger and bigger, a monument of stone.

But these were only dreams, until one day someone he looked up to more than anyone in the world except maybe his dead mother, came to speak again at his alma mater. And then he knew her words would be the scripture on which the legend of his life would be built.

10

Pen Pals

——

"Is he there for Dr. Hudson?" Andy sat near Helen in her study while he placed a call to Charles Mendoza, assistant warden of the Florida State Penitentiary, former home of the now deceased Ted Bundy and current home of other illustrious felons, including Danny Harold Rollings, fondly termed the Gainesville Ripper by the Florida media.

Helen's study looked like the war room of a city newspaper after a major event. Stacks of cardboard file boxes were piled up in front of her wooden bookcases. All three terminals in her homemade network were buzzing, two with e-mail communication to and from penal institutions around the country. The third was set up with a special program to collate data. Two fax machines were operating simultaneously, one for outgoing correspondence and one for incoming. The receiving fax was excreting an endless list of names that Helen was unrolling and preparing to scan into her system, where it would soon be visible on the terminal reserved as the "Serial Murderer Fan Club Data Bank."

Andy nudged Helen with his elbow; Mendoza was picking up. She grabbed the receiver.

"Hello, Helen. Long time."

"Yes indeed. How are you, Charles? You get my fax?"

"Yes, Helen. But we only keep files on correspondence if it's of a threatening or illegal nature. Like that fellow awhile back who sent Dahmer the strychnine cookies. It's only a partial list, but you're still looking at about forty pages."

"I'll be waiting by the fax."

Across town, in the homicide division squad room of the San Francisco Police Department, Inspector Mary Jane Monahan was pouring over the names of every living serial killer in North America, which was now cross-checked with the prisons in which they were currently residing. She had split the list with Helen, leaving the doctor to make the calls to the wardens she knew. There were many. Helen had traveled the circuit for several years, and had been brought in as a consultant on a pretrial and trial basis on a national level. She had needed favors in the past from many of these prison officials, especially when she was researching her book. And occasionally, they had needed something from her.

Gigi dumped a long fax sheet of names on M.J.'s desk: "The many admirers of Mr. Rifkin."

Up until about two years ago, Joel Rifkin had been a mild-mannered mama's boy who still lived at his parents' home in his old neighborhood. Friends and family who lived nearby repeated the clichéd story, that they always felt safe coming home alone because Joel was usually in the garage tinkering around. One summer day he was signaled to pull over because the license plate had fallen off his pickup truck. Instead of stopping, he sped away and the State Police chased him for over twenty minutes before they caught him. Then one of the troopers smelled the unmistakable stench of rotting flesh, which led to the lucky capture of one of the most prolific prostitute murderers in the history of the state of New York. Joel was so relieved to be caught, he gladly led the police to the many shallow graves that cradled his seventeen victims. Like Peter Foley, Joel was a bumbler when it came to women. He never had a date, unless it was a paid one. And most of the unlucky prostitutes he spent time with ended up dead. Now, he had the legions of perverse fans that exist only in America—that particular brand of lonely heart who likes to write to men in prison, the sicker the crime, the more appealing the pen pal.

M.J. was on the phone waiting for the warden who had Richard Ramirez under wraps. She crossed Rifkin's name off and nodded to Gigi to put his list on the pile with the others.

Helen spent several hours that day scanning

names and writing a program to cross-check and break down the lists. Beside her sat the proverbial cognac, a plate with a half-eaten sandwich of smoked salmon and capers on rosemary bread, and an ashtray of half-smoked cigarettes. The sandwich had been there since noon. It was close to 5:30 P.M. Helen worked in the semidarkness with only the light from the terminals, oblivious to the setting sun outside.

" 'Bye, love!"

Andy appeared in the doorway with his friend Hal, who was tall, dark, and handsome if a little absurd, in a white Nehru jacket, white pants and shirt with love beads, sort of a nineties take on a sixties look. Andy had costumed himself à la the seventies in a jacket that he must have been keeping at the back of his closet for twenty years. It was a patchwork of bright orange, yellow, and red triangular and circular patterns. He wore love beads, too, but they were irrelevant in light of the jacket's statment. Helen was glued to her computer screen and Andy was determined to get a rise out of her.

"Say good night to Hal."

" 'Night, Helen."

She finally looked up. "You're not actually going out in public looking like that."

"Festival of Love, man. Power to the people and all that." They flashed her the two-fingered peace sign."

"Well, have fun you two. I'll say a little prayer that you don't get nabbed by the fashion police."

They left her alone with the Serial Murderer Fan
Club. M.J. had faxed her the list of names she had
gathered. Helen scrolled down the thousands of
names. She was nervous, excited. She lit a Marl-
boro. Something in her gut told her they were
close.

Helen ran the program that sifted out the
names of all the correspondents who had written
to more than one prisoner. From that list, she
eliminated any with female given names. Then
the columns reformed. Helen scanned the remaining names. When she got to the "K" names,
one name caught her off guard: PETER KURTEN.
She stared and shook her head and mumbled,
"Ah, for Christ sakes." And then she picked up
the phone and called M.J. ·

M.J. was there within twenty minutes, peering
over Helen's shoulder as she justified her theory
that they had found their boy, or at least an alias.

"Obviously, Kurten's not his real name. He's
playing another game."

"But why would he use the name of a killer in
Germany back in the thirties."

"Probably 'cause the real Peter Kurten changed
his MO from time to time, too. Just to throw off
the police. He killed women, but he'd go after
men, children, animals, whatever."

"Another gentle soul."

"Not for nothing he was called the Monster of
Düsseldorf."

M.J. nodded to the screen and petted the terminal. "Can this little hootigator tell us who Kurten's written to and how often?"

"Hootigator?"

Helen was amused by M.J.'s primitive computer experience. She smiled. The rough waters between the two women were starting to calm and Helen was feeling back on her game.

She types in a command:

"PRISONERS RECEIVING MAIL FROM PETER KURTEN."

Almost immediately, a new list appeared:

CULLUM 5
DAHMER 1
GACY 2
MANSON 1
RIFKIN 2

They stared at the first name and M.J. stated what they both understood. "We might wanna find out why he and Daryll Lee Cullum are such good pen pals."

Helen flinched. "I can't. I can't do that."

"I'll talk to him."

It took some doing to cut through the layers of bureaucratic red tape, but by 8:00 P.M, elaborate plans were made for a video-monitored hookup with Daryll Lee.

After the first few months of her self-imposed incarceration, Helen paid for the extra software and surcharges required for televideo communication. She had used it only a few times since her professional obligations had dwindled. Once her mother, who Helen rarely spoke to, desperately had wanted to communicate on Helen's birthday. Their relationship over the last twenty years had been awkward, especially since her brother Matt's suicide and her marriage to Carter. Helen didn't speak to her father at all. After Helen had separated from Carter, her mother came back into her life. Mrs. Ashland had to sneak behind her husband's back to call Helen or write her as he had never forgiven Helen for her left-wing politics and left-wing husband. So Caroline Ashland went down to the local copy center, which was online and hooked up with one of the long-distance companies for televideo, and she had a novelty conversation with her only living child. Helen was relieved that most of their exchange was consumed by her mother's oohing and aahing, cheap thrills over the wonders of technology. Caroline actually thought Helen looked good on the video monitor, despite the fact that her daughter was housebound with an extreme panic disorder. The small victory of their exchange lay in Caroline's revelation that she was thinking of leaving Helen's father after all these years. . . . "Mind you, I'm only thinking now." Helen was elated and as supportive as she could be under the circumstances. Her mother was sixty-five years old.

The conversation with Daryll Lee would be the first time Helen had used the option since her birthday. But, this time the camera would be only one way: they could see him, he could only hear

Inspector Monahan's voice. Helen fully intended to sit back and let M.J. do the talking, despite the morbid itch she felt at the thought of getting Daryll Lee under the microscope again. Theirs was definitely a love/hate relationship that bound them together with the tenacity of belligerent ex-spouses connected for life by their children.

Helen and M.J. sat side by side staring at the center monitor in Helen's study. On view was a high-security holding area in San Quentin. There was no one in there yet. Helen chain-smoked and rocked her leg. The speaker phone was one, the only sound an empty crackling. Their conversation would be recorded on video and audiotape.

Suddenly, a mix of voices and footsteps were heard, with the unmistakable good-ol'-boy twang of Daryll Lee pitched above the others. The midsection of a man in prison grays and shackles appeared, flanked by two guards. Then Daryll Lee Cullum sat into full view of the monitor.

The off-camera voice of the warden advised Darryl Lee to look into the camera. He cocked his head right and left the preened for the camera. His hair was combed back with some gel that he'd copped off one of his buddies from Bible class. He was looking good for Helen.

"She can see me on this thing? Cool! Hey, Doc! How you doin'?"

"This is Inspector Monahan. Dr. Hudson's asked me to speak for her."

"I'm hanging up. I ain't talkin' to no cop."

He tipped his chair to the side and leaned off-camera to the unseen warden.

"Hey man, you lied to me. You said . . ."

M.J. cut him off. "Peter Kurten, you know that name?"

"I surely do. But that's all I'm sayin' if the lovely lady don't get on the horn."

M.J. looked at Helen. She didn't need to plead with her. Helen knew she would be acting like a selfish child if she refused to assist in getting the information they needed. She steeled herself and spoke.

"Hello, Daryll Lee."

"Hey, Doc. So tell me, one author to another, how d'ya like my book?"

"Your book?"

Daryll Lee was indignant; he thought she was insulting him. "My book. The one I wrote. Sent it to you special by private messenger. You didn't get it yet?"

"I got it. I just haven't gotten around to reading it yet."

"It's real well written. You should read it. You're in it."

"I'll look for it. Right now I want to talk about Peter Kurten."

"Is that guy botherin' you? He was supposed to just bring you the book and leave you alone."

M.J. looked at Helen. They'd hit pay dirt. Helen remained calm on the surface as she interrogated Daryll Lee.

"Sort of. Now I need to get hold of him. Any ideas, Daryll Lee?"

Daryll Lee was getting a little jealous of Peter Kurten, even though he had manipulated him to get to this point. But he was also genuinely thrilled to be of service to Helen. He wanted to milk this for what it was worth, which was a break from the oppressive routine of San Quentin and a little glory back on the North Tier.

"Listen, you want my advice? Steer clear. The guy's a freak! He says he's gonna give me five hundred bucks for some of my . . ." He hesitated, then looked down at his crotch. "You know . . . spirit. He says he can make me immortal if he has some of my . . . spirit. You know what I'm saying? This is kinda embarrassing. I don't want to say it right out."

"I think I know what you're referring to. What did you do about it?"

"Well, right away I smell freak. What I did, I sent some liquid soap in a sandwich Baggie with a message from Jesus to mend his ways. You hear I found Jesus?"

"How were you going to contact Kurten?"

"A buddy of mine from here, who's out now. Kurten was gonna hook up with him."

M.J. leaned over and whispered to Helen. Helen attempted to remain cool, but she could not keep a hint of urgency out of her voice.

"When? Do you know how they're hooking up."

"I think they're supposed to meet at 10 o'clock

Friday night at Danver's Meatpacking, the loading docks."

"What Friday?"

"What day is this? In jail you lose track. This week. Friday."

M.J. leaped to the other phone and called the station to try to track down Ruben. Daryll Lee continued to ramble on to Helen.

"So, Doc, how is life, you okay? Come see me, talk to me. I think about you, worry about you all the time. You know, you're blessed by Jesus."

M.J. pulled her stuff together and started waving to Helen to hang up. The psychologist had taken over. Helen was mesmerized by the man on her monitor. She had tugged a pad over and was jotting down notes as he spoke. M.J. shrugged and left for the station.

"That's why you need to come talk to me, because Jesus kept you alive for a reason, and I was his sacred instrument. Satan was in my heart raising my arm to kill you, but Jesus took my hand to spare you. I am death and life to you, Doc, death and life. . . ."

Helen kept up the back and forth with Daryll Lee for another ten minutes. Then the warden pulled the plug.

Daryll Lee was escorted back to his cell on the North Tier of the Adjustment Center, past the jeering inmates in South. He wanted to prolong his moment in the limelight as long as possible, but none of the guards wanted to hang around to listen to his exploits.

Joe Dellums was busy picking the dirt out from under his toenails with his fingernails. He would follow up each toe by cleaning the fingernail tool with his teeth and mouth. This was all-consuming activity and he couldn't give a cockroach's butt for Daryll's braggadocio. As a matter of fact, Joe's next planned activity involved the torment of three pet cockroaches he had been saving under his bed in a shoebox for three days for his biweekly "Torture Theater." The show had to go on tonight because he needed to flush his soon-to-be dead actors away before inspection tomorrow. Joe was a wiz at filling the empty jail time with unusual and entertaining projects.

The guy in the next cell over from Daryll Lee had managed to get himself sent to the mental wing for observation by screaming for twelve hours straight and scratching the skin on his arms and legs bloody. He had replaced Conrad Chow who had been a really good listener and a friend while he'd been next door. Connie was on his way to meet Peter Kurten now as a favor to his old neighbor. So poor Daryll Lee would have to celebrate the triumph of his recent video performance alone.

He picked up his Holy Bible and his copy of Helen's book, both his eternal comfort. He ran his hands over the smooth finish of the jacket cover and he flipped to the back and stared at Helen's picture on the inside flap. Daryll Lee thought Helen was incredibly beautiful and it really tickled him that he was getting so much special attention from her. He looked around to make sure there were no guards or stoolies peeking into his cell and he took off the jacket cover. Taped to the inside of the cover was the last letter from Peter Kurten. Since the knife incident in his Bible class, they had searched his Bible regularly. For some reason they had not gone through his other books as carefully. He had thrown out the first few letters from Kurten thinking the guy was a crackpot, but the last ones had gotten interesting, and he had started writing back. His most recent letter was typed on a rented computer in a copy center in Oakland.

Dear Mr. Cullum,

Thank you for your brief note and your understanding of a kindred spirit. You will not be able to write back after this one because I had discontinued the post office box.

I continue to appreciate and admire your work as my understanding grows. You have been lucky enough to have had a relationship with an extraordinary woman. I must say that I am envious that you have achieved such an intimate range of contact with her than was possible for me up until now.

I have read and reread pages 246 to 252 in the Book as you requested. I know now where your work was leading you and what has to be done to continue it.

Now I must broach an indelicate subject that I mentioned briefly to you before. If there is any way you could oblige me with a sample of your semen, I can make it very worthwhile for you . . . $1,000 payment at least, half up front. I cannot tell you what it's for now, but I assure you the cause will become clear ultimately, and you will thank me. It will absolutely not be used for fertility purposes.

If follow-up arrangements can be made, someone can contact me either Monday, Wednesday, or Thursday of next week at the following number (415) 822-7603 between 1:30 P.M. and 1:50 P.M. After that, it will be impossible. Please know that you will be extremely pleased when I am finished, even if I cannot fully explain everything now.

Could you please destroy this note as you did the others. I cannot thank you enough for everything you have done already and this thing I leave you to think about. My apologies for not being more clear, but I know you will understand in the end.

Very truly yours,

Peter Kurten

Daryll Lee liked the fact that Peter Kurten called him Mr. Cullum even as their correspondence progressed. He also appreciated the flattery and the fact that Peter had done his homework in Helen's book as he had directed him. He figured Kurten was a pretty educated guy from the prissy way he wrote.

The fact that Peter Kurten was obviously a creepy weirdo had not really bothered him, despite what he had said to Helen. Freaks and creeps were the cogs that made Daryll Lee's new pen pal world turn. Daryll's intuition told him this guy was after a piece of glory that had once rightfully belonged to him. He figured that if Kurten was up to going after Helen, Daryll Lee might help by opening a few doors, making a few suggestions. It would be entertaining for him to see his own little touches show up in the Copycat's work. However, if Peter Kurten wanted to screw around with Helen's head, which he apparently had done, that was fine with Daryll Lee. However, he drew the line at his own sperm, his "valuable holy seed" as he liked to think of it. Daryll Lee figured Peter Kurten was probably impotent.

He kind of liked throwing out the information about the meeting that night. Let's see if old Peter squeaks by without getting busted. This will be a nice test for his favorite pen pal.

Daryll Lee peeled the letter off the jacket cover and tore it up into tiny pieces. Over the next twenty-four hours, each time he used the toilet, he flushed down a few fragments of the letter.

The phone number on the letter was a pay phone in Ghirardelli Square that Peter had routed through ten other phone exchanges before bouncing it back to three different pay phones, one for each day mentioned, on the campus of San Francisco State near the clinic where he worked. The complicated phone-number hopping was accomplished by hacking into the international phone system, a feat Peter had learned from subscribing to *The Phreak Phantasy Phanzine*, an underground hacker magazine. If anyone copped his

letter to Daryll Lee, it would be impossible to
find him on the other end of the line before the
conversation finished. On the following Wednesday after he had sent the letter to Daryll Lee, at
1:45 P.M., the man who called himself Peter Kurten
had received a phone call from Daryll's old tier-
mate, Conrad Chow.

11

Chinatown

The number 30 municipal bus travels the heart of Chinatown along Stockton Street. That is the way the Chinese, not the tourists, enter their village within a city. Visitors are all told to wander down colorful Grant with its elaborate gate and expensive shops hawking silks, gems, clothing, furniture, and antiques geared to tourist prices. Chinatown proper is a twenty-four-block radias bound by Kearny, Bush, Powell, and Broadway. In the predawn hours, the streets come alive as produce and seafood vendors shuttle in the ingredients that will be transformed by evening into a cacophony of exotic smells that Kerouac once called "that panfried chow mein flavored air." Pushcarts brimming with tangerines, hairy melons, mustard greens, ginger, and cabbages roll along the market streets of Stockton and Broadway still littered with last night's detritus. Merchants

pour fresh-shaved ice into troughs that will soon
become a chill bed for newly caught whole fish.

The cellar full of Asian figurines and antiques at
the Canton Bazaar on Grant hasn't opened yet.
One or two lone vendors pad in their soft embroidered black slippers through their semidark shops
weighing roots, fungi, and odd exotic potions in
the tea and herbalist shops on Washington. And
old man and his little grandchild chat quietly in
Cantonese as they make noodles in their tiny shop
on Beckett Street. On a playground off Hang Ah,
five men and women, all over seventy gather to
perform their slow-motion ritual of t'ai chi that will
guide them to good health, long life, and spiritual
awakening. High on the fourth floor of 123 Waverly
in the Tin Hau Temple, a few worshipers including
a young couple mourning the passing of a grand-
father make offerings to the Queen of Heaven in
a sea of incense smoke under the soft glare of
hanging lanterns.

For a long time in its early history, Chinatown
was a bastion of vice and vulgarity. The brutal
Chinese Exclusion Act prevented the predomi-
nantly male Chinese population from bringing
wives over from the old country. Prostitutes and
sex slaves were brought in illegally. Opium dens,
gambling, and violence flourished. The legitimate
brotherhoods, or tongs, also had their dark criminal side and they controlled and expanded their
tawdry ghetto of crime until the great fires of 1906
demolished Chinatown almost completely. Out of
the ashes, rose a modern Chinatown slowly rebuilt

to attract the tourist trade with curio shops, fake temple roofs, and ornate dragon lanterns.

At least 25 percent of San Franciscans are Chinese, the largest Asian population outside the Orient. Chinatown runs its own newspapers, financial institutions, and government, and the mystical tongs, or brotherhoods, have a hand in everything, including the village's dark side that has never disappeared.

By evening, the bustling of daytime shopkeepers, tourists, and schoolchildren is replaced by the draw of hundreds of Chinese restaurants from dim sum shops to spicy Szechuan and expensive seafood houses. The infamous Li Po Bar with its deep red door and dark interior will draw in the drinking crowd. And after night has swallowed the power of light, a black alliance of Tong and Triad will dump a shipment of frightened illegals in the cold bay like sacks of dead fish. The lucky ones will make it to shore. The weak will sputter and cough and cry till their lungs are filled with filthy water and their bodies are sucked down into the maw of the bay.

About the time the Hong Kong ship pulled into port, Nicoletti had assembled his arrest team. He had gotten the call from Kwok Tung yesterday morning notifying him that tonight was the night. Ruben stood in his black SFPD windbreaker and tried to blend in with the other cops, just another soldier. He didn't want to get into Nikko's way tonight. He remembered the story of David and Bathsheba. David had become obsessed with Bathsheba, so he sent her husband to the frontlines of the battle to be killed. Nikko just grunted at him as he walked past and then pointed to one of the vans. They would not be riding together tonight. The cops piled into three vans and a few cars. Then they caravaned up Market Street toward Stockton.

Ironically, the rendezvous point, the place where all the illegals who survived their evening swim would gather was the New China Buddhist Temple on Ross Alley, one of the seamier streets in Chinatown devoted to the rag trade and the manufacture of fortune cookies, including the X-rated variety. The temple was only the fourth floor of a converted fabric warehouse, but it had all the accoutrements of worship, including a saffron-robed priest who chanted prayers for the wealthy brethren from Hong Kong who had been so generous at helping them fund their new home. The New China Buddhist Temple was endowed almost completely by the Wo Ho To who didn't mind the extra insurance to have the good spirits on their side. In Southeast Asia there were more than a few ashrams and temples that were funded by drug money.

The local Tong gang leaders and their soldiers had gathered the illegals in the temple and handed out fresh dry clothes and a day's ration of food. Depending on what each had paid up front at the beginning of their journey, some were handed small amounts of American money. A few had relatives who had come to pick them up. Some of them were to be shuttled to the back entrances of some of the restaurants controlled by the Tong to be low-paid kitchen help. Many would sleep on the floor of the temple at night until work and homes could be found.

The two Wo Hop To boys were the last to arrive. They had come in on the ship. They had valid traveling papers. Neither had ever been arrested before.

The priest knelt in front of a placid jade Buddha and continued to chant.

Below them, the police vehicles had arrived and taken out the guards that were posted in the alley. One managed to run up the stairs and warn the others. There was a minimum of gunplay and no one was injured. No one escaped.

◆

Nicoletti's arrest team crowded into the station with their bounty. Gigi and the other station clerks were unnerved by the chaos of tough gang thugs wired with anger and the hyperkinetic fear of the illegal immigrants. The uniforms who staffed the station were used to seeing all manner of victims; most of the flotsam and jetsam of humanity washed up on the shores of the local police at one point or other in their unfortunate lives. But they were unprepared for the filth and squalor of the illegals who crowded the station. They were undernourished and trembling with paranoia, and most did not understand a word of English. The arresting cops were herding them through the station by grunts and physical threats. There were only one or two bilingual Chinese officers available. No one had been prepared for the onslaught of humanity this operation would unearth. The room sounded like the Tower of Babel.

On the other hand the local Tong gangsters and their teenage gangbangers, were fit and well-fed. Among them, the two young men from Hong Kong recently indoctrinated into Wo Hop To kept silent, blending into the background. The other illegals were just as afraid of them as they were of the police. They huddled together like orphaned children. The smell of guilt and fear permeated the atmosphere. They knew they could be exported back to mainland China, and this was a chilling notion.

Some of the gang leaders were already demanding to see their lawyers, and a few of the guys were laughing and kicking, performing fake little kung fu moves and mocking their captors.

M.J. was trying to work her way through the maelstrom of bodies to reach Ruben. He had grabbed a Chinese police officer, Sergeant Ng, and was trying to enlist him as a translator for a family of illegals.

"No can do, bro. I speak Mandarin. These folks are Cantonese."

"How am I supposed to get a statement?"

"Wish I could help."

Ng removed Ruben's hands and walked off to another area of the squad room. M.J. had to yell to be heard above the mob.

"I need you. We've gotta go down to the docks. Can you do it?"

"You get Quinn to release me from the curse of the Fu Manchus here. I'll do anything you want."

"Anything?!"

He laughed and watched her as she pressed her way through the bodies. He thought to himself how unlucky he was. The two sexiest women he knew right now were by conventional standards, off limits.

Ruben grabbed a young thug from the line of suspects.

"Over here, you." On the way to find Quinn, M.J. passed Nicoletti's desk. He unholstered his gun and placed it in his desk drawer. He fumbled in his pocket for his key while he kept an eye on the young Chinese kid next to him. The kid wore an expensive-looking white turtleneck and tailored gray jacket. His thick black hair was long and trimmed in a bowl shape. He looked like a Chinese mod rocker gone bad. He was the Wo Hop To soldier who had grown up in Los Angeles.

"You speak English? You speakee *English*?"

The kid scowled at him and refused to answer.

"Well, screw you, too, Boo Boo."

M.J. rolled her eyes at Nikko's unenlightened to communicate. He shrugged at her as she headed into Quinn's office. Quinn was on the phone screaming to the chief.

"I didn't want the fuckin' illegals. I just wanted the bastards dumping them in the bay!" He grimaced in frustration at M.J. and waved her in.

"Look, sir, just tell those prissy little shits in Immigration to get down here ASAP, will you? Hold on a second . . ."

A disturbance had broken out in the big squad room outside. M.J. and Quinn watched from the door to Quinn's office. Ruben had been questioning one of the Tong lieutenants, a bad boy with long rastalike hair and dark sunglasses. The thug went berserk. He kicked another cop who fell back into Nikko's desk and knocked the turtleneck kid Nikko was processing off his chair. Nikko got up to help subdue Ruben's charge.

Ruben broke out of the melee and dragged the Wo Hop To soldier who fell out of the chair off the floor and pushed him back out of the way against Nikko's desk. The kid, his back to the desk, opened the drawer. Nikko had never had a chance to lock it in the bedlam. With his hands still cuffed, the kid rifled the contents. His hands touched the gun. Then he closed the drawer and sat down quietly.

Quinn could sense things were under control and he and M.J. went back into his office. He dry-swallowed a couple of aspirin while M.J. lit into him.

"I gotta have Ruben . . ."

Suddenly, Quinn remembered the unattended phone and reached over his desk. "Hello, sir? No . . . everything's fine . . ."

He turned to deal with M.J., but she had walked out into the hallway, impatient to get away from the squad room tumult. She also hated to see her boss play the obsequious lackey to the commissioner, when she knew Quinn was twice the man. The lieutenant finally came out looking for her and she resumed her argument to pull Ruben back on to the copycat murder.

Inside the squad room, Gigi handed Ruben a box of donuts and a plastic cup of lukewarm coffee.

"Ah, Gigi. You're a lifesaver."

He took the box of donuts and leaned over the turtleneck kid, who sat calmly in his chair and stared straight ahead. The back of the chair was still leaned up against Nikko's unlocked desk drawer. Ruben uncuffed him from the chair and offered him a donut. The kid scowled at him.

"Behave. You refuse my hospitality, I'm putting you to bed."

Ruben reached over and grabbed the kid's arm and pulled him to his feet. The kid shook him off and yanked on Nikko's desk. The drawer flew across the floor; the kid had Nikko's gun in hand. He slipped behind Ruben and put a skinny arm around his neck and jerked him upright. Ruben still clutched the donut box in his left hand. In the reigning confusion that consumed the other cops, it took several moments for the others to see what was happening. Finally, the room grew absolutely still. Somehow, Ruben managed to speak.

"Take it easy, kid. Nobody's gonna do anything. Just let the gun down, so it don't go off."

Inspector Ng repeated his words in Chinese. The kid spoke for the first time, in English.

"Nobody comes through the door."

The kid, with Ruben as hostage, started to ease his way backward toward the door. His eyes flitted around the room. The adrenaline pumping through him pounded his nervous system, already wired by the methamphetamine he'd swallowed earlier that night.

Through the glass double doors opposite the door they were backing into, Ruben could see M.J. running down the corridor toward the squad room. She jerked to a stop when she realized what was happening.

M.J. drew her gun and braced herself in firing position, arms extended in front of her. She realized she would have to move forward slowly and was edging to the right to get a bead on the kid. Ruben was still directly in her line of fire, as were several of the cops in the room. They started to scramble out of the way, but she still didn't have a clear shot.

Ruben and his captor backed into the hallway toward the front exit of the station. The kid hadn't seen M.J. yet. She yelled across the room.

"Hey, you!"

The kid turned, and exposed his right side to her. M.J. had a clear shot of his head, his neck, and upper torso. She aimed and fired, hitting him directly in the right shoulder. Brachial nerve. Donuts flew helter-skelter. The bullet sent him reeling onto the green marble floor and twisted around by the impact, he landed behind Ruben, out of M.J.'s view. She couldn't make another shot. Nikko's gun had fallen from his hand when he was shot, but it slid to a stop right beside the kid's left hand. He grabbed the gun and Ruben reflexively reached for his sneaky gun at his ankle, but it wasn't there. He had given it to Helen. The kid shot Ruben in the back with Nikko's gun. With the singular power of an old woman's curse, the bullet burst through his chest in a great rosette of blood. Ruben's body arched at the impact and then slammed foreward onto the floor.

The kid immediately threw the gun away and stood, his hands up in surrender. He grinned like a madman. A crimson patch of blood stained the shoulder of his expensive white turtleneck and gray jacket. A bevy of cops rushed him and flattened him on the floor. He started screaming, "I'm a juvenile! I'm a juvie!"

Quinn moved quickly over to Ruben and laid a hand on his shoulder. M.J. rushed over and leaned over his body. He was dead, his lung and heart shattered by the bullet. Blood poured from the wound. M.J. kneeled into the spreading pool of crimson and held her partner. "Oh, God," she mumbled over and over. "Why didn't I kill him?" Quinn gently eased her gun out of her hand. Nikko stood nearby in shock, numbed enough that he could not yet comprehend the depth of guilt and sadness he would soon feel. He reached down and put his arms around M.J. and gently lifted her up so that when the paramedics arrived they could move in beside the body and complete the required drill, as futile as it was. Nikko edged her over to

Quinn's office from where she watched the kid taken away.

For several minutes, she sat frozen in time and space. She tried to focus on her breath, to remember to keep breathing. These sensations, the feelings had been there once before. They got all crossed up with that memory. Sitting in the hospital outside her father's room after his coronary. Waiting for death. An unknown country. People moved around her—Quinn, Nikko, Pachulski. Was her mother there? Karen, little sister? No. That was Gigi. Someone brought her water; someone handed her some pills. *When somebody dies, all you can do it attend the living.* The generous urge to sleep passed over her body in a great, heavy wave.

Then somewhere inside her the cop rose up and started to fight its way to the surface. For a few moments, the curtain of sadness parted, and a small voice pushed its way into her consciousness. Then she remembered the rendezvous with Peter Kurten. She forced herself up and out into the squad room and called to Gigi.

"Call dispatch. I need all available units to drag the area round Danver's Meatpacking, China Basin, now! Look for a male, probably Caucasian, aged twenty to thirty-five. Uses the alias Peter Kurten."

It was 10:30 P.M.

◆

In the black cavern of a loading dock, hidden in the shadows, Peter Foley held vigil for Conrad

"Connie" Chow, former prison buddy of Daryll Lee Cullum and messenger of his "spirit." Looming up beside him was an immense door with a large number two painted on it. Occasionally, he would pace outside the shadows and walk a few feet out on the silent dock in front of the door. He would look up and down the pier and disappear back into the shadows.

Peter wore a beige trench coat over his trousers and dress shirt. His hair was slicked back off his face in a vague attempt to look chic. He was going dancing tonight.

He had already picked out the disco. It was a gay club in the heart of the Castro district, the Sound Factory. He had actually gone there because there was someone special he was interested in and that's where they had gone that night. Peter had sat in his car and watched him go in with his friend. Peter didn't want to spoil his plans for later in the evening by following them in now. The excitement was held inside him like the chocolate cookie a little boy saves in his lunch box for an afternoon treat.

At 9:15 P.M., Peter Foley had left the disco and driven over to Beale Street and parked his car north of the Embarcadero. He prepared himself for the twelve-minute walk down to his desination in China Basin.

As he waited on the dock, he watched the fog settle in on Treasure Island. The red warning signals on the base flashed and sparkled through the mist like Christmas tree lights. Thousands of cars, like tiny fluorescent ants, scuttled across Interstate 80 and the Bay Bridge northeast to Oakland and Berkeley. He thought about all the nobodies inside the little ant cars going to and fro. He used to be one of them, but not anymore.

Not far from where he stood, only an hour or so earlier, dozens of Chinese men and women had swum in the cold murky water to temporary refuge.

Today, he had burned his white lab coat in the basement. The smoke almost got Georgette out of bed. Instead, she yelled down to him that the house was on fire. He walked upstairs and told her that he had just been burning some old notes of his. Then he went back down and completed the ritual destruction of the lab coat and a few other items from his old life. After he fanned the smoke out of the basement, he stood on the ladder and reconnected the smoke alarm.

He would never go back to his old job again. It meant nothing in light of his new life—the important work he was doing now. He would not miss the swirling mists of frozen nitrogen that could burn the skin off his fingers. The person who had stored the vials of milky white semen did not exist anymore. Fertility clinic. Couldn't they see the absurdity of it? They were not supposed to have more babies. Creation time was over. Now it was time to give life away—or take it. The sperm could only be a symbol. *A symbol.*

That's why he could never use his own. He had to keep it sealed inside his body. His power and the meaning of everything he was doing now was reserved in that liquid and he could not give it away. Especially to a woman. Daryll Lee would make that sacrifice. Then Peter would complete the job that Daryll Lee had left unfinished.

He looked down at his watch. It was 10:25 P.M. Where was Conrad Chow? Peter's thoughts went back to Daryll Lee. *Perhaps, he failed to see the importance of what I'm doing.* Or perhaps, something had happened to Conrad Chow. Peter looked down at his watch again. He felt uneasy. Something wasn't right. And if he waited much longer, he would foul up the more important work of the evening.

In the instant he looked up from his watch, a dark figure approached him from the far end of the pier. As he came closer, Peter saw that he wore black jeans and a beat-up leather jacket, just as Daryll Lee had promised. The man had a baseball cap pulled down low over his face. From a distance, he looked and walked like a young man. Up close, Peter saw his face was battered and leathery with hard times, and his right cheek in the shadow of his hat was crisscrossed with knife scars—war wounds from a lifetime in prison.

Peter let the man come to him. Wordlessly, they exchanged packages. Peter handed off a small envelope of cash; Connie Chow passed him a wrinkled paper bag that held a plastic Baggie full of dishwashing detergent. The next day, when Peter realized the truth of its contents, he would release his rage domestically, a departure from his usual pattern. Georgette would take the fall for Daryll Lee's little practical joke.

Peter slipped out of the shadows and started walking back to his car. He patted the slight bulge in the pocket of his jacket where the precious Baggie rested. As the distance increased between himself and Conrad Chow and Gate Two at Danvers Meatpacking, he heard the sound of sirens in the distance heading toward China Basin. He smiled to himself knowing that his vision was intact and they would not find him tonight.

No. Peter would be found when he decided they should find him.

◆

The sat together in Interview Room Four. Barred windows and white walls stained with nicotine. Their hands rested on the wood table discolored by pencil and pen scribbles. There were little grooves on the top of the table in front of her where someone had anxiously dug their fingernails and scraped. Two mugs of police station coffee sat cooling on the table.

Interrogation and confession. When you sat in Interview Room Four, those were the currents that carried you. Not much else could exist outside that territory, except the raw emotion that was its waste matter.

She could not look at her old lover as she spoke. "Quinn will be here any minute. What are you going to say?"

"Christ. I didn't lock the fucking drawer! You

spend twenty years thinking some bad guy's gonna whack you. Or you'll crash your car. But what happens? You fuck yourself."

He laughed, a choked laugh.

"You can't imagine how many times I saw you two . . . fooling around, laughing at some dumb shit, and God I wished him dead. Every time. But you want to hear something weird? I feel like I'd give my life to bring him back."

"You're in terrible trouble, Nikko."

He began to weep silent tears.

"Who gives a fuck?"

"I give a fuck." Now she fought back the tears, but they came anyway.

"All the years I've known you, I never seen you cry." He stared at her and she finally looked up to him. "D'you love him?"

"Who gives a fuck?"

Quinn walked in and found his senior officers in tears.

"Nikko. My office? M.J., I wanna see you after."

Nikko stood and walked out with Quinn. M.J. walked over to the window and looked down. Outside, on the street below, the paramedic ambulance pulled away and drove off down the street. She closed her eyes and repeated the memory of the shooting from the time she stopped in the corridor to the moment she knelt over Ruben's body. She punished herself with the play-by-play, as if she were strapped to a chair and forced to watch the video of her loved ones being tortured over and over. She had to know why her instincts failed her. Yes, a good cop doesn't shoot to kill; a good cop shoots to save lives. But in that moment, she realized she had programmed herself into a gesture that had blocked her intuition. And that was not the action of a good cop. Her self-righteous approach had cost her the life of her partner and saved the life of a piece-of-shit lowlife killer gangbanger. Now, she knew how Beryl Ann had felt and her heart welled with compassion for her old friend, a compassion she could not extend to herself. Again, she rolled back the tape and played it over in her mind. Would she have done the same thing again? *Oh, God, Ruben, please forgive me. Hail Mary, Mother of Grace . . .*

Quinn walked in. She followed him silently into his office. Quinn watched her eyes travel to his desk. Nikko's gun and badge lay there.

"He's on leave with pay. I talked the commissioner out of no pay."

M.J. pulled her badge out and laid it down beside Nikko's.

"You take his, you take mine."

"So I'm gonna lose three good cops?"

"Sir, I tried to control the situation. I tried to control it . . ." She held back the tears again. "I made a choice. It didn't work out . . . An officer got killed."

"Mary Jane. You made a decision. It was the right decision. You got the wrong result is all. Now go get drunk. I am."

◆

M.J. went into her office and took off her blood-stained clothes and changed into the extra slacks and blouse she kept hanging on the back of her office door. Then she drove to Helen's to give her the night's bad news.

At the apartment door, M.J. was greeted by Mike, the new uniformed bodyguard, Burt's replacement. He was the young rookie who had been first on the scene when Jennifer Lyle had been found. M.J. had remembered his diligence and ingenuousness and had suggested him to Quinn after Burt's screwup.

Mike started to thank M.J., then he realized she was preoccupied; it looked like she had been crying. He stepped aside as she walked into the foyer. M.J. didn't know what she would tell Helen first until she opened the door. Mike moved away from the two women, sensing they needed privacy.

"We missed him."

"For God's sake—how did you let that happen? I don't believe it!"

"It's my fault. So stupid. We had a problem at headquarters. A crazy kid . . . and—Ruben's dead."

"Oh, dear God! What . . . come inside. Come in . . ."

M.J. was making a valiant attempt at stoicism.

"No, really, I'm okay. I just thought you ought to hear it from somebody and not see it on the news. I know you and him . . . You and he . . . had a thing."

Tears started running silently down her face. She brushed at them angrily. Helen looked at her tenderly. She sensed that M.J. was sitting on a long-unrecognized well of feelings for her dead partner. There is always that person whose affections you take for granted until it is too late. Helen knew M.J. knew and needed Ruben much longer and more profoundly than she ever had.

"Ruben and me? I think he felt sorry for me. He let me flirt with him and he was sweet enough to flirt back. He was a darling man."

"I thought he was a boy. This last Christmas was the happiest Christmas I had in six years. You know why? It was the first Christmas I was not in love." She started to pace as she told Helen things she had never said to anyone. "Son of a bitch married men! Who cares about marriage. The bed just gets crowded and noisy. Your phone is ringing. I've got to go."

M.J. started to head for the door, hoping to leave Helen's before she broke down altogether. Helen had no intention of picking up the phone while M.J. needed her attention. The answering machine clicked on in the background. Andy's voice on Helen's outgoing message echoed across the apartment. While the message played, Helen tried to ease M.J. into the living room and offered her some brandy.

"If you dialed carefully, you've reached the right number. Now you know what to do."

Helen asked M.J. "Who's the married man?"

The machine beeped. As the called began to leave a message, M.J. shrugged.

"What does it matter? Answer your phone."

Abruptly, a recording of the Village People singing "YMCA" interrupted them. The two women stared at each other. It seemed so absurd at this moment, on this night. Then over the song, loud and clear, the sound of Helen's voice came through the answering machine.

"All right, girls. What d'ya see? Some pretty cute guys. If one of them invited you out for a beer, you might go. Maybe dinner, dancing. Maybe even a dirty weekend in Big Sur . . . Well, let me tell you something. Ninety percent of serial killers are white males aged twenty to thirty-five just like these . . . Would you know if one of these cute guys is addicted to murder? Anything in their faces give you a clue?"

As the haunting message echoed through the loft, Helen and M.J. moved toward its source. They both began to run for the office. As they entered they heard Helen's voice continue to speak.

"Albert DeSalvo, Bianchi and Buono, Berkowitz, Dahmer . . . Ted Bundy. They were quiet, unassuming, even sweet. They held down jobs, made good neighbors. Their victims trusted them."

Helen grabbed the receiver.

"Peter Kurten."

Peter Foley hung up the phone as soon as he heard Helen's voice. He slipped the Walkman tape player back into his jacket pocket. He turned around to walk back into the club. A mass of swaying men in an odd mix of sixties- and seventies-styled paraphernalia, with a drag twist, danced to the tail end of the Village People. A few straight women and an occasional lesbian couple were sprinkled in the bunch. Overhead, garish-colored lights flashed and a mirrored ball spun slowly in the middle of the room, suspended from the ceiling. The disc jockey segued into Lou Reed's "Walk on the Wild Side."

Peter headed for the bar and bought two cocktails, a martini and a piña colada. Before he headed for his destination, he stopped at a side table, turned his back to the crowd and spilled a small quantity of white powder into the piña colada. He moved through the crowd toward a table in the corner, and almost bumped into a tall black man wearing a huge afro wig and striped gym pants. Sitting at the corner table in front of a large iron net screen were Andy and Hal, Peter's new friends. Peter handed Hal the martini and Andy the spiked piña colada. Andy downed the drink; he was pretty plastered already. Then Peter gave him a come-hither look and stretched out his hand. Andy took off his ridiculous jacket with a flourish and dumped it into Hal's lap dramatically, and then he turned and winked at Hal as he followed Peter onto the dance floor. Hal sat forlornly nursing his drink as he watched his date shimmy on the dance floor with the cute young stranger.

Peter and Andy danced one more dance, when Peter happened to glance over and see Hal drumming his folded leg, looking angry and impatient.

As the dance ended, Peter planned to steer them back to the table. At that moment, Andy started to weave and grasp his stomach and almost fell into Peter's arms. Peter cringed as the sick man grabbed on to him; this was no dance step. Andy looked at Peter, slapped his hand over his mouth and shook his head fast in apology as he ran for the bathroom.

Peter smiled to himself. This was working perfectly. He glanced over at Hal who was staring at the wall in defiance; surprised at the twinge of jealousy he felt over his friend's catch. He looked up as Peter strolled to the table.

"Where's Andy?"

"Didn't you see? Somebody cut in on me. They headed out the back way. I have a feeling you've seen the last of your friend tonight."

Hal stared at his martini. This really wasn't Andy's style to dump him without a word, but he had been drinking all night. Suddenly he felt Peter's arm slip around his shoulder. Hal looked at Peter, who smiled at him. Hal thought how charming he looked; he had that boyish bookworm thing that always used to turn him on.

Peter asked, "Hey, you feel like a drive up to Sausalito? It's a perfect night for it."

Hal nodded his head and stood up; he stumbled slightly, a little more drunk than he had anticipated.

They walked out in the alley toward the younger man's car. Hal carried Andy's jacket over his arm.

Peter pressed his hand lightly on the small of Hal's back as they walked. Hal liked the feel of it.

They got into the alley and Hal slowed down. They were alone. Now was a good time to test the waters. He turned in toward Peter and slipped his arm tentatively around him. Peter smiled and responded likewise, as if he were moving closer to kiss Hal. He let the moment hang between them for a breath, then he looked into Hal's eyes and punches his fist hard into his stomach.

◆

M.J. called the Task Force immediately after Peter hung up. While she was on with the station, Helen played back the answering machine and sat down at one of the terminals and started banging commands onto the keyboard.

"This is Inspector Monahan. Get the tap on Hudson's phone. See if it backtraced a call about two minutes ago." She checked her watch. "Yeah. Just this second he hung up. Don't fucking argue with me, just do it, now!"

"You were right. That's the connection. He must have been some kind of student of mine."

"Where did you give that lecture?"

"I gave it dozens of times. All over the country. It was my star turn."

"When was the last time you gave it in San Francisco?

"In Berkeley last year. Just before . . ." Helen was distracted. She stared at the monitor with the text of the lecture they had just heard. Then she highlighted the names of the serial killers. "There's the order. I gave it to him."

M.J. read it out loud over her shoulder. She still had the phone receiver glued to her ear while she waited for the results of the trace.

"DeSalvo, Bianchi and Buono, Berkowitz and Dahmer . . . It's going to be Dahmer next."

"Which means he'll kill a man. And after that . . ."

"Bundy. That's the last one in your speech." She backed up and focused on the phone; she was finally getting some news from the Task Force. "Yeah. The Sound Factory! Perfect. No, I know where it is. I'm going straight there, gimme some backup." She hung up. "Christ, Helen. Maybe, just maybe . . ."

M.J. ran for the front door. Helen sat in front of the terminal and dipped into her old teaching file. She started pouring over old course records.

◆

M.J. skidded to a stop in front of the Sound Factory and leaped out of her car. As she ran to the door, she saw through the tinted plate glass window that the place was closing. Waiters and bartenders were cleaning up.

She banged on the locked front door waving her badge at the manager who let her in.

"Why don't you guys just leave us in peace, man?"

"Where are your pay phones?"

She didn't wait for an answer because she saw

the Men's Room sign straight ahead, and peaking through a partition, the sign for Pay phones. She ran to the back of the club. A girl was on the phone in midargument with her boyfriend. As soon as M.J. saw her, she came to a dead stop. Her shoulders drooped. He had won again; there would be no decent prints tonight.

As she walked toward the exit, the backup uniforms started arriving. She shook her head. They didn't know who they were looking for. She instructed them to have somebody come down and take the prints anyway from the pay phone, although she knew it was meaningless.

She didn't remember driving home or taking off her clothes. When they called her at 6:40 A.M., she was dreaming about Ruben.

12

Fire

It was an Indian summer dawn in Sausalito by the bay. Last night's fog had dissolved in the late dark. When the sun rose in the east, the light shimmered and bounced off the green woods of Angel Island.

The regulars at Sarah's Bay-Side Diner and the guys fishing on the dock got a dilly of a sunrise. When they found the body, there was only old Tommy still eating inside the joint, a greasy burger ordered at 5:45 A.M. smothered in onions. He had dumped a load of ketchup and mustard on top of the oily brown onions. With all that lubrication, it was a wonder the meat didn't slide out of the bun and shoot across the room and land back on Sarah's grill. He was halfway through it when he saw the commotion down by the boats. Tommy put the burger down and went out to the water. He figured maybe one of those killer sharks washed up again with half a leg in its mouth. After he saw what it was, he never did go back and finish the burger.

Carl Woods stood in his rotting dinghy and gaffed it in. It was a big man's body, wearing the most bizarre jacket anybody there had ever seen. Nobody in Sausalito would have been caught dead in that jacket. Had to be from the city. Tommy joined the others staring at the corpse and making comments. "Hey, maybe that's why it don't have a head. Maybe he was too embarrassed for anybody to know who he was."

"Put a lid on it, Tommy."

◆

After M.J. got the phone call, she wished to hell that she had forced Quinn to take her badge. It had been the most godawful night she'd had in years and she knew she'd have to go tell Helen.

They'd found Andy's wallet and identification in the jacket. The copycat had done Dahmer, and he did it in a way specifically to get at Helen. M.J. tried to ground herself by going over the gestalt of everything she knew about the copycat killer. It all kept coming back to Helen. He had tracked down her Internet address and her phone number. He'd left the Son of Sam note specifically for her. He'd been to her lecture. He killed according to the order laid out in her speech. Now he had chosen to kill someone she loved.

Someone she loved. Within twenty-four hours, both women had lost a man for whom they deeply cared. Did this case have some weird karma? M.J. shook off the idea. There was no time for superstition. But she couldn't stop thinking about Ruben. She stuffed her grief down inside herself. She knew she would have to wait to feel it all when this was over. Then she would sit down and have a conversation with him, and tell him everything she had never said. She looked up at the ceiling for a minute and sat back in her bed. The longing to crawl back under the covers was immense. For a moment, she wished she could be a little girl again and snuggle up to her mother. Whenever she was sick as a child, which wasn't often, her mom would come sit with her on the bed and put her arms around her and whisper in her ear to remember her guardian angel. Her guardian angel was very small, but very powerful. She had long flowing golden curls and white gossamer wings. Sometimes she would sit on the headboard of her bed and sometimes she would perch on her shoulder.

M.J. picked up her gun and slid it into her holster. She looked up at the ceiling again. *I need you, Rube. Please stick around for a while. I need a guardian angel.*

Then she stood up, put on her jacket, and went out to her car and drove to Helen Hudson's.

◆

Helen sat sobbing, her face buried in her hands, willing herself quietly not to fall apart. M.J. held the bottle of Xanax.

"Helen . . ."

"I don't want to talk about it."

"How many do you need to sleep—really sleep? I hate to leave you like this, but I have to go. Helen?"

M.J. put the bottle in front of her. Helen just stared at it. Through the tears, she looked up at M.J.

"He's going to do Ted Bundy. Bundy was the last on the list." She forced herself to give everything she was capable of to M.J. "And he'll pick the most extravagant murder. The song talked about a threesome. Bundy killed three girls in one night at a sorority house. Chi Omega, I think. Bundy faked injuries, wore a cast on his arm, used crutches, and would ask girls for help. He drove a very distinctive car. What was it? Oh, God, I can't think . . ."

Helen rubbed her forehead. The shock of Andy's death on top of Ruben's and the stress of the case were clouding her mind. A migraine had moved in to share the same territory with her grief and guilt. She pulled herself up and beckoned M.J. to follow her into the study. She tapped the keyboard for a few seconds and up popped the Bundy profile she had finished after M.J. had left her the night before. Executed in 1989, Bundy was believed to have killed at least fifty young women and girls in possibly a half-dozen states during the seventies. She had taken all the essential elements of Bundy's modus operandi and distilled them into a list for M.J. Then she had created an appendix of all the murders, a description of the victims, times and places, etc. M.J. stood in silent gratitude as Helen printed it out for her. They never spoke again before M.J. left. Both women felt a primitive desire to hold each other the way women have comforted each other through the ages after they've lost a son or husband or father to war. It seemed they were losing everyone.

But they were the soldiers now. They did not touch each other. M.J. walked out clutching the notes on Bundy, praying that she held the key.

◆

"We're looking for a gold Volkswagen bug. We need to get onto the DMV. We want records on all gold or yellowed colored VW bugs, any year. I want an in-person check on every registered owner."

Inspector Mary Jane Monahan was briefing a full assembly of homicide inspectors, uniformed policemen and women. A lot of suits were mixed in around the table. A few of them were press relations. One or two local FBI had finally joined the game until the heavies from Virginia could fly in. They were jammed into the Task Force Room, standing room only. The big tabletop was littered with yellow pads, IBM notebooks, telephones, and Coke cans.

M.J. stood framed next to the projection screen and the glass brick wall. She wore her brown suit jacket with its matching skirt and her long hair was down, pinned up behind her ears. Despite her youth, femininity, and small frame, she radiated an intensity and power that was magnified by her anger and determination. Intelligence and command. It was almost as if the energy of all the deaths that had surrounded her over the last several weeks had built up inside her and were focused to a laser point of action. Behind her was a blackboard with a few details about Ted Bundy on it.

"If it's rental—check rental first—get names and locations of who is driving one now. Contact campus security at every college within fifty miles."

Lieutenant Quinn walked in and stood at the back of the room and watched M.J. She made eye contact with every essential player in that room as she moved through her checklist. Every one was suitably awed at her focus and intensity. They all knew about the shooting the day before, the tremendous loss she had experienced. Every cop has a sense of the deep connection between partners. Your partner on the force is the person whose life depends on yours day in and day out, and vice versa. They are your life's blood.

One by one, over the last fifteen hours, most of the cops who sat in front of her had approached M.J. and said a few words about Ruben. To a man or woman, the ones who had seen her shoot the kid had told her she'd done the best she could. There was nothing she could have done better or different. It was Ruben's time.

"They need to warn all female students, especially those with long, straight, dark hair parted in the middle—that's who Bundy went after—to avoid any contact with males they don't know. Also to report any man with an injury or handicap who asks them for help . . . carrying books, groceries, anything like that."

Quinn watched her knowing he had done the right thing by picking her to head the investigation. She didn't need Nikko. She'd gone way beyond him. This girl . . . this woman had the kind of guts and brains he had only seen in a few cops in his lifetime, and one was her father. He needed to know this because he'd spent the last hour staving off the clowns from Internal Affairs who were itching to get into yesterday's shootout. He'd had to throw Nikko to them, knowing it was inevitable. But he couldn't afford to lose M.J. from this investigation. He had that feeling in the pit of his stomach that the Copycat Murders were about to break wide open.

"We need to arrange a press conference to get this out to TV and radio, particularly the college stations. Can we get a police spokesman up here so I can brief him? Contact law enforcement and every neighboring area that has a Chi Omega chapter and have them post a security detail. That's probably where he'll make his move."

Quinn also knew she had disobeyed his direct orders to cut Helen Hudson out of the investigation. He turned this around in his mind. Once again, M.J. had been right. Nevertheless, he knew he was going to have to go head to head with her on that one.

Quinn watched her after she finished her speech. The folks she still needed in the room huddled in pockets. She was talking to Pachulski, Kerby, and Landis. Quinn referred to these guys as the Three Stooges. They were good detectives, but the biggest goofballs in his department. He eased up behind them as M.J. laid out their orders. She needed them to cover Andy Friedman's murder, the Dahmer one. Kerby and Landis were to go back to the Sound Factory and canvas the staff. She wanted Pachulski to track down Andy's date. They hung on her every word.

Respect. No matter how smart or driven or ruthless a detective, they don't make it up through the ranks without it. He gave her less than five years before she had his job. He knew that if she were a man, it would be sooner.

For a moment, she made eye contact with him. He smiled at her, a thumbs-up smile with a dose of pride. She took it in and went back to work.

◆

Dr. Helen Hudson sat in her dark study ringed by her triad of terminals, all a dead gray. She leaned over and booted up the center hard drive and monitor. She closed her eyes and let her mind drift and clear while the computer went through its wake-up process. A few dozen icons popped up against the pale magenta background, each representing a piece of software or program or CD-ROM. She opened her eyes, and in a slow, deliberate gesture placed her hand on the smooth, round turbo mouse that nestled beside her keyboard. Gray plastic, cool and hard. The only sound in the loft was the low singing of the terminal. Her face was set. A sad, high priestess poised for some kind of dark ritual.

She rolled the mouseball slightly toward a little icon with a camera and scissors, and clicked. She had rarely used this graphics program.

In her mind, she locked onto the man she thought of as Peter Kurten—a contemporary incarnation of an aberration. He had this software, too, or something equivalent. This was how he had made all the lovely Valentines he had sent her out of season. Now she would make one for him.

She culled through all the graphic images that were stored on her system, thousands of them. She knew exactly what she was looking for and where to find each one. This was not a systematic search. It was as if the unseen force of purpose that was driving her guided her directly to the specific images she needed. A photo of a bride and groom in the classic wedding cake pose filled the screen. A death's head skull materialized next to it. An image of her own face pasted itself over the bride's. The skull floated into place atop the groom's neck.

She turned to the terminal on her right, the one on a modem with the Internet and turned it on. As it came to life, under the assemblage, she typed:

PETER KURTEN. I'M READY.
HUDSONHEL@UNIVOLD.COM

Then she tapped the keys to send her wedding invitation out onto all the open bulletin boards.

She sat and stared at the collage in the silence. Then she heard the unmistakable sound of her front door opening. Feet were moving toward her, cautious and deliberate.

Attempting to make as little noise as possible, Helen's eyes and hands searched her office, looking for anything she could find to defend herself. She tried to keep her breathing quiet. It was fast and hard, but she managed to push the panic down. Her right hand settled on the cool metal handle of a letter opener, almost buried under the mound of notes and papers scattered over her desk. She had not opened her mail herself in months. Andy had handled that.

Helen grasped the sharp paper knife and eased herself out of her chair. She moved to the door and raised the weapon and waited. The footsteps grew closer, the heavy imprint of a man.

Then he turned into the office. She lunged at him and brought the knife down. Just short of stabbing him, she jerked the knife back in midair and screamed.

"Andy." Then she screamed and screamed.

"Stop screaming!" She screamed again and then she hugged him and kissed him all over.

"For God's sake, stop! My head. I have the mother of all hangovers. Very quiet in the hospital zone, please."

She clung to him. "Where have you been? They

said you were dead. Oh, thank God you're not dead."

"No, I didn't get home till 3:00 A.M. I was so sick and drunk, I've been passed out all day. Who are you talking about? And why would they think I was dead?"

"Oh, God, Andy, do you know where Hal is?"

He looked at her and he was very afraid. Andy started talking very fast, explaining that he thought Hal had gone home with the cute guy he had been dancing with. Maybe, he was even a little jealous. He had chalked it up to all's fair in love and war. But Andy couldn't figure out why Hal didn't leave him his jacket. Andy had waited for a while by Hal's car, but he never came back.

Helen got him to shut up finally, and told him about the headless body that was found with Andy's jacket and identification. It fit the Dahmer copy-killing they had been too late to stop.

This time it was her turn to comfort him, payback for all the times he had held her in his arms. Andy knelt on the floor and lay his head in Helen's lap and wept for his friend. Helen allowed him a few minutes of grief, then she bent down to him and spoke gently.

"You've seen him, Andy. You've met him and talked to him. You've got to go to the station now."

He lifted his head and nodded. Then she helped him up off the floor.

◆

". . . Then he gave me this piña colada and I started to feel really wild . . . and sort of stoned. Then I got really nauseous. See, I'm allergic to painkillers and sleeping pills and all that kind of stuff. Anyway, I had to really race for the john. I was horribly sick. Over and over and over."

Lieutenant Quinn sat almost knee-to-knee with Andy and M.J. stood behind him. They were in the Task Force Room listening to Andy's story. Pachulski sat nearby working the phones.

"You were sick. What happened then?"

"I have to tell it my way." Andy paused to let them know who was boss. Despite the fact he was feeling lousy from his hangover and the death of his friend, he was enjoying his star turn in front of a captive audience. "I was in there a very long time. And when I came out, they were gone. So was my jacket, which I gave to Hal when I was dancing. Hal was my . . ." He dropped his head and choked a little. How do you explain this kind of friendship to a couple of heterosexual law enforcement officers?

Andy and Hal weren't lovers, but they had been very dear friends. It was the kind of deep loyalty and caring that was now commonplace in the gay community—friendship born of a continuous chain of shared grief. If a gay man in San Francisco were alive in the nineties, chances are he had seen a lot of his friends die. This had been the case with Andy and Hal.

"Could I have a glass of water?"

Gigi walked in with a sheaf of printouts of drivers' licenses with copies of their photographs.

"M.J., DMV printouts on guys who sold or rented gold VWs in the last six months."

M.J. handed them to Andy. He took a while to look through them and then he saw Peter Foley's picture.

"That's him."

Quinn jumped up. "Okay. Let's go. Patch, call the SWATs, will you. With this little shitkicker, I'm not taking chances."

Everybody got moving to prepare for the raid. On the way to the squad room, M.J. called out to Gigi. "Get a hold of Helen Hudson and let her know we tracked him down."

M.J. came into the squad room to grab a bulletproof vest. Nicoletti was cleaning out his desk across the room. They were alone. She went to her desk, pulled out the vest, then went into an empty office off the room and took off her crisp white cotton shirt to put the vest on underneath. She tucked her shirt into her black slacks and walked back out to gather a few last-minute things at her desk. She glanced over at Nikko; he looked out of place and vulnerable in his casual civilian clothes.

"Kinda defeats the purpose of my Miracle bra. But who's looking?"

"I hear you're onto him. Good work."

"Just horseshit luck."

"I don't think so. You take care out there."

"Don't I always?"

She sat down at her desk. He had moved closer

to her. He stood behind her and leaned over to almost touch her hair with his lips.

"I love you, you know."

"Yes, I know."

He left her. Alone in the squad room, with the echo of Nikko's voice and smell, the fury and the sorrow over Ruben's death rose up inside her again. Despite the fact she needed to move quickly, she waited one of the longest minutes of her life. She wanted to make sure Nikko would be out of sight completely before she walked out of the station.

◆

On the coast just barely south of San Francisco, a little ways past Lake Merced, sits a little town called Daly City. It's in a pocket of land set off by the spots where Skyline Drive intersects the Pacific Coast Highway on the left and the 280 crosses it on the right. The huge Olympic Country Club golf course creeps right down to Daly City's northern border and Thornton State Beach lies under it to the south. Plenty of residents are lucky enough to have a view of pieces of the Santa Cruz Mountain ridge spread out in the near distance.

Peter and Georgette Foley rented an old frame house up on a gentle rise in a nice middle-class neighborhood surrounded by trees, oak and eucalyptus. It was a little shabby on the exterior, but neither one of them cared. Outside appearances weren't of great importance to either of them anymore.

As she sped down the 280 and off onto John Daly Boulevard, M.J. wondered what kind of house they were going to find. *What kind of home does the average American serial murderer live in?* As they turned off Daly onto the side street that led up to Foley's neighborhood, she observed just how normal everything was. This might be the kind of place she would pick to live in if she ever met a guy she could settle down with.

She followed the SWAT bus up the hill and watched it park. Then she pulled up much farther down the street, away from what she knew would soon become bedlam. It was a trick her father had taught her when she was a rookie. If you know it's going to be a big raid with a lot of press and CSUs afterward, park a few blocks away. That way you can get out of there easily.

As she ran back toward the bus, she saw its doors open. One by one, the SWAT boys disembarked from their sleek jet black transport, bouncing down silently onto the street like Indians to the hunt. They were all in black, with heavy arms and full body bulletproof vests. Several wore helmets mounted with inset lamps, which made them look like coal miners gone to war. They took up their positions, silently ringing the house.

M.J. climbed onto the SWAT bus and found Quinn close to the infrared surveillance monitor setup. The SWATs showed up as fuzzy shadows on the heat-sensitive infrared. The radio crackled with whispered communiqués.

M.J. thought she saw the outline of a man in a

cellar window as one of the armed silhouettes passed across the lighted window to camouflage himself in the trees. She pointed it out to Quinn on the monitor just as the light in the window went out.

Outside the house, the SWAT guy near the cellar heard moaning. Then he could vaguely see a man pick up what looked like a gun. He whispered all this into his radio wire pickup. The SWAT commander picked up his bullhorn.

"Peter Foley, this is the police. Please come to the front door and come out with your hands above your head."

The barrel of the gun in the cellar lifted up and flames shot out; it was a propane barbecue lighter. A smoke alarm went off inside. Flames flickered in the cellar.

The commander gave the signal to move in. M.J. watched as the lethal shadows broke down the front door and kicked in windows, busting in all over the house.

A few neighbors started trickling out on their front porches. Lights were flipping on all over the block. Some residents were afraid enough and smart enough to stay inside.

As the SWAT team poured into the house, it began to fill with smoke. The house was completely dark in the living room and hallways. The helmet lights were turned on. The smoke particles in the shafts of light swirled like ghosts and made the air appear thick and alive. Weapons were lifted and sighted. Narrow red beams of laser light crisscrossed the smoky room. The men could smell gasoline everywhere and at least three reports of gasoline-soaked furniture and carpets went out over the wire.

M.J. looked at Quinn. The house was a bomb waiting to happen.

A couple of the guys reached the bedroom. They kicked in the locked door. Georgette sat in bed with her dinner tray in front of her and the television on. A small red hole in her cheek marked the place where the bullet had entered. A dark splash of her blood had skidded across the precious wallpaper with the pale pink roses behind the bed.

One of the commandos poked the bathroom door open with the barrel of his assault rifle. Sweetie was strung upside down from the shower rod, her rusty fir soaked in red.

The fire was beginning to spread rapidly throughout the house. The men in the bedroom were given the order to pull out.

They heard screams from the cellar door, the source of the smoke. A brave SWAT team member in the kitchen kicked the door open and looked down into the wall of flame. Suddenly, as if borne out of hell itself, a man on fire from head to foot burst up the stairs screaming. He made it halfway up, then the basement stairs collapsed and he was sucked down the inferno. The blaze began to suck the air out of the kitchen; the SWAT guy felt himself pulled into the hot vacuum. Two of his comrades grabbed him and everyone ran for the doors.

M.J. watched on the monitor as flames began to lick out of the lower windows of the house. She heard the command to evacuate. Quinn looked at her; he knew she was about to blow just like the house. M.J. got up and before Quinn could grab her, she ran through the bus and out to the scene outside.

As the men ran out of the house onto the lawn, several doubled over coughing. The shriek of fire engine sirens blistered the night. The house that Peter and Georgette rented ever since their honeymoon, exploded in a massive fireball. M.J. watched her case go up in smoke.

As she stood in the street watching the firefighters move up the hill, and the SWAT team coming down, M.J. let her mind take a survey of her feelings. She felt nothing but a general numbness, as if someone had washed her body in anesthetic. Quinn came over and patted her on the back. "Good work, kiddo. It's all over."

Pachulski, Kerby, and Landis all walked over and hugged her. "Way to go, M.J.!" Somebody said something about Ruben, but she didn't really hear it. Now she knew the meaning of anticlimax. *Oh, yeah, We caught the guy. Killed at least five people. Burned himself to death.* Maybe, she just wanted to see him once. Look him in the eye, face-to-face, like he had looked at all those girls trapped and helpless. She wanted to make him feel what it was like. And she knew it was a ridiculous notion. She wished Helen was there. Most of all she wished for Ruben. She kept expecting him to show up any moment with a box of Chinese take-out, the weirdest stuff on the menu.

The KXBU van pulled up and the Mouth emerged looking impeccable. She had a full crew with her. Other local news stations were beginning to arrive. This one would make the national networks tonight.

Susan Schiffer was in an excellent mood. She had dogged this baby from the beginning and she swooped down on Quinn before the other vultures were set up. Susan snubbed M.J.—retaliation for all the stonewalling she had put up with. That was fine with M.J. She was reveling in her numbness.

"I am here with Lieutenant Quinn of the Homicide Division. Can you tell us what happened here tonight?"

Quinn was more than happy to reply. The brass had been all over him like white on rice for the last few weeks. He'd been living on an alternate diet of Alka-Seltzer and Pepto-Bismol. This was a moment of glory he thought he'd never see.

"The San Francisco Police Department developed evidence the killer, known as the Copycat Killer, was an individual named Peter Foley who resided at this address. Upon being asked to step out of the house to be interviewed, it is believed Mr. Foley set fire to his residence. Perhaps to destroy evidence of the murder of another woman found dead by gunshot wounds, possibly his wife."

M.J. saw Commissioner Petrillo arrive. He would conduct the press conference. Of course they expected her to stay, to stand in the back with the SWAT commander and accept their kudos. All she wanted was for one moment to feel the sense of relief she had expected, to feel the elation that comes from finding the bad guy. She couldn't get to that feeling.

"Hey, Patch." M.J. grabbed Pachulski who was taking to one of the SWAT guys he'd come up with from the academy. "Let Quinn know I'm outta here."

"Where you going, Mary Jane? This is your moment of glory."

"Tell him I'm going to Disneyland."

She headed up the street toward her car, a few blocks past the chaos. The neighborhood was lit up like a Christmas night. A helicopter buzzed overhead. M.J. couldn't wait to get away from the cacophony of sounds: the roar of the fire and the screams to the men fighting it blended with the bullhorns of the police trying to control the crowds and the bustle of the news crews. The noxious effluvia of the firefighters' chemicals wafted through the haze. Blue-and-red lights spun and flashed and smoke blackened the air. As M.J. reached her car, salt-and-pepper ash began to rain down around her. A suburban Vietnam.

She unlocked the car and shut the door against the disorder. For a moment, she breathed in the relative silence and welcome smell of musty vinyl. She was still uneasy, unsettled inside . . . as if she couldn't believe it was really over. She turned on the radio. The press conference had begun and

Quinn's familiar voice disrupted her little refuge like a rumor of impending death.

". . . A number of witnesses saw Mr. Foley in the burning building. However, their attempts to rescue him were unsuccessful. At this point, we believe he perished in the fire. . . ."

M.J. decided she couldn't take any more of this and she picked up the Motown hits cassette that she and Ruben thought of as their favorite driving music. Or as he would have said, "My favorite white-knuckle music." Marvin Gaye and Tammi Terrell came on midsong. "You're all I need to get by," were the first words she heard.

M.J. slammed her fist against the dash and twisted off the radio. The whole thing didn't sit right with her—the dramatic fire, the convenient body in the basement. The Copycat had wanted his moment with Helen more than anything, and that was the element that was missing. M.J. closed her eyes and her hand went reflexively to her stomach, and brushed against the tightness in her belly. She let her mind go there, the seat of her cop's intuition. Then she knew what she had to do. She picked up the cellular and punched in Helen's number.

◆

Helen Hudson had run from her office for a television after she'd heard the recent developments on her police scanner. She paced the den nervously as she aimed her remote control, channel surfing for the best coverage of the press conference from

Daly City. She stared longingly at a stray bottle of cognac, picked it up, and hid it in the bottom drawer of a cabinet.

She locked on to Susan Schiffer interviewing Lieutenant Quinn on television. Behind them, she could see the fire department hosing down the smoldering house. Quinn spoke with cocky assurance, a man finally off the hook, saved by the lucky cooperation of a dead man.

". . . A number of witnesses saw Mr. Foley in the burning building. However, their attempts to rescue him were unsuccessful. At this point, we believe he perished in the fire. . . ."

"Idiots!" Helen blasted the room, empty of other life save for the flickering blue light of the television. She would have to try to track down M.J. Only she would understand that the Copycat couldn't possibly be dead. He had unfinished business with her.

The buzzer sounded. Disgusted with the news conference, she muted the television and headed for the front door. She gazed through the peephole and thought she saw Mike, even though his face was turned away, distorted by the fish-eye glass. He turned toward her and she was relieved.

"Mike?"

Captured in the strange window of the tiny peephole she caught sight of a second man hovering close to him, another uniformed cop. His badge glistened, bouncing the light off the yellow walls of the massive hallway. His face was obscured beneath the shiny black brim of his hat.

Helen squeezed her eye close, but all she could see was an abbreviated picture of the two men waiting for her to open the door. It seemed that they were conferring quietly, but their conversation was a blended murmur through the heavy door.

Helen unlatched the door at the same moment the phone started to ring in the background. She was distracted momentarily as the door swung open and she looked back toward her living room and began to address the two policemen.

"I just saw on the news. Tell your people it's a mistake . . ."

She stopped midsentence, shocked silent by a spray of war liquid. Helen looked down and saw she was covered in blood. She reeled back screaming and saw Mike sink to his knees, a fountain of blood pouring from his sliced carotid in a brilliant red fan.

The other cop leaped over him, sailing through the door like a giant black bat, the wet blade glittering in his outstretched fist. Helen turned to run, but the man in the cop uniform broadsided her, slamming her facedown into the floor with a flying tackle. She tried desperately to twist out from under him, but he kept her pinned with the advantage of weight and surprise. Helen continued to struggle frantically like a trapped animal, so he pounded her brutally in the face three times for good measure. She blinked up in terror, dazed and nose bloodied, and she attempted to focus—to pull her wits about her. In that moment, the answering machine clicked on and she heard M.J.'s voice through the throbbing pain in her head and the manic sound of her own breath:

"It's M.J. I'm sure you heard on your scanner. Something doesn't sit right. I know it's late, but I'm on my way over. We need to talk."

The machine clicked off and Peter Foley grinned down at Helen Hudson. Helen's eyes darted back and forth in panic, but she caught sight of the hypo in his hand, which seemed to materialize out of nowhere, long and awful.

"Company's coming," he whispered to her.

He raised his arm and jammed the needle into her bicep. She screamed in pain and was swallowed in moments by merciful blackness.

13

Endgame

M.J. drove up to Helen's apartment building and pulled in behind Mike's black-and-white police cruiser parked near the entrance. She glanced inside the police car as she walked by; cold coffee in a paper cup sat on the dashboard.

She entered the building. Once in the stairwell, M.J. knew something didn't feel right. Alert to the smell of blood and fear she called out, "Mike?"

Halfway up the stairs she froze. Rivulets of drying blood stained the steps before her. She unsnapped her holster and faded against the wall, gazing up, straining to listen. She heard nothing but the pulsing of her own blood pounding in her ears. She drew her sidearm and bounded up the steps.

She found the hallway several yards from Helen's door awash in blood. The walls were streaked and spattered; she stepped over a long smear that crossed the floor from one corridor to the other. Thinking the worst for the young cop, M.J. whispered to herself, "Fuck." And then she moved on inexorably toward Helen's, choking down her fear with each step. She walked slowly down the hallway, gun leveled, riveted on the open metal door. Her eyes traveled down to the foot of the door. A wide, sticky pool of blood lay at her feet, the source of the trail down the hall.

M.J. stepped gingerly over the dark mess. She pushed the thought of the sweet young cop to the back of her brain and let the juice of her anger refocus the fear that threatened to jerk her back and out the door. Something told her that Helen was still alive and that thought kept her going.

She lunged into the apartment, swinging her gun in all directions, trying to cover a two-hundred-degree radius. There was only darkness and silence.

M.J. glanced down at the floor. There were bloody shoe prints everywhere. Someone had tracked Mike's blood all through the apartment. She followed the bloody tracks farther in, flinching at shadows and the hidden demons that dwelt in their darkness like the closet monsters of every child's nightmare.

Something flickered out of the corner of her eye and she spun to shoot and found herself face-to-face with her own image. She stood still breathless and pointed her gun at herself, projected in the gray box of a television monitor. Her image expanded on the screen as she grew closer. A camcorder rested on top of the television, wired in to her live image. Attached to the camcorder was a Post-It note carefully hand-lettered that read: "Press play."

She hesitated, tracking the shadows with her gun, taking no chances, blinking sweat from her eyes without touching her face or losing focus. She fumbled her walkie-talkie from her belt and raised it to her mouth and spoke softly.

"Monahan requesting backup at Pier One Fort Mason. One officer missing, over."

The voice crackled back over the walkie.

"Copy request for backup."

M.J. pressed the play button on the camcorder. An image popped up on the screen. Helen was sprawled unconscious in an easy chair wearing the special red suit she had warn the day Daryll Lee had confronted her at Berkeley. A dark figure moved into frame, humming tonelessly as he arranged her limp form.

With dread fascination, M.J. glanced at the very same easy chair some eight feet away, now empty. Her eyes were drawn back to the screen as the dark figure backed up toward the camera as he appraised Helen, his body a dark unfocused blur shifting right and left, arrogantly wiping against the lens itself. Abruptly, he turned, stooped down, and stared directly into the lens from a foot away. The autofocus grabbed the image of his face, monstrously close and distorted like the fish-eye of Helen's peephole. Peter Foley, the Copycat, had created this little performance especially for M.J.

"Hi, there. We join our program already in progress." He backed up at this point. "Inspector Monahan. Don't you ever get tired of being a day late and a dollar short?"

Peter circled behind Helen, crouched down, and started buttoning up the front of her dress, maintaining his conversational tone.

"So what do you think? Should I just slit her throat right now? Cut my losses, so to speak?" He seemed to look directly at M.J. "I mean, I couldn't do Ted Bundy, you people saw to that. Was it the car? Yeah, the gold VW I bet. I guess even cops can't help tripping over the obvious from time to time."

He finished buttoning Helen's dress, then he fiddled with something in his hand. He was using the camcorder remote to zoom in to a tighter two-shot, his face close to Helen's.

"So what to do? Finish it here and now? What would Helen say, if she could talk? What would her professional opinion be?" Peter patted the unconscious Helen on the shoulder and smoothed the fabric of her red jacket. "She'd probably say, naw, Peter's got another agenda. She'd toss in some happy crap about my deep need for attention, the damaged child within. I've got insight, see, 'cause I read all her books."

He looked at the camera again as if he were interviewing M.J. before his next move. "But what might that other agenda be? Skip Ted Bundy altogether? Go on to some thunderous grand finale?

Finish off where somebody else left off, maybe. That sound about right to you?"

He stood up, widening the angle at the same time with the remote. "Who am I to argue with a smart lady like her? Okay, quick impression . . ."

Peter whipped a gleaming bowie knife out from his belt and let out a redneck rebel yell, "Ooooo-weeee! Me and this here foxy lady gon' have some *fun!*"

He paused, looking to the camera as if he were due some kind of reaction. None forthcoming, he shrugged. "Okay, so maybe I'm not ready for Vegas . . ." He approached the lens as if ready to share a secret. ". . . But I think you get the idea, am I right? If you're a smart cop, you'll come alone . . ." He leaned in very close to the lens and whispered intimately, ". . .'cause if you storm in with the troops, I'll see she dies in incredible pain. Sincerely."

He aimed the remote, pressed a button, and the image vanished. M.J. was left staring at herself on the live feed, dwarfed by the silent apartment, witness to Helen's kidnapping.

M.J. ran through the apartment, jumped the pool of blood, and left the door open as she'd found it. She took the stairs three at a time and hustled for her car. She'd already run three red lights before she slapped the emergency light on the hood. The blue unmarked Chevy headed east out of Fort Mason down North Point a few blocks to Columbus Avenue, which ran in a southeast diagonal that would cut her way almost directly across town to the 80 and access to the Bay Bridge. M.J. sped through the night and barked and swore her way through three police radio operators before she could get Quinn on the line; he was still wrapped up in the business at Daly City. Quinn's voice came through garbled by overlapping dialogue and radio static.

". . . You are not to go in alone, you got that? You are to wait for proper backup."

". . . Just make goddamn sure all units respond code two."

". . . And you make goddamn sure you acknowledge my goddamn direct order! You stay out of that building until help arrives! Copy that, M.J.? *Copy?*"

"Yeah, yeah." And she floored it through another intersection as she headed for the entrance to the Bay Bridge.

◆

Helen awoke smothered in blackness. As she regained consciousness, her claustrophobia kicked in; she was encased in some kind of black cloth that clung to the skin of her face with every in-breath. This effect was compounded by her building anxiety, which caused her to hyperventilate. She couldn't open her mouth, something smashed her lips together, probably tape.

She prayed for instant death, preferable to the ordeal she imagined was yet to come. There were probably only a handful of people on the face of the earth who understood and anticipated the rituals of the lust killer better than she. Peter

Foley's was one of the most elaborate and brilliant minds she had encountered, and she rightly deduced that he had probably borne the most horrible of tortures himself. She had become the repository of all his resentment, all his blame, all the great cruelties and indiscretions that had been visited upon him his entire life. Helen knew she was his vision achieved. He had come to unlock the tomb of his pain and shower the sum total of those horrors on her. Tit for tat. Then he could die and nothing really mattered beyond that.

In the moment Peter Foley slipped off the black hood that covered her head, Dr. Helen Hudson knew she faced a more horrifying death than any living being, no matter how cruel, could deserve to endure.

She pretended to be unconscious still, which was easy as she was still groggy with the drugs he had given her. He crouched in front of her and cracked a vial of ammonia directly under her nostrils and she gasped, flinched, and turned her head away. She squinted against the assault of bright light around her.

Peter whispered to her in mock soothing fashion. "Easy, Helen. You'll be okay. That stuff keeps you groggy for a while."

He was charged by their intimacy, her name like a sweet liqueur in his mouth, expensive and delicate. He couldn't believe he could say it and be this close to her.

He rose and left her, a dark smudge fading past her hazy vision. Helen blinked rapidly, her eyes dry from the drugs and darkness. She forced herself to focus; to grasp her surroundings. Everything was white, cold, hard. She was closeted in a narrow space with metal sides. *Oh, God.* She sucked in her breath and cried with realization, a horrible moan trapped in her throat by the duct tape that covered her mouth. She shut her eyes and saw Daryll Lee laughing at her, ridiculing her. His voice penetrated her, loud and vulgar. *"It ain't over yet, Helen. This little fucker has plans for you. And I'm sitting at the back of his mind holding the strings."* Then she saw the terrible blade of his great knife slice Joe Shields's neck. In that moment of horrific déjà vu, just as she realized where she was, a loop of steel wire dropped over her head and cinched tight around her neck. It jerked from above. She felt her hands lifted above her head as she struggled and slipped on the porcelain. The wires wrapped around her wrists and her arms were jerked up in the air and pulled tight to the same wire that descended to the loop around her throat. Then he hoisted her, kicking and choking, gasping for breath through her nose. Her legs drummed the sides of the stall until they found their purchase on the toilet seat.

From her new vantage point in the air, she saw Mike's body slumped against the far wall, posed exactly as Daryll Lee had left Joe Shields. A smear and spatter of blood were theatrically re-created by Peter's hand.

After securing the wires that held her on the overhead pipes, Peter came back into her stall. He stared up at her terrified eyes and smiled at his handiwork. Then in a flash, his expression changed to disapproval. His face assumed the frown of a parent who had just caught a naughty child in a forbidden act.

"No. This is wrong."

He entered the stall and Helen whimpered in horror. He pulled off her right shoe and let it drop to the floor just as it had a little over a year ago. Helen's mind reeled. How did he know that little detail? It was as if Daryll Lee had drawn him a blueprint, a master plan to re-create his Waterloo. But did he rewrite the ending?

Peter stepped back, studying the composition.

"Better," he pronounced.

He turned from the stall, moving to the sinks where a camcorder waited on a tripod. He popped the lens cap off and peeked through the eyepiece and squared up the shot.

"You have any idea how valuable this tape's gonna be? *Hard Copy* . . . *20/20* . . . *America's Grisliest Home Videos*, whatever the hell it's called . . . shit, they'll be killing each other for the rights to air it. Talk about a ratings grabber."

He focused the camcorder up at the first stall and glanced up at Helen. "Smile, Helen. You're gonna be the most famous victim of all time."

He pressed the RECORD button and a red light came on. He grabbed a roll of tightly wound fabric from the silk and moved toward her. It looked like some kind of dark felt material.

"And me? If this were an Olympic event, they'd

have to give me the gold medal. If this were football, I'd be winning the Super Bowl." He walked into her stall and continued to lecture his captive audience. "You know more books have been written about Jack the Ripper than Abraham Lincoln?"

He dropped down to one knee, as if to propose, and slowly and ceremoniously unwrapped the roll of fabric onto the floor. Sewn into the sterile felt were patched sleeves, each of which held a glistening surgical tool, polished and needle-sharp—an eclectic sampler designed to carve into human flesh in a variety of ways. Peter gazed up at Helen with a strange mixture of desire and bravado.

"Sick fucking world, isn't it?"

Peter's whole demeanor had transformed over the last few weeks. Despite the morbid urges and sadistic cruelty that had raged in his soul for years, he had always preserved a persona of normalcy on the outside. He rarely cursed or spoke in vulgar colloquialisms. As his adventures into killing expanded and succeeded, a new personality emerged. Perhaps even his correspondence with Daryll Lee had added to the fire that had facilitated his transition from dreamy Walter Mitty to contemporary de Sade. Peter had finally found himself. He threw off the constricting costume of boy-next-door and assumed the mantle of the showman.

Earlier that night he had savored his time alone with Helen at her apartment, sharing the afterglow of fresh kills with her, even though she was unconscious at the time. He had laid her out on her bed and stripped off her jeans and sweatshirt, down to her camisole and panties. He admired their reflection captured in the full-length mirror on the inside door of the closet—Peter and Helen together. He savored the image of him in his bloodied police uniform crouched over her seminude body. He had wanted to touch her more intimately, perhaps even make love to her. But he knew there was no time. He was focused on his goal and he knew he had to get to Berkeley long before Inspector Monahan in order for everything to be set up perfectly.

Then he dug through her closet to find the red suit. She had buried it as far back as she could after the night she had found it on the bed from the first time he had broken in. He had some trouble putting her arms into the red jacket and pulling up the matching skirt. He chose some pumps that he thought she might have worn that day. It irked him that he didn't know the exact pair of shoes. Detail was so important; he wanted Daryll Lee to be impressed. Nevertheless, dressing Helen calmed him, relaxed his mind, and prepared him for the next more complicated stage of his plans.

He had to get Mike's body into the car without it being noticed. For this he had brought a furniture dolly, a garbage bag, and an empty cardboard box that had housed one of his new television sets. He had rented a brand-new dark green Nissan pickup that day. His own car would be out of the question; it had to remain near the house to be found after the fire. After he put Mike in the car, Peter carried

Helen down the back stairwell uninterrupted by any other tenants. Lifting her up into the front seat was more difficult, but the adrenaline high that kept him afloat all night pumped him through the strain. He slammed the truck door and smiled. Piece of cake.

Then they were on the bridge. The familiar humming that only a bridge and cars make together resonated through the truck. They passed through the Yerba Buena Island tunnel. He pretended briefly that they were a married couple on a car trip; she slept while he eased them through the night.

Now in the big white bathroom, they were approaching their final moments together. Once again he imagined that they were destined to be together, some bizarre variation of Romeo and Juliet—star-crossed and meant to die in a blaze of poetic glory . . . this time captured on videotape and broadcast live.

Peter chose a scalpel and pulled it delicately from its felt pocket. He approached Helen slowly, as if to ask her to dance. He gently lifted the fabric of the red skirt in his hands. Helen looked down, her eyes bulging with terror. He began slicing upward with a sinewy whisper of parting fabric. The white skin of her stomach was unveiled, convulsed with the shallow breath of panic.

"Careful. Careful," he cautioned softly. And just then the scalpel nicked her skin, drawing a single drop of blood. "See? Now you've gone and cut yourself."

The scalpel continued to ascend in its journey up her body. Helen could not help hyperventilating, her rapid and shallow breath able to move only through her nose. She clamped her eyes shut, her only means to cut herself off from the image of the nightmare that held her captive.

"Don't do that. Don't shut your eyes. Helen?"

She refused to respond.

"Helen. Open your fucking eyes or I'll slice off your eyelids like Kemper did to that one girl so she'd *have* to watch."

She forced her eyes open and peered down at him. His eyes were like shiny glass marbles behind his spectacles, ice blue and gray. Tears flowed down her cheeks.

"We have an understanding?"

She hesitated, then nodded yes.

"See, I know all the tricks. I've done my homework. Question is, have you? You know what I'm gonna do, don't you? You read the book, right? Daryll Lee's book?"

She stared at him blankly and shook her head no. He pulled a dog-eared paperback from his back pocket. Daryll Lee stared up at her from the author's photo. She knew the book. She had found it in her bed, a gift from Peter, but she wasn't giving him an inch tonight. Peter riffled the pages until he found the spot he needed.

"Let's open our hymnals to chapter twelve. This makes for fascinating reading . . ." Peter assumed an exaggerated imitation of hillbilly speech. "My daddy taught me how ta hunt. That's all I ever wuz good at." He glanced up at Helen for emphasis. "Daddy also taught him how to take it up the ass starting at the age of four, but never mind." He skimmed the page. ". . . It's the hunting part that counts. See, what Daryll Lee had in mind . . ." On this he proceeded to rip her dress apart from the cut he had already made, baring her entire stomach within inches of his face. ". . . What he really wanted to do—is dress you like a deer. That's when they string the animal up . . . cut off all its skin . . . slice open the belly."

She shuddered as he lay his face against her stomach, nuzzling her skin. ". . . And then they pull out all the soft stuff . . . all the entrails . . . it's like a striptease, only it goes to the bone. You won't have anything left to hide . . . not from me . . . not from anybody."

At that moment, a distant electronic beeping sound could be heard. Peter pulled back from her and laid the surgical knife on the floor at her feet, as if making an offering to the gods. Helen looked down, surprised at her reprieve.

"Ah, that's the sound I've been waiting for. This will have to wait." He waived the fabric package of tools at her. "Our final player enters from the wings. Cop Number Two, come on down! See, here's where Daryll Lee fucked up. He didn't know there was a second cop. But I do. And this time, we're going to get it right."

◆

M.J. sped as fast as she could through the campus
toward McCluskey. Finally, it loomed into view
through the shadowy trees. Lit from below by
small spotlights placed in the ground, it was an
impressive building with a concrete, stone, and
steel facade, one of the newer additions to campus.
It would be quiet tonight, deserted for the most
part, save for the last few pawns on the board.
She parked beside the green truck that Peter had
driven; the rest of the parking lot was deserted.

The building was unlocked and M.J. walked in.
Suddenly, she heard a loud beeping noise. At her
feet beside the door was a cheap plastic Radio
Shack motion detector, and she lunged for it and
shut off the gizmo, but she knew it was too late.
Peter would know she had arrived. Her footsteps
on the marble floor were magnified in the empti-
ness. The huge lobby with its oak benches was
dark, except for the soft light that streamed in from
outside through the cathedral windows. She crept
slowly through the shadows, her skin itching with
fear. She froze as a sound echoed from the auditorium.

M.J. opened the doors to the lecture hall and
looked around. She took a few steps in, but she
knew it was empty. She knew where they would
be waiting for her.

She walked back out into the lobby and turned
down the long, dark corridor that led to the ladies'
room. Her breath was coming fast and hard. Her
hands groped along the wall for light switches, but

there were none. She edged her way forward in the darkness.

Around the corner, M.J. approached the alcove that housed the ladies' room. She leaned against the bathroom door to listen, but she heard nothing. She willed herself up and forward and shoved the door open.

The lights were on, brilliant against the sterile white, blinding her for a moment. She stepped in and adjusted her eyes. The room seemed empty and cold, a makeshift charnel house waiting for the dead to arrive. A trickle from a faulty tap dripped and reverberated off the white tiles that spread out before her like an infinite grid of slippery stone. To her left was the broom closet. The stalls were to her right. She inched forward, holding the gun in front of her.

All the stall doors were shut except the first, which swung open slightly. M.J. looked up and saw Helen strung up, forcing herself to stay balanced on the toilet rim, her mouth taped shut and her hands captured up above her head by the same wire that threatened to strangle her. Helen was trying desperately to communicate with her eyes. M.J. could only read the tremendous fear.

The detective motioned her to be calm, but Helen kept indicating the floor with her eyes. M.J. scanned what appeared to be the empty bathroom, save for the bloody corpse in the corner. She saw the uniform and realized Peter had dragged Mike's body to Berkeley with Helen. She understood that Peter was completely insane, but somehow he had managed to outsmart all of them and had carved a trail of death that had led them to this nexus. She had to find him now. He maintained the element of surprise like a lethal trump card.

M.J. looked over to the stalls, then suddenly, she remembered the janitor's closet. She spun around and blasted four rounds through the closet door in an even pattern of ragged holes.

The room was dead still save for Helen's labored breathing. M.J. moved slowly to the closet and jerked it open. Mops and pails thundered onto the tile floor. The last mop, anchored in a pail leaned down to her. Andy's friend Hal's head was impaled on top, his skin a bloodless blue and eyes open, accusatory. She lurched back. Helen moaned, kicked and jerked, panicked to get her attention. M.J. turned and looked at her; Helen shook her head. She knew Helen was trying to warn her, but she could not translate her frantic looks.

M.J. yelled across the room. "Come out of the stall with your hands above your head!" M.J. raised her gun and blasted the second stall; it was empty. She caught her breath and faced the third and shot again. Empty. Still crouched down in perfect shooting stance she aimed at the fourth and shot. Quickly, she aimed at the fifth and last door and hesitated as Helen's muffled groans became more intense. Mistaking them as a warning, M.J. blasted several shots into the final stall and kicked it open.

M.J. stared in horror and disbelief at Mike's

body, white and drained of blood crunched up on the toilet seat. She spun around, realizing far too late that the corpse on the floor had been Peter.

He grabbed her from behind and the gun flew out of her hands and spiraled across the cold tiles. He held her tight around the neck with his left arm and jammed a bowie knife against her throat, turning her simultaneously to face Helen. Then he dragged her to the center of the floor and scooped up her gun with his right hand. There was a heartbeat of eye contact between the two women, both stunned and hopeless.

"C'mon, Doc! Do I stick her or shoot her, shoot her or stick her?"

M.J. fought desperately to break free, smashing her heel down on his instep, in no way ready or willing to give her life up to this monster. Peter bellowed in pain, pushed her away and reached straight out with his right arm and shot her through the collarbone with her own gun. The impact slammed her against the wall and blood spurted and flowed from her wound. For good measure, Peter aimed dead center at her chest and shot her again. M.J. slid down the wall leaving a long red smear.

He spun around to Helen and called triumphantly, "*Two* in the chest! Two points! All we need to do now is cut her throat . . ." He raised the bowie knife in victory. "Then it's just you and ol' Daryll Lee."

Peter turned back to look at his handiwork. M.J. was bleeding profusely, going into shock, dropping into unconsciousness. He inched toward her, the blade gleaming in his fist. A shard of broken mirror crunched beneath his heel.

Helen attempted to scream under the duct tape, a high, keening, helpless whine.

Peter loomed over M.J., grabbed a handful of hair, and slammed her head back against the wall to expose her throat. Her eyes rolled back in her head.

"I'm not gonna lie to you. This is really gonna hurt."

Helen was devastated by the horrific prospect of her friend's impending death. Action was the only antidote to the terror that raged through her system. As long as she had a purpose, she could battle the demon of fear that threatened to suck the breath from her body. She thought to herself, *Oh, God, not M.J., got to save M.J.* In the split second before Peter brought the knife down, Helen believed that somehow she was at the core of everything that had happened. So many had died. Guilt, disgust, and fear battled to claim her senses. She had to save M.J. She would do anything within her power to keep one more from dying . . . to redeem herself. The heart of the matter that had kept her imprisoned for the last year rose to the surface, and shuddered over her skin like a thin, poisonous membrane. She felt it shrinking and tightening over her body, claiming her. It whispered of her original sin: she was inherently evil. Bad things would happen to anyone who touched her or got close to her. She knew what she had to do.

Helen's eyes went cold, calculating. She stepped off the rim of the toilet seat, hanging herself.

Peter immediately sensed what she was doing and he whipped around screaming, "Nooooo!"

He left M.J. and lunged for Helen's stall and threw his arms around her, trying to hoist her back up.

"What are you doing? Get up there! Get your feet up there!

Helen remained limp, choking, willing herself to die.

"Helen, I mean it! Stop fucking around!"

Now she was truly strangling, her face was turning dark blue, the skin mottled. The pain of dying was excruciating, but she endured. Panicked, Peter backed up into the middle of the room, raised his gun and blasted the wire directly above her hands. Helen crashed to the floor in a tangle of steel wire and shattered porcelain. She yanked her hands free from the mess of wire, ripped the tape from her mouth, and tugged at the loop around her neck, gaining precious inches of slack. She sucked a great ragged lungful of air down her bruised windpipe, battling to remain conscious. Then she pulled the wire over head and she was free. Still crouched on the floor, she saw Peter's feet exit the next stall. With only a millisecond to act, she snatched the gleaming scalpel off the floor.

Peter came barreling into the stall screaming at her. "Goddamn it! You're ruining everything!"

He found her slumped against the wrecked toilet, gasping and weak. He leaned down to help her, petrified that she would die before he could complete his business with her.

Suddenly, she lunged up at him with a furious cry, straight-arming the scalpel at his eye, but he jerked his head away at the last instant. She buried the blade deep in his cheek.

Peter reeled back howling with pain. He fell to the floor with the scalpel still stuck in his face. "Oh, you fucking bitch! It hurts!" He jerked the scalpel free and writhed in pain, hands reflexively covering his face, blood pouring through his fingers.

Helen jumped to her feet, leaped over Peter, and ran for the exit. His hand lashed out and grabbed her ankle. Her body slammed onto the floor and Peter tried to grab her flailing legs as she fought to scramble away.

"You wanna play? You wanna play?" Peter cried hysterically at her.

She closed her seeking fingers around a jagged shard of mirror, slicing her hand. Oblivious to the pain, she twisted around and slashed the shard deep across Peter's face, sending his glasses scuttling across the floor in a streak of blood. Then she slashed him again, ragged across his jaw, whipping his head in the other direction. He batted the shard away, shrieking with terrifying rage, grabbing at her and pounding her as she crawled away.

His hand brushed against the bowie knife and

he grasped it triumphantly, waving it in the air. Simultaneously, she reached for a glass bottle of Pine Sol that has spilled out in the janitor's closet. She hurled the bottle against him and it hit him full in the face, an explosion of glass and ammonia. Peter released a bloodcurdling scream and fell back, convulsed with agony, clutching his ruined face.

Helen pushed to her feet, slammed out the door and rushed into the hallway as Peter hurled himself to the sinks. He jammed his head under the spigots and let the water flush his face.

Helen moved as fast as she could down the corridor, limping slightly from her battle with Peter. In moments, he burst out of the bathroom, raging and half blind. She pressed on, twisting and turning through the hallways half in confusion and half in an attempt to lose him. She found the entrance to a stairwell and yanked the door open and ran up the steps. She turned at a landing and kept going up till she reached the end of the stairwell and an emergency door. She shoved the bar handle and the door swung open onto the night. She burst outside and found herself on the roof.

This was her first conscious moment in the outside world for long over a year. A blanket of city lights sparkled against a vast sea of blackness. Helen froze; panic threatened to shut her down. The world just outside the door began to weave and dance before her eyes. The freedom of space without ceilings or walls was black death itself to her, a thousand anxieties spun around her in the open air. She threw herself back inside the stairwell and slammed the door against the infinite night. She leaned against the wall and thought for a false moment, *safe now. Safe.*

Then she heard the echo of Peter's footsteps coming closer. His breath was heaving with effort and pain. She turned and backed herself into the corner next to the safety door. In a second, his shadow spilled up the wall from below. Soon he came into view on the landing below, a dark silhouette with a shiny knife in hand. The EXIT light reflected off the lenses of his glasses, now bent and askew. His eyes flashed as if they were a tilted pair of glowing red holes, like the eyes of some kind of crippled demon.

He stopped for a moment, exhausted. He slid down the wall and sat on the bottom steps to catch his breath. He laughed weakly, a slow, raspy chuckle.

"That was some trick you played on me . . . hanging yourself . . . and I fell for it."

"It's called using psychology." She felt silly as soon as she said it, as if she were succumbing to his insane and childish game of one-upmanship.

"Good one for you, but what are you gonna use now?"

He pulled himself up and continued to trudge up the steps, using the wall for support. He laughed again, an empty, desperate laugh. "This is some funny shit, you know? I mean, all you gotta do is go out that door. But you can't, can you?"

He was right. She pressed herself back against the wall, her arm dangling beside the bar of the emergency door, unable to touch it.

"Has it occurred to you, Helen, you might be the first person in history to die of agoraphobia?

He laughed weakly at his own irony and kept coming, closer and closer, one slow step at a time. He was almost within reach now.

Measuring terror against terror, she closed her eyes. Hands trembling, she reached for the emergency handle. Just as Peter lunged for her, she slammed the door open and threw herself into the night. She tried to run, but the ingrained panic hit her like a sledgehammer and her knees buckled. She crawled across the thin gravel of the rooftop, scraping her knees, hellbent on freedom.

Peter burst from the stairwell, his face a tattered and bleeding ruin, and he stumbled to catch up to her. He inched toward her like a nervous lover.

With all her remaining strength, she pulled herself up and started staggering a few steps right, and then left and back, trying to fake him out.

"You can't do that, Helen. You can't win now."

They continued this cat-and-mouse game, both of them wounded, taunting each other. She would spin toward him and he'd swipe at the air with the knife, just barely missing her. Then she would stumble back at the last moment, and he would lose his balance as he lunged, jousting at windmills.

"Come on, Helen. You know it's inevitable. We're meant to be together." He was backing her up farther and farther to the edge of the roof. She slipped and started to fall back and he grabbed her, not willing to lose her just yet, not willing to give up the last blow to the earth below.

Then she was down and he kicked her savagely in the ribs.

Suddenly he stopped, finally realizing that the trees surrounding them down below were pulsing with red-and-blue lights. He moved to the edge of the roof and gazed out to discover police cars everywhere, with more converging from the outer rim of the campus. A SWAT team was deploying. They were surrounded by a full-scale tactical alert.

Peter stood in awe. He had created this. This was his moment, perverse in all its glory. "Wow. Look at 'em all."

He faded back from the parapet and turned to Helen.

"You can never trust a goddamn cop."

Helen was gasping, struggling to keep her senses, still defiant. "What's the world coming to?" she quipped back to him.

They stared at each other, a brief truce for war-weary gladiators, both knowing that an infinite possibility of tragic endings awaited them.

Suddenly, a brilliant spotlight erupted from the sky above their heads, probing, turning night into day. The glare was harsh, incredible, surreal. The clatter of rotors pounded the sky. They shielded their eyes, as the helicopter roared overhead, pinning them in a circle of holy white light.

Peter gazed up. "Whoa, look at that." He grabbed Helen and hauled her to her feet as if she were his bride in death. He spun her around and around as the copter churned in slow, lazy circles above.

"Look, it's a news copter. This is *perfect*. Fucking perfect. It's even better than tape, 'cause it's going out *live*."

He raised the bowie knife to her throat for the finale, one quick, violent slash to go out . . . "Live and prime-time."

Neither of them heard the gunshot above the helicopter noise. The bullet sheared through his shoulder, leaving a gaping, bloody hole. He dropped the knife and sank to his knees, his head turning and searching in confusion and shock. Helen turned toward the rooftop entrance and saw M.J. in the shadows, shivering. The gun trembled in her textbook two-handed grip.

The three of them hung there motionless on the roof for a moment, a tragedy frozen in time and space. In the darkness overhead, the helicopter swooped down like a massive vulture ready to scavenge the remains of another's kill.

M.J. looked at Helen and beckoned her to come toward her to safety.

Helen forced herself to move toward M.J., slowly limping, tripping slightly on the tiny gravel, willing herself to freedom.

Peter called out, "You bitches are all the same."

She turned around and saw him groping for

the knife with his good arm. Unbelievably, he struggled to rise.

Helen screamed, "Don't." Despite the thousand cruelties he had foist upon her and all his victims, she willed him to live. Perhaps it was the last vestiges of the scientist in her; perhaps it was the remains of her humanity.

He called back, "You're like all the women that ever tried to suck the life out of me!" With that, he lunged to his feet and hurtled toward Helen with a prolonged wail of lunatic rage.

M.J. started firing, emptying the clip into him. All nine rounds.

Helen slammed down on the rootfop floor and rolled away from him.

Peter took every single round, screaming as the bullets chewed through him and jerked his body through space. The last few shots sent him reeling back across the roof. M.J.'s final shot took him between the eyes, splitting his glasses and snapping his head back, driving him clean off the edge of the roof to plummet in freefall. He was dead before he hit the roof of the patrol car waiting below. The light bar exploded in a grotesque shower of blood and multicolored plastic as the body hit. It was a final moment befitting Peter's elaborate dreams.

Cops descended on the dead man from all directions, encircling the corpse with guns drawn like anonymous toy soldiers drifting in a surreal kaleidoscope of swirling red-and-blue light.

It took a few minutes for the SWAT team,

Quinn's group, the CSIs and the FBI tagalongs to
get up to the roof. They got paramedics over to
M.J. and Helen immediately. They carried the two
women down to the auditorium on stretchers for
preliminary treatment.

On the gurney, M.J. trembled and tried to lean
up to help the paramedics hovering over her. She
was covered with blood from the wound in her
collarbone. A paramedic lifted her Kevlar vest
away, revealing a massive bruise where Peter's
second shot to her was deflected. Dopey with
shock, she was unaware of how gravely injured
she was.

"I think I maybe busted some ribs."

The paramedic nodded to his partner. "Gimme
a pressure pad here."

Together they ministered to her wound, easing
her back on the gurney.

"Thank the Lord for Kevlar," she whispered to
the ceiling.

M.J. blinked up, seeing Quinn. Her voice came
out small and tentative, like a little girl caught
disobeying her daddy's strictest orders.

"I fucked up."

"You did great."

"I kill him?"

"Don't you give that shit-stain another thought,
M.J. Not another thought. You hear me? There's a
beach towel with your name on it somewhere
south of here. You'll take a couple of weeks. You'll
feel fine. You'll come back to work."

Helen was giving a preliminary statement

nearby to a uniform while a paramedic patched up her cuts and bruises. She never took her eyes off M.J. Helen's neck was bloody and discolored from the noose. In a few hours it would be black and blue from the bruising.

The medics lifted M.J.'s gurney and rushed it to the waiting ambulance and loaded her in.

Helen walked up to Quinn. He felt awkward in her presence, momentarily ashamed at the way he had underestimated her.

"Can I ride with her?"

"Of course." Quinn smiled and took her arm and guided her through the crush of bodies. "Let the lady through."

He lifted her up into the ambulance. The doors slammed and they took off, moving fast beyond the glare of minicam lights, the pop of flashguns, and the bustle of the video news teams.

At the back entrance to the auditorium, generally used for goods and garbage, Commissioner Petrillo stood nearby, surrounded by the press. At the forefront was the indomitable Susan Schiffer, as perfectly coifed and radiant as a Barbie doll, despite the long night.

"We're coming to you live from McCluskey Auditorium and Berkeley University and . . . yes . . . here it comes. The body of the alleged Copycat Killer is being taken away and you can hear the reaction of the crowd."

As the yellow bag was carried toward the waiting ambulance, catcalls and cheers emanated from the strange gathering, mostly cops and press actually.

"And now Police Commissioner Petrillo is about to make a statement."

Petrillo stepped in front of the microphones waving in front of him.

"I have just been informed that the individual believed to be the Copycat Killer has expired from wounds sustained in a gun battle. The largest manhunt in this city's recent history has come to a conclusion with no further loss of life. I want to congratulate Lieutenant Quinn and the brave men of the Homicide Squad for the excellent work they've done. . . ."

Just as Petrillo was lauding "the brave men" of the SFPD, Helen and M.J. were on their way to a nearby hospital. Helen sat next to M.J. protectively. It was quiet in the ambulance after the long night of violence and confusion. M.J. looked up out of her grogginess and recognized Helen. She managed a smile.

"Hey. You got out of the house."

Helen laughed, choking back her impulse to cry.

"Yeah, I guess I did."

M.J. took Helen's hand and gave it a little squeeze, the best she could muster under the circumstances.

"Gonna be okay?"

"Gonna try." Helen laughed again. This time the release caused the tears to flow down her cheeks. It felt good.

"You're way above average, you know . . . for a cop."

"Well, for a paranoid ex-agoraphobic shrink . . . you're not too bad yourself."

With that, M.J. closed her eyes and drifted off into druggy sleep.

Helen strained to peer out the windows of the ambulance.

The Bay Bridge rose into sight over the blue-black water as they rounded the hill. The lights of San Francisco faded with the dying mist, the last remnants of an Indian summer night. A narrow band of orange red glowed low in the eastern sky. Helen held M.J.'s hand and smiled at the thought of the sun on her skin again.

EPILOGUE

Jack

Daryll Lee lay back on his narrow prison bed, his head propped up on a pillow and he watched the aftermath in front of McCluskey Hall. *Damn*, he thought. *That Peter Foley was one tough motherfuck. But, Helen, boy, he would never underestimate her again.* Anyway, Foley'd given her a run for her money, and that's all that counted. Daryll Lee was no fool. He hadn't put all his eggs in the Copycat basket. *No-siree*. He had all kinds of potential waiting in the wings.

Daryll Lee got up from the cot and flipped off the little TV. Then he pressed his fingers to his lips, puckered up, and brushed a tiny newspaper cutting of Helen he kept taped to the side of the television. "Girl, you must have had just about nine lives to start out with. Well, I think we've whittled a few of 'em down."

Then he grabbed his Bible and slipped a letter

out of the back he had just received yesterday. He flipped it open, perused it again, folded it up, and placed it back in his Bible. Then he picked up his felt-tip pen and a pad of paper, sat hunched over his tiny makeshift desk, and began an answer.

Dear Jack,

Got your letter, and can't tell you how much it meant to hear from you. I can see you're a very sensitive and worthwhile person, which is why most folks don't understand you. They underestimate you, and I know how that feeds your pain.

I'm also pleased you share my keen interest in Dr. Helen Hudson. It just so happens I have a pair of her undies that she autographed personal to me, and which I am delighted to send to you. Think of it as a special gift from a special friend. Now if it ain't too much trouble, there is something I'd like you to do for me in return . . .

Daryll Lee wrote a few more lines, then he reread the letter. Pleased, he set it aside. Then he lay back on the bed and listened to the jailhouse screams and grunts of pain, the angry pleading, the groans of boredom. Daryll Lee was an island of calm in this sea of torment, a kind of zen jailbird. He had learned to channel his anger, and he could honestly say he was never bored these days.